THE

Empty

JAR

a novel

By

M. LEIGHTON

A NOTE FROM THE AUTHOR

This book is not a fairy tale. Yet, it's the most romantic story I've ever told. It's a journey of pain and loss, of hope and happiness. It's both achingly tragic and exquisitely beautiful. It's a love story. A *true* love story about *real love.* The kind that sees you through the night and holds you when you cry. The kind that won't give up and never lets go. The kind we all dream about and few find. But it's real. I promise you, it's real. I've seen this kind of love, and I've seen this kind of heartbreak. I got to see it up close and personal, and quite honestly, I will never be the same. I hope it changes you as much as it changed me.

Dedication

To my wonderful father, TEM,
who used to catch lightning bugs with me when I was a little girl.

The world is a lesser place without you in it. But my jar is no less full. You made sure of that while you were alive.

I love you, Dad. Always.

Until I see you again…

And to all of you who have lost someone you loved,

This is for you.

Death is not the opposite of life, but part of it—*Haruki*

PROLOGUE

Save a Prayer

In the attic, one day in the future

The dusty box lies open at my feet. The scent of ancient memories and dampness wafts up to tickle my nose. I hold back a sneeze as I rifle through Dad's things, looking for the old Mason jar. It's at the very bottom beneath an old baseball mitt, a Barbie doll, and a red puffy vest I can remember wearing a thousand years ago during one of my first snows. Carefully, I pull out the container, the glass cold against my palm, and I twist the lid. At eighty-six, my strength isn't what it once was, but it's my gnarled, arthritic fingers that can't budge the rusted metal. I give up and stare into the empty jar for several long minutes, imagining it full of lightning bugs, a colony of brightly-lit bellies that lulled me to sleep more nights than I can count.

I glance back down into the box, looking for the note that went with this jar, but I don't see it anywhere. Not that I really need it. Even after all these years, I can still recall what it said. I still remember the promise of the empty jar.

When you look at this jar, don't think of it as empty. It's not. It's full of promise, promise of all the bright and beautiful things that it will hold. Your life is the same way. It won't ever be empty if you can see the beauty that will fill it. You are full of promise, baby. Just like this empty jar.

Just as I remember the words of that note, I know exactly what I'll find when I turn the jar up on its end. A message from a lifetime ago, etched into the glass.

I love you, baby girl. More than I could ever tell you. Don't go to bed with dirty feet or an empty jar. Say your prayers, every night and never stop chasing the lightning bugs.

1

Bed of Roses

Nate

"Welcome to the next three months," I announce with a flourish as I walk through the door. From behind my back, I produce a pair of plane tickets in one hand and a bottle of champagne in the other. My jacket is unbuttoned, my tie loosened and I've worked on schooling my smile into "casually relaxed" since I turned onto our street five minutes ago.

I knew that's what my wife would need.

Helena crosses the kitchen toward me, pulling her robe tighter around her waist. I recognize the gesture for what it is—insecurity about her weight gain. She is deeply bothered by it. But me? I've hardly noticed. I love her every curve whether she does or not.

Over the years, I've watched her transform from a young woman coming into her own into a *real* woman who knows exactly who she is and what she wants. The changes have been both emotional and physical. She hasn't been as fond of the physical ones as I have. I've loved the rounding of her hips and breasts, and I've appreciated the graceful aging of her oval face. Lena is one of the few who is actually getting better with time. Its passage is only *enhancing* the incredible beauty she's always had. Or at least that's how I see it.

Her cheeks have slimmed as the fullness of youth gave way to the leanness of maturity. Her lips spread more readily into a smile as the shyness of her younger years waned. And now the smooth skin around her eyes is crinkled with the lines of a thousand laughs, a sure sign of the life she's lived. She calls them "badges of courage". She even laughs when she says it. I think every one of them make her even more beautiful.

"Nate, are you sure this is what you want? We don't have to…"

As she approaches, I see the uncertainty etched on her features. It's there in the concerned pleat of her brow, the worried redness of her lips and the woeful brown of her eyes. My gorgeous wife is troubled.

I know every subtle nuance of her thoughts and her moods. They shine on the landscape of her face like a movie projected onto a blank white canvas.

I know that face.

I know it and all its hundreds of expressions like I know the vein work on the back of my hand. She's never been able to hide what she was thinking or feeling.

Not from me.

I set the tickets and the champagne onto the corner of the spotless black granite island and take Lena gently by the shoulders.

"I swear it," I pronounce firmly before she can rehash her million reasons why this isn't a good idea. "They'll be the best three months of our lives."

"Well, maybe not *yours*," she clarifies.

"Yes. Of mine, too. Promise me you'll stop worrying about this."

Lena drops her eyes and turns her expressive face to the side, no doubt in hopes she can hide the lie from me. Which she can't. "Okay."

With a curved finger hooked under her chin, I urge her face back toward mine and I lean in until we are forehead to forehead, nose to nose. "Liar," I whisper, brushing her lips with my own.

I know my battle is just beginning. It will take time and a lot of distraction to convince my wife not to fret about our trip. I'm determined to make it the best it can possibly be, though, even if it means wearing myself out reminding her that this *is* what I want. In the end, it'll be worth it. There is no question of that. If I can give her nothing else, I will give her this.

"My heart," I murmur, rubbing the tip of my nose back and forth over hers, wishing I could make things right, make things better. Change them.

But knowing I can't.

"For yours," she replies, as she has since the night I proposed to her just over sixteen years ago. One of the best nights of my life, and they've only gotten better with time.

Time.

I squelch the thought that erupts like an acidic volcano, spewing destructive lava through my mind. There are some things I won't allow myself to dwell on. Not until I absolutely have to.

"We'll celebrate our anniversary on the banks of the River Thames and we'll celebrate every day after that someplace new. The French Riviera, Rome, Prague, Vienna, Belgium. Everywhere we've ever wanted to go, we'll go."

"What if the only place I've ever really wanted to be was in your arms?"

My chest tightens painfully as the still-new fear wraps its cold, black fingers around my heart. Quickly, before Lena can notice, I wrestle it into the background, just like I used to wrestle our skis into the hall closet every spring. I'd press them in with one hand, in among the other various debris of our life together, and then I'd close the door as fast as I could before they fell out. Both Lena and I both know to open that door with caution. We joke about it often and use it as our go-to analogy for awful situations.

We both know that one could easily be hurt by what rests behind it.

Summoning a smile, I reply, "That's the one place that will always be available to you. They're open twenty-four seven. Day or night. Rain or shine. As long as we both shall live."

"As long as we *both* shall live?"

"As long as *I* live," I explain.

I feel the slight shake of her head before she buries her face in the curve of my neck, trying unsuccessfully to hide her emotion from me. She does it often—tries to hide what she's feeling. At least she does these days. And I let her. I know she needs to feel as though she's somehow sparing me from her devastation.

But she isn't.

I know. I always know. *I* am actually sparing *her* by pretending that I don't.

They say ignorance is bliss. I think I might just have to agree. There are many, many things I wish I didn't know because once you know, you can't *unknow*.

I'm aware of the moment that she rallies, the moment when she, too, stuffs the skis back into the closet to be taken out only when they must. Or when the latch gives way and the door flies open unexpectedly, dumping those damn skis out onto the floor. I'm aware because she runs her hands up my arms, over my shoulders and then laces her fingers behind my neck, leaning into me in that way she's always done when she wants more than just a kiss.

If I weren't trying so hard to guard the closet door and those damn skis, I'd probably growl.

"Then let's get this party started the right way."

When our lips meet again, there is hunger. And desperation. And sadness. It rings like an inaudible bell in every touch, every whisper, every one of her soft moans. Within seconds, our tongues tangle in a sweetly familiar dance that is followed closely by sure fingers that undo buttons, tease skin and incite nerves.

She excites me.

She always has.

It isn't until I sweep my wife into my arms and carry her, naked, to our bed that our lovemaking slows to the careful memorization of body and movement and moment. Even in the throes of our shared passion, the truth—and the future—is there.

It's always there.

In the background.

In the closet.

With the skis.

Waiting…

2

Bitter Wine

Lena

"Mimosas for breakfast? Who are you and what have you done with my best friend?"

I smile at Nissa, my neighbor. She and her husband, Mark, are our only really close friends. Since neither Nate nor I have many living relatives, and none that are actually close to us (emotionally or geographically), our neighbors are like family.

She is my best and only close friend and has been since Nate and I moved in next door to her. We bought this place two years after we got married, when Nate landed his first job as a financial analyst at a big bank in Charlotte, North Carolina. On our third night in the house, Nissa came to the back door, like we'd known each other all our lives, carrying an armload of casserole dishes containing every Southern-fried family recipe she could make. She was as different from me as night from day and we took to one another like bees to honey. Or like flies to shit, as Nissa is fond of saying. She never specifies who the shit is, though.

"What? A girl can celebrate, can't she?"

"Of course," she responds, enthusiastically draining most of her flute in one long gulp. "I'd just like to know *what* we're celebrating. Since it includes *champagne*, I know you didn't bring me here to tell me that you finally got pregnant. Although, as weird as you've been acting for the last few weeks, I wouldn't have been surprised." I swallow the lump in my throat, making sure to maintain my placid expression as I watch my friend. "So, what's going on? Spill."

I hold Nissa's blue eyes with my own light brown ones, committing to memory the way this feels—to be sitting in my kitchen on a quiet morning, chatting with my friend as effortlessly as leaves fall from the trees in autumn.

It would be so easy to tell her. We've always shared that type of relationship—open honesty, no holds barred—but this is different. I won't give my sweet friend this burden to bear. Because it *is* a burden and I love Nissa too much to hurt her.

I've spent the majority of my life protecting others from pain in any way I can. Some things never change. Not even when I've so desperately needed someone else to help carry the load.

"Nate brought it home last night so we could celebrate. We just didn't drink much of it."

Memories of our lovemaking drift through my head, easing the tension in my mouth and turning my smile into a genuine curve of the lips.

"Celebrate what?"

"He left the bank," I say carefully, my eyes darting nervously from Nissa's sharp periwinkle eyes down to my untouched mimosa and back again.

I knew Nissa would have a thousand questions—she knows Nate and me too well *not to*—and I thought I was prepared to field them all. I only have a couple of days before we leave and I thought surely I could keep the truth from Nissa for that long.

Maybe I was wrong.

I've always been a terrible liar. But this is so important…

"Left? Left like quit-his-job left? Or left like I'm-taking-a-long-lunch left?"

I chuckle. Three months would be a *very long* lunch. "Left like quit. Left like *left* left. Permanently left."

"Why?" Nissa asks, seconds before her eyes widen in understanding. "Oh God, he's not sick again, is he?"

I gulp down the wave of nausea that swells behind my tonsils and I shake my head. "No. He's taking me to Europe. For three months."

Nissa's mouth catches up with her rounded eyes and she squeals. The sound is so loud enough it sets Mr. Johnson's dog, Radley, barking.

"Shhhh," I chastise lightly, unable to stop my grin. "You'll wake the neighborhood."

To understand Nissa, you have to know that she's vivacious, outspoken, and Southern to the bone. And *loud*. *Very* loud. She's the type of person who is of the opinion that if she is awake, everyone else should be, too. Although normally she keeps her decibel level in check so as not to disturb her children, there are times when she simply can't contain her exuberance. Right now—when an impending extended dream trip abroad has just been announced—constitutes one of those times.

"I don't give a damn!" she exclaims. "If we have to be up, *everybody* should have to be up."

I laugh outright. As I suspected.

That's Nissa for you. But I love her like family.

Nissa and I have suffered from insomnia for years. We have this routine where we watch for the other's kitchen light to come on. It's a silent invitation to come on over and enjoy *not sleeping* together. We alternate houses and today was my turn. And just as well. I'd hesitated in turning on my light *at all*. If it had been up to *me* to go to *Nissa's*, I'd probably have chickened out altogether. But I'd done it. I'd turned on my light and forged bravely ahead because it's not my nature to take the easy way out. I've always been a fighter. A quiet, steady, reliable fighter.

"We leave on Friday."

"Friday, as in the day after tomorrow?"

"Well, this is Wednesday," I say, counting on my fingers, "tomorrow is Thursday, which means the next day must be Friday. One, two, three..." I tease.

I'm not surprised when Nissa slaps my fingers playfully. "Don't be a smart ass," she says gruffly. Her smile doesn't fade, though. If anything, it broadens in excitement.

My best friend and I have always lived vicariously through each other's life. Since high school, Nissa has wanted a career and a life of travel, but an early pregnancy shattered her dreams, and she's never quite been able to pick up the pieces. I, on the other hand, have enjoyed just such a life. I graduated from college with a master's degree in nursing and have become one of the most experienced nurse practitioners at Franklin Osborne Cancer Center, something I'm incredibly proud of. Considering my home life, it wasn't easy to make *anything* of myself, and the fact that I did what I set out to do makes me feel more than just accomplished. It makes me feel *whole.*

Travel has just been a bonus. Nate and I have enjoyed the resources to be able to travel all over the country, and even to some of the Virgin Islands. But never to Europe, even though it's the one place we've both really wanted to go. We just never made it a priority.

While I've enjoyed the travel, it was never *that* important to me. Unlike Nissa, my biggest aspiration has been to have children with my wonderful husband. Or at least have *a child*. But fate never took our side, never helped us out. Neither had modern medicine with its infertility treatments and in vitro fertilization. Nothing had worked.

We've discussed adoption, but I wanted to hold off until I turned forty. Being a nurse, I know the risk of birth defects increases at that magical age. By then, I thought I'd be willing to concede and go another route. "At that point," I'd told Nate a dozen times, "I'll happily explore adoption." Until then, however, I'd been unwilling to give up on my dream of giving birth to a child that would, in my eyes, be the best of my soulmate and me—my dark blonde hair, Nate's jewel-green eyes, my ready laugh, his sharp mind. But now, at forty, I wished I'd chosen more wisely.

If only I'd known...

"Europe. God, this is a *huge* deal, Lena! Europe?"

I nod, pushing my melancholy aside. I'm perfectly content to let my best friend's enthusiasm drown out all that plagues my mind. Or at least muffle it to a tolerable gurgling sound in the background of my every thought. I know there is no escaping it while I'm conscious, so I have to settle for as many short-term distractions and mufflers as I can get.

As we chat about the plan, Nissa finishes off the majority of the '81 Dom Perignon Nate brought, along with a half gallon of orange juice, while I nurse my single flute. It's nearly eight o'clock by the time Nate stumbles into the kitchen, his attractively graying hair standing on end all over his head. He looks like a perfectly rumpled version of the man I've loved for over half of my life.

"Did you sleep here?" he asks Nissa, his voice still rough with slumber. I've always adored that sound. It's sexy and intimate and so totally Nate that it makes my heart ache like ancient bones on a cold day. But then, when he turns his gaze to me, one side of his mouth twisting up into a grin, memories of last night's endless lovemaking brings warmth rushing in to chase away the chill.

"No. I don't sleep. You know that."

"Then is Mark home?"

"No, why?"

Nate shrugs. "I just figured you'd have an army of mouths to feed by now."

Nissa gasps. "Holy Lord, my kids! I forgot my kids! They'll burn the house down trying to work the toaster!"

Nissa hops up so quickly she nearly upends the table. With reflexes peculiar to mothers of small children, she somehow manages to steady both of our glasses as well as the mostly-empty champagne bottle before they do much more than rock on their bottoms. "Whew! That was close," she exclaims, gingerly releasing the glasses as she bends to kiss my cheek. "I'll be back over later to help you pack."

"You told her?" Nate asks from in front of the refrigerator where he's lazily sifting his way through closed containers of leftovers, peeling back lids, and sniffing contents.

"She did," Nissa chimes from half in and half out of the door. "You just leave it to me. I'll make sure she packs something sexy. She'll turn every head."

"We're going to Europe, not a swinger's club."

"Nothing wrong with a few strange eyes on a man's wife to make him appreciate her."

At that, Nate turns and pins Nissa with a frown. "I *do* appreciate her. More than anybody on the planet."

Nissa nods. "Well, you'll want to appreciate her *naked* when you see what I'm sending. Things from *my* closet."

"You're bringing me clothes to wear?" I ask, surprised. Nissa does a lot of shopping and buys a lot of clothes that Mark, her husband, doesn't really take her anywhere to show off. My friend is beautiful and sexy even in her terry cloth robe, but Mark never seems to be quite as impressed by that fact as everyone else. I think Nissa buys the clothes that she does in hopes that her husband will see her the way he used to, but so far it hasn't worked. At least not that I can tell. Nissa is just as desperate, and Mark is just as oblivious as ever.

"I am. It doesn't look like I'm ever gonna get to wear 'em, so somebody should. I'd like to see them on a *body* rather than a *hanger* before they die a lonely death in my closet. You got a problem with that?" she asks Nate, throwing a little stink eye his way.

Already bored with the conversation, Nate shrugs and returns his attention to the makings of breakfast.

"What's his deal?" Nissa jerks her thumb over her shoulder to indicate Nate.

It's my turn to shrug. "Dead-headed. I don't think he got much sleep last night."

Nissa's eyes narrow on me. "I'll stab him if he's mean to you."

At that, a bark of laughter bubbles from my lips. I can't help thinking she has no idea how *way off track* her thinking is. "Duly noted."

"I heard that," Nate mumbles from what sounds like the inside of a cabinet at the island.

Probably in search of a pan.

Nissa sticks her tongue out at Nate then tosses a sassy wink over her shoulder at me before darting out the back door. She makes her escape before any further commentary can be made.

I watch her cross the short span of grass that separates my patio from hers and see her disappear into her own house.

"Did you decide to tell her?" Nate's question comes as he reappears in front of the stove, sauté pan in hand.

"No. I'll tell her after we get back. By then..."

I turn toward the window, my mind racing in a million directions yet always ending up back at the same place—the diagnosis.

The scruff of Nate's cheek scrubbing lightly over mine brings my attention to him where he has materialized behind me. He wraps his arms around me, enveloping me in his scent, his protection, his love.

"I love you," he mutters tenderly, his lips moving against the curve of my jaw.

"Are you sure this is what you want, Nate? I need you to be sure. You know I'll do whatever you want."

"This *is* what I want. I promise."

I close my eyes and let his reassuring words and the certainty in his voice soothe me. Well, at least as much as *anything* could soothe me at this point.

3

Take Back the Night

Lena

"And I brought this one for a night out on the streets of *gay Paris*," Nissa says with a flourish, holding up a red sheath that fastens over one shoulder, leaving the other one bare.

"Will that be warm enough? According to Google, September temperatures over there can get pretty chilly at night. "

I don't mention that I've Googled information about the countries we'll be visiting at least a dozen times and can never seem to retain what I've read. My mind always drifts back to our somber reality.

"That's why I brought this to go with it," she explains, her smile proud and satisfied as she holds the dress in place with one hand and reaches behind her with the other. From the pile of clothes on the bed, Nissa produces a red silk shawl with a fine silver thread running through it. It's beautiful. A beautiful shawl for a beautiful dress to be worn in a beautiful place. "And the clutch and shoes that match."

I take the wispy drape from her, letting the slippery material run slither across my palm. "I never thought it would be like this." My whisper is unintentional, the words out before I can stop them. They weigh so heavily on my heart, it's as though my tongue is a flap too flimsy to hold them inside.

Of all the times I've fantasized about a romantic trip to Europe with Nate, I've never once considered that it might be under these circumstances. I guess no one plans for disaster. Not really.

"Be like what?" Nissa asks.

Startled, I glance up guiltily from my perch on the bed. "I-I just meant that I never really thought I'd get to go. I mean, Europe! After all this time. *Finally!*" I add the last with as much dramatic flair as possible, smiling widely to better sell my lie.

Nissa's sharp blue eyes narrow on me, our friendship too old, our relationship too close for her to miss the slip and believe the lie. "Is something else going on?"

"Of course not." I shake my head and frown, my expression clearly accusing her of being silly.

At least I hope it is.

Nissa lets the red dress drop over her folded arm then pushes the pile of dresses and blouses and lingerie out of the way so she can sit on the bed to face me. "Are you sure? Because you can tell me. Do you think something is going on with him? Him and...and someone else maybe?"

I stare at my friend, noticing for the first time that she appears to be ill at ease. Nervous almost. But why? What does she have to be nervous about?

As I study her, Nissa begins to worry her bottom lip with the point of one tooth, something she often does when she's uncomfortable. I think back to the past few weeks, to all the times she's seemed about to say something and then suddenly made an excuse to leave, or when she's abruptly changed the subject to one of random unimportance. Behavior like that isn't entirely out of character for my bubbly, eccentric friend, so I've never suspected that it really *meant* anything. But now, in retrospect...

Fear knots my stomach and questions fly through my mind.

What is this about?

What's going on?

The longer we sit watching each other, the more uncomfortable my oldest friend seems to become.

I finally prompt her when she seems hesitant to continue. "Nissa?"

Nissa tucks a strand of blonde hair behind her ear, her gaze sinking to her lap where her trembling fingers are fiddling with the red material puddled there. She clears her throat before she begins. My heart pounds with dread "Lena, I..."

She seems to quickly lose her courage, and when she stops again, my palms grow damp with increasing anxiety. What could be *this* bad? What could she have so much trouble telling me?

"I think Nate might be...might be seeing someone."

In the space of a few seconds, a reel of memories from the past plays across the screen of my mind. Millions of happy moments that I've shared with Nate race by in a flash. Tropical trips and glamorous parties, erotic showers and quiet dinners, heartfelt truths and teasing lies—it's all there, stored in the ridges and valleys of my cerebral cortex. But more importantly, they're stored in my heart, right alongside the knowledge that my husband has and will always be faithful.

Yes, there were some tense times in our past—fights I wasn't sure we'd make it through, arguments that had seemed unending. But never once did I ever consider that Nate might cheat on me.

We have our differences, just like everybody else. And we have our faults. I'm stubborn as hell and Nate has a temper if he gets poked the right way. But we love each other. Deeply. Truly.

We share the kind of love that picks you up when you stumble, the kind of love that catches you when you fall, the kind of love that rescues you when you need saving.

The *real* kind of love.

And I believe that it will last long after the door of life closes on one of us. I believe that more than I believe anything else.

What I can't, what I *won't* believe is that my husband is capable of risking all that for a fling. It's not part of the Nate I know. And I *know* Nate.

Nate is my "in sickness and in health".

Nate is my "until death do us part".

Nate is the staying kind.

He proved that beyond the shadow of a doubt when he quit his job so we could spend the next three months together living out one of our dreams. He gave up everything so we could have this one last big adventure. Those aren't the actions of a man who isn't fully committed.

Those are the actions of a man who is fully *devoted*.

"Lena?"

Nissa's voice jars me from my thoughts, bringing me back to the conversation. "What? Sorry. I zoned out for a second. What did you say?"

"I was just telling you that I'm sorry to have to be the one to tell you. And it's probably nothing. I mean, I *know* how much Nate loves you. Anybody can see that. But I know how men are, too. I mean, even my dad…" Nissa stops midsentence and shakes her head as if ridding it of an unpleasant memory. "Anyway, it's probably something completely innocent. But even so, I couldn't *not* tell you. Not for one more day. You're my best friend. If it were me, *I'd* want to know."

That's it in a nutshell. Poor Nissa lives her life *expecting* news such as this. That's what happens when you marry an asshole.

She deserves so much better.

"How long have you been carrying this around?"

I feel as much as hear Nissa's sigh when her warm breath fans my cheek. "About a month, I guess."

"What makes you think he might be seeing someone?"

"I saw him. With a woman. On two different occasions. Both times they were at a little bar off 7th Street."

"Maybe it was someone he works with."

"It could very well have been. I just thought it was odd that they were at a *bar*."

"Maybe they had to work late and went out for a bite. Nate works late a lot."

I can tell Nissa wants to argue. Her brow furrows, and her mouth opens and closes a few times. After a few attempts to quell her urge to rebut, Nissa finally manages and she gives me a watery smile along with a weak, "Maybe so. But I wanted to tell you. Just in case."

Pity and compassion coil behind my chest wall.

I know my friend's suspicions about *her own* husband are playing a role in her thoughts. It's only natural for Nissa to include other men in her doubts, to sort of lump them all into one unfaithful heap. I, however, just don't believe that's the case.

At least not with my Nate.

I reach for Nissa's hand and squeeze, giving her my broadest, most genuine smile. "I'm glad you did. That's what friends do. They tell each other the hard things."

"Yes! Exactly!" she exclaims, looking pointedly at me. I ignore the remark. What I don't tell Nissa is that sometimes *not* telling the hard things is the *kinder* option.

When I don't take the bait, Nissa moves on, asking instead, "So, what will you do? About Nate, I mean."

I shrug, unconcerned. "I might ask him about it."

"Might?"

"Yeah. Might."

"Don't you want to know for sure?"

I turn my sad eyes, sad because my best friend in the world doesn't have this assurance, and I tell her, "Honestly, I already do."

Nissa is thoughtful as she considers me. For long minutes, she simply watches me before she finally nods. "I'm glad, Lena. I'm glad that you two have that kind of relationship. The kind where you know. I wish Mark and I had it, but…"

She doesn't have to finish. She knows they don't. And I know they don't.

I say nothing, mainly because I can't offer words of comfort. Mark and Nissa have a troubled marriage. It's no secret. It's because of their children that the situation just gets politely ignored. It's still there, though, like an underlying medical condition. Nissa treats it with a healthy prescription of expensive clothes and shiny baubles. Mark treats it with ambivalence.

I squeeze her hand again and give her my quiet support. For my friend, I'm as solid as the floor beneath our feet. "I hope that one day you'll be able to say the same thing about your husband." *Even if you have to get a different husband,* I think the last rather than adding it aloud.

Nissa only smiles, visibly skeptical. "Well, at least now I know you can enjoy your trip. Your *dream* trip. I just can't believe that you let Nate plan it."

I smile. Nate has always teased me about being a neurotic planner. A control freak. And, for the most part, he's right. Before this, I would never have dreamed of taking a spontaneous trip to Europe. Never. Not in a million years. That would've been out of the question. But things change. Circumstances change. And dreams aren't what they once were.

These days, dreams are desperate attempts to pack as many memories and intentions and as much *living* as we can into a few short weeks.

These days, there is no time for planning.

Time.

I smother my sigh.

Time isn't what it used to be either.

"I'm not going to let anything ruin this. Not even my obsessive need to plan everything a year in advance and right down to the last minute. It's time to follow the lightning bugs and just...go with it," I pronounce resolutely, clinging to the tiny bit of calm that thought infuses into me. It's been a long time since I've thought of them.

"Follow the lightning bugs? Do they even *have* lightning bugs in Europe?" she asks dubiously.

I snort, "Not literally, silly girl. It's just something my dad used to... It's something my dad mentioned once when I was young, after we said our prayers."

"*You* said *prayers?*" Nissa scoffs disbelievingly. "I thought you didn't believe in that sort of thing."

"I don't. Not anymore. But he did. Not that it did him any good."

"Well, you don't need prayers for this trip. It's going to be perfect, which is why I brought you *this* for those long, Tuscan nights," Nissa says brightly, discarding the red dress in favor of a slinky black negligee. She holds it up and waggles her eyebrows suggestively. "Can I pick or *can I pick*?"

I reach for the lingerie. "You can *definitely* pick. Nate will love this!"

"He absolutely will," Nissa agrees, smiling sweetly at me. It seems her suspicions have been put to rest.

I just wish *all things* could be put to rest so easily.

4

Seat Next to You

Lena

The hour is late and everyone on the airplane has settled in for as much rest as can be had at thirty five thousand feet. Nate chose a flight that left late so we could sleep in the makeshift beds in first class. His idea was to thwart jet lag by arriving in London in late morning. I admire his efforts, but I'm skeptical. I figure the best chance we have of this working is our level of exhaustion when we departed. We were both running on steam by the time we boarded.

In the quiet, I let my mind drift wherever it wants to go in an effort to calm myself. My insomnia is bad enough on a regular basis, so if there is any disturbance in my life's rhythm, it throws me into a tailspin.

I consider this—this trip, this circumstance, this time in my life—a disturbance. If one can call a Category Five Hurricane a "disturbance," that is.

I've always hoped my sleep patterns would get better, but they never have. Now I can only assume they won't *ever*. At least not until medication is introduced. Once it is, I won't be aware of much of anything at times. But at least I'll finally be able to sleep.

Pushing that thought aside, I turn my head to look out the window. I left my shade up so I could see the puffy clouds below us. They're illuminated only by the moon, which gives them a silvery appearance, like the white caps of waves in the ocean. They stretch as far as the horizon—a sea of shimmering curls, dancing lazily below the plane. I can almost *feel* the beauty of their glow, like a whisper-soft kiss on my cheeks.

As I stare out at the radiance, willing a dream to come for me, I'm reminded of the way I was ushered into dreams as a child—by a different kind of glimmer, one just as gentle, just as soothing. A jar full of lightning bugs.

My father has been on my mind a lot lately, for good reason. And where my father is, there are lightning bugs. And where there are lightning bugs, there is my father.

"Goodnight, stars. Goodnight, moon," I murmur, reaching out to brush my fingertips over the thick plastic of the window. "Goodnight, lightning bugs. Come again soon."

"What's going through that gorgeous head of yours?"

Nate's soothing voice is near my ear, his tone so as not to disturb the other passengers in first class.

"Just thinking about Dad. This little thing he used to say every night when he put me to bed. A ritual, after we'd caught lightning bugs."

"Lightning bugs? You caught *lightning bugs*?" My husband's expression is quizzical.

I roll my eyes. "You're such a Yankee! You probably called them fireflies."

"I know what lightning bugs are, babe," he snorts. "We called them that, too. But why would you want to catch them? What did you do with them?"

I shift my shoulders so I can better look into my husband's handsome face. I'm bemused. "I guess I never told you about that, did I?" He shakes his head. "For a lot of years, it was an almost painful memory. And I suppose when you put a memory away long enough, it sort of…fades."

"But you remember it now?"

"Like it was yesterday," I reply quietly, a dull ache squeezing somewhere deep behind my breastbone.

"Tell me."

"It was just something Daddy and I used to do when I was a kid. We'd poke holes in the lid of a Mason jar so they wouldn't suffocate and we'd put a bunch of lightning bugs in there. I imagine it started out as just a little game, but for us, it ended up being so much more." I smile as I step back in time to some of the only sweet memories I have from my childhood. "I remember twirling through the backyard on a night a lot like this, catching the bugs I could reach and pointing out the ones I couldn't. My dad would get those. Sometimes we'd spend a whole hour out there."

I close my eyes for a moment, recalling one of the nearly perfect nights spent with my father, doing what I loved most as a child.

"Daddy, get that one! Get that one!" my younger self cried, indicating one stubborn firefly that had made its lazy ascent to a place just beyond my tiny fingertips. The sky was littered with dozens of the insects. Their luminescent bellies winked on and off in a staccato rhythm, as if to a tune only they could hear. Catching them, with my sweet daddy by my side, was my favorite part of every warm summer night. For that one hour, my dad and I would dart in circles all around the yard, rounding up the beautiful bugs to put into a wide-mouthed Mason jar.

I open my eyes and smile over at my husband. "My heart would pound so hard. I'd hold my breath as he'd try to catch the ones I wanted. So many of them were out of my reach, like they would find a spot right beyond my fingertips and dance there just to tease me."

Nate smiles, too, resting his temple against his little pillow, content to watch me as I reminisce. "Did he always catch them?"

"Always. And I'd squeal every time, I think." I can remember with absolute clarity the sight of my father's hand sweeping in from above to capture the tiny creatures, nudging them gently into the opening until the jar was too full to hold anymore. Now, the memories of doing something so simple with Daddy are just as delightful as the excitement of catching them was when I was a girl.

"What was the rest of the ritual?"

Happily, I recount our every step after that jar was full. "Daddy would take my hand and he'd say, 'Let's go get those feet scrubbed up, doodle bug. Time for bed and these little fellas have a job to do.' Even now, I remember exactly how his calloused palm felt against mine. There was something so comforting about that scratchy hand of his."

I sigh deeply, my soul filling with a subtle sadness that I haven't thought of this in so, so long.

"He'd take me inside, to the bathroom—it had this awful avocado colored sink and toilet—and he'd plunk me down on the lip of the tub while he got the water *just* the right temperature. When he did, he'd loop his arm around my waist and pull me down to him. He'd make this *vroom* noise like a car going really fast. I think I giggled every night when he did that. Every. Night."

A knot begins to throb at the base of my throat. Memories of my father are all I have left, all I've had for a long time. And even though I haven't retold this one, it's as precious and clear as if it just happened. Just as precious and clear as everything else about my father.

"What was the big deal about having clean feet?"

I shrug. "I don't know. He just didn't want me going to bed with dirty feet."

"Interesting. Okay, sorry. Go on."

"Daddy would tuck me against his chest and wrap his arms around me, press his scruffy cheek up against mine, and he'd lather his hands with soap. We always had this pink soap that smelled like flowers and bleach, but even over that scent, I could smell him. My dad. He smelled like smoke and pine. Like love," I declare on a laugh. "At least that's how I always thought of it."

"So *that's* what love smells like," Nate observes, a playful quirk tugging at one side of his mouth.

"Yes. Love smells like my father. You should write that down."

We grin at each other, falling easily into the lighthearted humor we've shared from practically our first meeting, over nineteen years ago.

"Duly noted. Now, proceed."

I turn my eyes up, toward the airplane ceiling, looking at the seatbelt light, but not really seeing it. I dive back to my childhood, swimming in remembrance with all my senses, basking in those memories.

"When his hands were pink and foamy, he'd reach down and pick up one of my feet and he'd scrub the bottom until the lather turned green. He'd even get in between my toes, and you know how ticklish I am." From the corner of my eye, I can see Nate nodding enthusiastically. "As he washed my feet, he'd tell me stories about where the lightning bugs came from, how far they'd traveled to get to me."

"I bet these came all the way from California," Daddy would say. *"They laid low all day long, storing up that bright sunshine in their bellies until they could fly through*

the sky and make it to our backyard in time for you to find them."

"God, he was charming! I hung on his every word. And he knew it. He knew I loved every second of it. It was our thing. I guess since Janet was so sick most of the time, he had never been able to do things like that with her. Or at least I don't remember it if he did. Catching lightning bugs was always *our* thing."

My childhood was littered with heartache and sickness. When I was too young to recall, my older sister, Janet, was diagnosed with acute lymphocytic leukemia. Childhood leukemia. She was sick for as long as I can remember. Our lives had revolved around Janet—her prognosis, her medications, her doctors appointments. Keeping her healthy. Getting her better.

Only she didn't get better.

She died when I was only six.

That had been blow number one to our family.

"So your father hated dirty feet and gave elaborate backstories to the local insect population. I'm getting a mental picture."

I reach over to lightly smack Nate's arm. "Stop it. He was a wonderful man."

"That's a given. Look at his daughter. He couldn't have been anything *less than* wonderful." Nate's eyes take on that warm, loving sheen that stole my heart nearly twenty years ago. I'd known the instant he'd fallen in love with me. It was there, on his face, plain for all the world to see.

Just like it is now.

If I could bottle that look, I would. I would eat it, drink it bathe in it. I'd breathe it in through my pores, draw it into my cells. I'd soak it up until it became a part of me, an inextricable part of me. I'd drown in it until I could feel it with every breath I took. Until I couldn't see or hear or feel anything else. That's how much I love that look.

"I wish you could've met him. He'd have loved you."

"I do, too, baby. I do, too."

Nate reaches for my hand and laces his fingers through mine. Such a simple gesture, but such a profound one sometimes. It speaks volumes to me. It tells me of our inseparable bond, of Nate's compassion for my loss, of his appreciation for a man he never knew. It reminds me that he loves me so deeply that he often feels my pain as if it were his own. I know this because I do the same thing. That's why I worry so much about the future. I *know* how it will affect my husband.

I *know* how much it will hurt my Nate.

"So what did you do with your clean feet?" he asks, prompting me to get back to my happy memories rather than getting lost in the sad ones.

"He'd dry them off, my clean feet, and then he'd carry me and that jar of lightning bugs to my room. He would set them on the nightstand and kneel beside the bed while we said our prayers."

"*You* said prayers?"

I roll my eyes again. "It was a long time ago. And that's how I figured out that no one was up there listening. He prayed for me every night, and after he left my room, I would pray for him. I knew he was sick. They didn't have to tell me. I knew. And I begged God to make him well so we wouldn't lose him, too. But He never listened. Not even to the prayers of a little girl."

Even after all this time, I feel the bitterness well within me. I don't know what kind of God my father prayed to, but I hope there's another one, one who wouldn't give a child leukemia, one who wouldn't take away both parents from a little girl. If there *is* more than one, though, I've never seen Him.

Shaking off my dismal thoughts, I let out a breath and continue. "But, after that, he'd tuck me in between my Holly Hobbie sheets and he'd tap that Mason jar and say, 'Watch 'em close, doodle bug. Watch 'em close and count to a hundred. They'll be gone when you wake up.' One time I asked where they went. He said to heaven, to a beautiful place that my eyes had never seen. That night, I asked if I could go with them. He told me that it wasn't my time. He said, 'Just chase them, doodle bug. They'll bring you sunshine and sweet dreams.' And they did. They always gave me good dreams." I snort, adding derisively, "Too bad I can't get a jarful now."

"When we get back, I'll bring you a jar of lightning bugs," Nate vows quietly. "Only I won't kill them after you go to sleep."

"Oh, he didn't kill them," I clarify. "One night when I was older, I caught him sneaking back into my room and taking the jar. I heard the front door open, so I looked out my bedroom window. He took them outside and set them free. I probably caught the same ones over and over and over again, poor things."

"I bet every night they dreaded seeing you two coming."

I can't stop my snigger. "I bet they did. And we were out there every night in the summer. Without fail. Until…"

My thoughts sober.

Goodnight, stars. Goodnight, moon. Goodnight lightning, bugs. Come again soon.

"Until the night before he went into a coma. But up until then, as horrible as he must've felt, he'd drag himself out into the yard with me to catch lightning bugs. Every night. Until it was *his time* to say goodnight. Until he followed the lightning bugs."

I glance down at my hand, the one still joined with Nate's. For just a second, I can almost imagine it belonging to my father. I'd give anything to hold that calloused hand one more time. My heart aches with the residue of decades old grief. "God, I miss him!"

Wordlessly, Nate kisses my fingertips. The silence grows. Between us, around us, it yawns and stretches until we are enveloped in a tranquil cocoon.

Slowly, my eyes drift shut and I find my father again. I find him in the only place where he still lives— in my mind, in my heart.

In my dreams.

Where happiness will never die.

****

I startle awake when a warm, familiar hand touches my arm. My eyes flick open to Nate's handsome face, to his strong jaw, smiling mouth, and sparkling green eyes hovering above me. I focus intently on him. I *see* my husband, but for a few seconds I don't *feel* him. I'm still stuck in my dreams, engaged in a battle of fading sensations—the pleasure of catching lightning bugs with Daddy warring with the agony of losing him.

"Wake up, baby. I know you don't want to miss this."

It takes me a minute to shake the dream, and when I do, I'm speared with grief, a sharp lance that tears its way through and through. Dreaming of my father always leaves me feeling bereft when I wake, when I'm thrust back into a reality where he no longer exists.

Nate's face grows blurry as he leans toward me, brushing my lips with his. Calm floods me, washing me back into the now, the *immediate* now, and the trip my wonderful husband and I have embarked upon. We are on a plane, stretched out in first class, crossing an ocean to a foreign land. His words finally settle in to make sense.

I know you don't want to miss this.

My eyes widen sharply, realization dawning. "Are we on the ground?"

"Not yet, but soon," is his smiling reply.

He kisses me again, a playful smacking of the lips this time. It carries with it the mischief I've always known him capable of, even when the stresses of our life are rising up to drown us. I love that side of him—

his teasing, his wit, his ever-present sense of humor. I love his kisses, too. Especially the ones like this, that speak of excitement and love and something we will forever share so intimately.

I know I'd be perfectly content if I could be awakened in just such a way every day for the rest of my life. But some things just aren't meant to be. Already, I've seen enough tragedy in my life to know that those are the facts. Fate sometimes makes different plans. And most of the time, she can't be reasoned with.

Nate backs away and I sit up to flip open the shade that covers the window. Outside, I can see some of the drear I expected, but as the plane banks to the right, I see a wedge of sunshine illuminating the glorious, massive city of London as it comes into view.

Spread out as far as the eye can see is a tightly packed collection of buildings broken up by a thin network of streets. From our altitude, they look like veins on the back of a maple leaf. I watch the buildings grow larger as we descend, my excitement escalating as I begin identifying some landmarks I'd hoped to see from the plane.

The River Thames sweeps along the edge of the cluttered urban chaos like a lazy serpent, soaking up what little sun there is to be had in the city's renowned gloom. Its graceful path is interrupted only by bridges slicing across its width like dashes of Morse code. On either side of the river, the bank is casually littered with such famous sights as the London Eye, the Palace of Westminster, and Big Ben.

A finger softly strokes my cheek, and I turn to glance at my husband. Although he has his phone held up to video our arrival, his eyes are trained on me, eyes that glow with a love I know he feels as deeply as I do. I know Nate loves me. I can feel it as plainly as I can feel wind in my hair or water on my skin. *This* is how I knew Nissa was wrong. *This* is why I don't doubt my husband's devotion.

This.

This is what happiness is made of.

"What is it?" I ask of Nate's touch, half smiling.

"This," he replies, using his free hand to brush the corner of my upturned mouth. "I just wanted to see this."

"A smile? You see those all the time."

"But not *this* smile. This one reminds me of how you looked when we flew into Vegas that first time. Do you remember?"

I nod, the memory a sweet one despite its challenges at the time. "How could I forget? We'd only been married a few months, and I still hadn't changed my driver's license, which meant I couldn't board the plane as Helena Grant, which was who the ticket was for. Yeah, getting us stuck in the airport for nine hours until we could get a flight out to Vegas isn't something I'm likely to *ever* forget," I pronounce. I feel chagrin for just a few seconds before the dreamy memories of the remainder of the trip rush in to soften it. "But seeing Vegas from the air at night… That was spectacular!"

"Not as spectacular as you were when it came into view. This face and those lights…" Nate's emerald gaze glides over my features, one by one, as if memorizing every curve and line, every light and shadow. "Beautiful."

Looking back on that night—at the awe I felt when the dazzling city came into view, at the excitement I felt as Nate and I explored the casinos, at the intimacy I felt as we'd held hands on the strip and kissed in front of the floor-to-ceiling windows of our suite—I wish I'd done things differently. Rather than sticking to the strict itinerary I'd created, I would've been more spontaneous, laughed more. Simply enjoyed my husband more. I wouldn't have gotten so hung up on the details, and we wouldn't have fought on our last night there.

I want to apologize, to explain to Nate how I'd have done things differently if I had known, but I know if I bring it up, he'll say something flippant. He will pretend it's nothing, even though it might've been, because that's how Nate is. That's *who* Nate is. He's forgiving and tolerant. He's kind and thoughtful. He's the type of man who makes a woman better for just *knowing* him.

That's who my husband is.

Besides, it's bad enough that I began the trip with stories about my deceased father. That's why, rather than bringing any of that up now, I let him nudge my chin and turn me back toward *this* view.

The view of the present.

The view of London.

And, honestly, I'm sort of relieved to lose myself in something new.

It's all about the distractions.

I make mental notes of everything I see. I take it all in, catalog each sight alongside all the other incredible places I've visited with my husband. I know that before all is said and done, I'll take these memories out and revisit them over and over and over again, reliving the best moments of our life, one at a time until they're like the pages of my favorite Jane Austen book—all yellowed paper and curled corners.

I know, to the bottom of my soul, that no matter what *has* happened and what *will* happen, the best thing in my life will always be Nate. No trip, no scenery, no majestic landmark is quite as impressive as the man at my side.

We've been together for what often feels like a lifetime, but now it's beginning to seem like the blink of an eye. Nineteen years we've been in love, sixteen of which we've been married. There have been a few times through the years when we both wondered if we made a mistake, but most couples have times like those. The main thing is that we survived. Endured. We weathered the rough patches and came out better for having gone through them.

I can look back and say with absolute certainty that I wouldn't have wanted to travel the road of my adulthood with anyone else. I know without question that if I could live another two hundred years, and Nate lived with me, I'd want to spend every second of those years with him. He stayed when he didn't need to. He forgave when he didn't have to. He overlooked, held his tongue, held my hand, and now he's holding up his end of the bargain—in sickness and in health.

Because that's who Nate is.

And that's what love is.

"Where'd you go?" he asks from his place to my left.

I can't tell him what I was thinking. I don't want to dull this precious time. I don't want to remind him that our most challenging days are out in front of us.

Ahead.

In the future.

After Europe.

We both know it. I don't need to remind him of that.

We made our choice.

We are in it for the long haul.

Together.

No point in talking about it all the time. It only makes things more difficult.

That's why, as quickly as I can, I push the skis back into the closet and force the smile I'd been wearing only moments before back into place. Then and only then do I turn to look at him. "Nowhere. Just enjoying the view. And the company."

Nate's answering smile doesn't quite reach his eyes and only one side of his mouth turns up. He knows me.

All too well.

"I wouldn't want to be anywhere else."

He reminds me because he knows.

He knows.

I nod and turn back toward the view, working hard to keep my expression free from the sadness that burns at the back of my eyes. And I hope against hope that his camera didn't capture it.

5

It's My Life

Lena

The room is curiously bright, and I wake to a feeling of disorientation. After years of nursing, I'm not accustomed to sleeping until the sun is high. For a few seconds, I forget where I am.

For once, I'm not worried about today or tomorrow or next year. I'm not aware of my circumstance. I'm just...dazed.

I raise my head off the pillow and look at the window across from the bed. It's tall and wide, and the curtains are long and white. The view beyond the panes doesn't look familiar. All I can see is brick and the edge of another window. It looks like a city, but we don't live in a city. We live in the suburbs.

That's when I remember where I am.

I'm not in my room *or* my city. I'm in London. I'm waking in the middle of the day, in a foreign land, after being up for over twenty-four hours straight. This is the first full day of the best three months of our life.

Until the worst ones begin.

It's infuriating that thoughts like those seem always to be at the forefront of my mind, but I know it's normal, too. Anyone in this situation would be the same way.

Consumed.

But I never give up trying *not to be,* so resting my head back onto my pillow, I let my mind wander instead to the previous evening. The suite Nate arranged for us is beyond anything I could've hoped for. Every posh amenity I can think of is at my fingertips.

When we arrived, we were shown to our room right away, and it made quite an impression. It was cleanly made up in stark white and jet black. The only splash of color was the rose petals, laid out in the shape of a heart, on the crisp duvet. It had made my lungs constrict when I saw them. The scene was befitting of a couple who was just beginning their life together. I understand Nate's reasoning for having the room set up like that, though. The bed had been adorned in just such a way when he'd carried me across the threshold on our honeymoon so many years ago. He was reminding me of his love, of how it hadn't changed, of how it wouldn't die just because one of us will, and I appreciated it for that reason alone. That's why, when I saw it, I forced a grateful smile rather than shed my bitter tears.

Turning my attention to today, I note the fact that I'm in bed alone. I neither see nor hear any evidence of Nate, which leave me free to take stock of my body in complete privacy.

Gently, I push the covers off and let my hands skate over my bare skin. Some part of me expects to be able to *feel* what's going on beneath the surface, even though I know I won't.

"Don't get started without me," a deeply familiar voice says from behind me. I jump guiltily and crane my neck to look at my husband where he stands in the doorway that leads out to the living area. Between his fingers, he twirls a single red rose. On his lips, he carries a smile that's *allll* man.

A blush stings my cheeks at his insinuation.

"I...I wasn't..." I begin to explain.

Nate pushes himself off the doorjamb he'd been leaning leisurely against and walks slowly to the bed. Bringing the rose to his nose, he inhales and then sets one knee on the edge of the bed, stretching out across it until his face is inches from mine.

"You weren't? Then what were you doing?" he asks suggestively, tickling the tip of my nose with the velvety petals of the blossom.

I hate to admit it to him, but I'm caught. To lie at this point would only make things worse.

"I...I guess I expect to wake up one day and be able to *feel* it."

Nate's eyes hold mine for several long seconds before he drops his forehead onto my shoulder. My chin trembles once as I reach across my chest to thread my fingers into his hair, whispering, "I'm sorry."

God, how I hate to hurt him!

"What do *you* have to be sorry about?" he inquires softly, his voice as tortured as I know his expression would be if I could see it. He tries to hide it, but like I've come to realize, it's nearly impossible to hide very much from the person you've lived with and shared your life with for the better part of two decades.

"I just wish you hadn't seen that."

Nate raises his head and brings his glassy green eyes up to mine. "Do you do this every day?"

Hesitantly, I nod, still opting for the truth.

He exhales on a sigh laced with grief and sadness. "I wish I could take it from you. I wish it had been me instead."

My heart squeezes with panic at the mere *thought* of such a twist of fate. Although I'd have wished that *neither* of us would ever get sick, I know I'm much more capable of handling sickness in my own body than sickness in his. "Don't say that. I couldn't stand it. I couldn't stand watching it take someone else that I love. It's better this way."

"Then don't shut me out like this. Let me carry it with you. Give me that. Please."

I stroke Nate's stubbly cheek with the tips of my fingers, memorizing every strong line of the only face I've ever loved. "It'll be easier for me if I bury it. It'll be easier for me if I put it out of my mind so that we can have as much *normal* as we can get for the next little while. There will come a time when normal will be a thing of the past. Remember, I've seen this before. I know how it works."

And I do. I saw something similar with my father. At nearly fourteen years old, I'd known that he wasn't well. I'd watched him wither with unexpected weight loss. I'd witnessed his unusual bouts of confusion. I'd seen him deteriorate over those few short months.

He'd done his best to hide the worst of it from me. He'd gone to work every day, made sure there was food on the table. He'd fought it so hard, refusing to give in until the very last. He'd even pulled himself out of bed to chase lightning bugs with me, begging me to come outside with him when I'd complained about being "too grown up" for it.

But he never gave up. Not for one second.

After my sister died, Momma grew distant, but not my father. He never neglected our time together. Daddy coaxed me outside to chase the lightning bugs right up until the day before he slipped into a coma. Taking that time with me, *making* that time *for* me when he had to have felt so awful, spoke volumes to me. His actions had whispered words of love and sacrifice that had reverberated through my life like the delicate ring of a sweet, beautiful bell. He never had to tell me that I was important to him, that he was fighting for me. Even then, I knew. His sacrifice was made clear in every breath he took, every step he made.

It just hadn't been enough.

I learned early on that fate is a cruel, cruel bitch.

And that prayers are a waste of time.

"Lena, I…" Nate clears his throat. "Ar-are you sure you don't want to reconsider treatment? I talked to—"

Placing two fingers over his lips, I cut him off.

"I'm positive. I told you what Dr. Taffer said. She was diplomatic about it, but the message was still clear. There isn't any hope. Trying would just be pure hell. For *both* of us. And I don't want that for you, Nate. I know what that does to a person, and you don't deserve that. Let's just enjoy our time as much as we can. While I still feel good. Can you do that for me?"

"I'd do *anything* for you. You know that." His answer is quiet, but strong. Steady and solid like hard wood. He would do anything for me. And I *do* know that.

"I know. It's one of the many reasons I love you."

There's a pause before he speaks. I know he's trying to rally, trying to put the somberness of reality on hold for a while.

Just a little while.

But it's so hard.

"Many reasons, huh?" His grin appears as Nate falls back on his sense of humor. That's his way. It always has been.

I can hear it in his voice—the mischief. But it's his tone that betrays what he's actually feeling. Beneath the lightness, I hear his exhaustion. He's still struggling to accept my decision, and the battle is wearing him out.

I wish I could help him with acceptance, but I can't. The only thing I can do is ease his pain as much as I can in the meantime.

Even if that means pretending right along with him.

"Yep. There's a list," I reply teasingly.

I let my lips curl up into an evocative smile, resolving to steer our every conversation away from the subject as much as I possibly can. It's like an ugly black stain on this trip, and I don't want to waste one minute of the rest of my life being unhappy or anxious. And I don't want Nate to either. I have to fight it because I want to give my husband some of his very best memories of me over the next few months. Moments and words and expressions that will one day override the horrible end when it comes for me, an end that he is bound to witness.

"A list? Does it begin with my engaging smile or my winning personality?" Nate is absently stroking his finger along the delicate skin beneath my chin.

"No, although both of those are *on* the list."

"No? Then what could be first? What could've caught the attention of the most beautiful woman I'd ever seen? Hmm, let's see. My sparkling green eyes?" His mouth is beginning to show the early signs of a genuine smile. I feel encouraged, my heart lightening noticeably. With a grin, I shake my head. "Lips that could charm the devil himself?"

"Nope," I deny, inching my way closer to him.

"Well, you hadn't seen me naked yet, so it couldn't be my—"

"No!" I hurry to say.

"Then what was it?"

I lift my hand and trail my fingertips over the contours of his face—the edge of his cheekbone, the hollow of his cheek, the dip of his chin. With Nate's eyes on mine, I skim his jaw and throat, brush his chest and belly, and then wrap around his waist to his tight butt. "Honestly? It was this ass," I confess with a squeeze of my fingers. "I'd never seen an ass this fine in all my years."

Nate succumbs to a cocky grin. "It *is* a mighty fine ass, I must say."

"That it is. Even after all this time."

"Wanna take it for a spin?" Nate flexes his hips, the muscle of his butt tensing under my hand. "I'm happy to oblige your every fantasy."

Desire ripples through me. As always, Nate can make me forget everything else. Our chemistry has been off the charts from our very first meeting, and time has done little to diminish it. We haven't always made taking the time to enjoy it a priority, but the spark has always been there. Like a pilot light, ever flickering, always ready. Now, like never before, I appreciate my husband's ability to blot out everything but the sun.

I just never would've guessed I'd have so much I want to forget, that so much fear and uncertainty could surround my world when I'm outside the safety of his arms.

****

"Is this the best tea you've ever had, or is it just me?"

"It's just you," Nate replies, smiling at me over his cup. "Because your company is even making *my* tea taste good."

"Then my company must be *very good*, O Ye Who Hates Tea." I grin and set down my cup so I can pick up my scone. I bite into the dense treat, sending a spray of crumbs in every direction. They pepper onto my upheld hand, the table, and even onto my lap.

As I chew, I take in the cake-speckled tablecloth and my now-dappled slacks. Sheepish, I glance up at Nate.

"Woops!"

"God, you're messy," he teases in a playfully mocking tone, watching me as I ineffectively brush away the debris.

"That's what you love about me," I tell him around my full mouth. "I'm so classy." I pause to take a sip of my tea and wash down the sweet bread.

"Yep. Lena Grant, making a mess, talking with her mouth full. Bringing classy back to Stratford-upon-Avon." His smile is all mischief.

I chuckle, still dusting bits of scone from my lap. It seems like the more I brush, the deeper the bits burrow. "How do you know Shakespeare didn't like his women a little on the common side?"

"There's nothing common about you. And Shakespeare better damn well keep his hands to himself."

"Awww, still jealous after all this time."

"Even of dead men," he adds.

"Even of dead men. How romantic."

Nate rolls his eyes, and for some reason Nissa pops into my mind. Nissa and her suspicions.

I clear my throat. "This morning you mentioned you'd talked to someone. What were you about to say before I so rudely interrupted?"

"Messy, classy, rude as hell. The list goes on. It's no wonder I fell in love with you."

I smirk at Nate over the lip of my cup. "I'm quite the catch, don't you know?" Before we can get off topic, though, I prompt, "So? Who were you talking to?"

Nate's pause and the way he watches his fingers as they toy with the corner of his white linen napkin make me distinctly uncomfortable. My husband doesn't fidget.

Ever.

"Nate?"

The quiet intake of his breath can be heard even over the bustle of sightseers as they stroll up and down the street. In this moment, in this one single moment, doubt assails me, and my pulse begins to dance in my veins, going from samba to salsa in half a second.

"Lheanne," he responds softly, hesitantly. "We met a couple of times at a bar not far from the office."

"Lheanne? Lheanne who?"

"Taffer. Lheanne Taffer."

"My oncologist? *That* Lheanne Taffer?"

"Of course, *that* Lheanne Taffer. Do you know more than one?"

I frown. "Why were you meeting her at a bar?"

Nate continues avoiding my eyes, still toying anxiously with his napkin. "I wanted to meet with her off the record."

"Off the record?" *Thud-ump, thud-ump, thud-ump.* "Why?"

Finally, Nate raises his eyes to mine. I feel a momentary stab of panic at the guilt shining from the emerald depths. "I wanted to talk to her about your treatment."

"But I'm not taking treatment."

"I know. You'd already made up your mind, but I guess I just wanted to know more about the options."

"There are no options, Nate. You know that."

His breath hisses angrily through his vocal cords. "Maybe I…" he begins harshly. The muscle along his strong jaw tenses as he grinds his teeth together, a tell of the temper he's had for as long as I've known him. "Maybe I just wanted to know what your chances would be if you *did* take treatment. I wasn't there when you got all the details."

"Is that what this is about? About me getting the results while you were out of town?"

"No, it's not that."

"Because I was just sparing you, Nate. When I saw the scan, I knew. I already knew it was bad. There was no reason for you to have to sit there and listen to her explain it. I didn't want you to have to go through that."

"But maybe I needed it. Maybe I needed to hear it. Maybe I wouldn't have even considered asking you to take the treatment if—"

My heart skipping a few beats, I fumble when I ask, "Is-is that what you're asking me to do?"

Fear grips me, stretching my every nerve as taut as the strings on a guitar.

He closes his eyes and shakes his head once. "No. No. I could never be so selfish. I just thought... I just... I wanted to know if there was *any* hope. *Anything* that could be done. Things she hadn't told you or things you weren't willing to discuss with her. Or with me." Nate sits back and scrubs a hand over his face. "I guess that was just *me* hoping, hoping you'd missed something, hoping that I'd get different answers. I was just...hoping."

I sit silently across the table from my husband, twisting my hands in my lap. I knew he was hurting, and I did everything I could to keep this from touching him. But the truth is, there's no way to protect him from what's happening to me. The only thing I *can* do, I'm already *trying* to do—make the very most of every day, every hour, every second we have left.

And hope that's enough.

Reaching across the table with one hand, I curl my fingers around my husband's. For the first time I can remember, they're cold. Cold as ice. For years, I've teased Nate about being my own personal heater. I can curl around him on the couch or in the bed, at the drive-in or in the pool, and he keeps me cozy. It seems his body temperature is always at least a hundred degrees hotter than mine. He's always warm. Every inch of him.

Until today.

His cool fingers chill me to the bone.

"This is the best thing for both of us. I promise. Sometimes it comes down to quality over quantity."

Nate nods, his smile of acceptance tight and forced. "I know. Now, I know."

"This trip will probably be our last good times together. When the pain gets too much, there will be drugs and oxygen and hospice. But we have *this*. We have today. Now. Let's make this count. Let's love enough for the rest of my life," I suggest with a wry half-grin.

His next words stop my heart.

"No, let's love enough for the rest of *mine*."

I don't reply.

I can't.

I only rub the back of Nate's strong hand with my thumb. I know at some point I'll have to have the "you'll find someone else, and you have my blessing" conversation, but I also know he's not ready for that now.

Honestly, maybe I'm not either.

I want him to be happy. Of course, I do. More than anything. He's my Nate. My soulmate. His happiness feels like *my* happiness. But the thought of him laughing with someone else, the idea of him loving another woman, the mental picture of him putting his hands on my replacement...

I can't bear the thought of that.

Not just yet.

He's mine.

And I'm his.

At least for a while longer.

Neither of us speaks as we finish our tea and scone. Enough has been said. Maybe too much. There's such a thing as too much truth, and I think we're at that point. For now anyway.

Neither of us can shield the other from the pain.

Neither of us can change the future.

Neither of us can make the other unknow what we now know.

Our only choice is to go forward, one step at a time, one day at a time, into the future. No matter how brief that future is.

Enjoying the scenery and each other's company, Nate and I say very little as we tour the birthplace of Shakespeare and then the home in which he retired. We say even less when we visit the Henley Street Antique Centre. Neither of us wants to buy things for a future that seems so empty.

But we touch.

Every chance he gets, Nate touches me, brushing a strand of hair behind my ear, grazing my neck with his lips, rubbing the curve of my back with his palm. And I eat it up. I absorb it like nourishment for my soul.

We walk so closely that we bump shoulders, and when we stop, we stand so closely that I could fall over and never hit the ground. Nate would catch me without even trying.

He is a pillar of fire at my side—the heat I've always been drawn to, the one person in the world I've never wanted to leave.

As we walk the streets, hand in hand, I look around me and let my imagination take flight. Compared with tourist destinations in the U.S., being here is like being thrown back in time. Many of the buildings appear to be simply restored, still boasting their Tudor faces, as if time forgot to pass them by. The cool air carries with it the scent of literary history, smelling of old books, as though the spirit of Shakespeare himself is opening and closing books all over the cloudy sky.

Or at least that's how it seems to me. But I *want* to be in a different time, a time when my husband and I are enjoying rather than escaping, when we are running toward something rather than away from it.

So I let whimsy take my mind to another place.

Glancing around, I can easily envision the women who pass us dressed differently. I can picture them made up in Elizabethan finery—brightly colored, heavily padded, and bejeweled. And the men, I can imagine them laced up from head to toe, the ridiculous clothing of that time making even the smallest of movements a challenge.

I journey back with all my senses, back to a simpler time. Back to *before*. Even if it's just for a moment, for a moment that exists only in my imagination.

Because "before" *for me* means Before Diagnosis.

****

Later in the evening, Nate and I enjoy a quiet dinner at the Rooftop Restaurant and Bar above the Royal Shakespeare Theatre, overlooking the River Avon. Our conversation is soft and inconsequential, our gazes lingering and meaningful.

I manage to keep my contented smile intact even as I force food into a stomach that threatens to reject every bite. Silently, I pray prayers I don't really believe are going anywhere. But I pray them anyway.

Out of desperation.

Sheer desperation.

I ask that my nausea be a result of stress rather than the progression of my disease. Because if it's not...if it's progression...I won't last three months away from home. Our trip will be ruined.

So I pray.

I haven't suffered much with symptoms up to now, and I hold fast to the hope that I *won't*.

Surely the universe can give us three short months.

Surely Nate and I can have that.

is curiously bright and I wake to a feeling of disorientation. After years of nursing, I'm not accustomed to sleeping until the sun is high. For a few seconds, I forget where I am.

For once, I'm not worried about today or tomorrow or next year. I'm not aware of my circumstance. I'm just...dazed.

I raise my head off the pillow and look at the window across from the bed. It's tall and wide and the curtains are long and white. The view beyond the panes doesn't look familiar. All I can see is brick and the edge of another window. It looks like a city, but we don't live in a city. We live in the suburbs.

That's when I remember where I am.

I'm not in my room *or* my city. I'm in London. I'm waking in the middle of the day, in a foreign land, after being up for over twenty-four hours straight. This is the first full day of the best three months of our life.

Until the worst ones begin.

It's infuriating that thoughts like those seem always to be at the forefront of my mind, but I know it's normal, too. Anyone in this situation would be the same way.

Consumed.

But I never give up trying *not to be,* so resting my head back onto my pillow, I let my mind wander instead to the previous evening. The suite Nate arranged for us is beyond anything I could've hoped for. Every posh amenity I can think of is at my fingertips.

When we arrived, we were shown to our room right away, and it makes quite an impression. It was cleanly made up in stark white and jet black. The only splash of color was the rose petals, laid out in the shape of a heart, on the crisp duvet. It had made my lungs constrict when I saw them. The scene was befitting of a couple who just beginning their life together. I understand Nate's reasoning for having the room set up like that, though. The bed had been adorned in just such a way when he'd carried me across the threshold on our honeymoon so many years ago. He was reminding me of his love, of how it hadn't changed, of how it wouldn't die just because one of us will, and I appreciated it for that reason alone. That's why, when I saw it, I forced a grateful smile rather than shed my bitter tears.

Turning my attention to today, I note the fact that I'm in bed alone. I neither se nor hear any evidence of Nate, which leave me free to take stock of my body in complete privacy.

Gently. I push the covers off and let my hands skate over my bare skin. Some part of me expects to be able to *feel* what's going on beneath the surface, even though I know I won't.

"Don't get started without me," a deeply familiar voice says from behind me. I jump guiltily and crane my neck to look at my husband where he stands in the doorway that leads out to the living area. Between his fingers, he twirls a single red rose. On his lips, he carries a smile that's *allll* man.

A blush stings my cheeks at his insinuation.

"I...I wasn't..." I begin to explain.

Nate pushes himself off the doorjamb he'd been leaning leisurely against and walks slowly to the bed. Bringing the rose to his nose, he inhales and then sets one knee on the edge of the bed, stretching out across it until his face is inches from mine.

"You weren't? Then what were you doing?" he asks suggestively, tickling the tip of my nose with the velvety petals of the blossom.

I hate to admit it to him, but I'm caught. To lie at this point would only make things worse.

"I...I guess I expect to wake up one day and be able to *feel* it."

Nate's eyes hold mine for several long seconds before he drops his forehead onto my shoulder. My chin trembles once as I reach across my chest to thread my fingers into his hair, whispering, "I'm sorry."

God how I hate to hurt him!

"What do *you* have to be sorry about?" he inquires softly, his voice as tortured as I know his expression would be if I could see it. He tries to hide it, but like I've come to realize, it's nearly impossible to hide very much from the person you've lived with and shared your life with for the better part of two decades.

"I just wish you hadn't seen that."

Nate raises his head and brings his glassy green eyes up to mine. "Do you do this every day?"

Hesitantly, I nod, still opting for the truth.

He exhales on a sigh laced with grief and sadness. "I wish I could take it from you. I wish it had been me instead."

My heart squeezes with panic at the mere *thought* of such a twist of fate. Although I'd have wished that *neither* of us would ever get sick, I know I'm much more capable of handling sickness in my own body than sickness in his. "Don't say that. I couldn't stand it. I couldn't stand watching it take someone else that I love. It's better this way."

"Then don't shut me out like this. Let me carry it with you. Give me that. Please."

I stroke Nate's stubbly cheek with the tips of my fingers, memorizing every strong line of the only face I've ever loved. "It'll be easier for me if I bury it. It'll easier for me if I put it out of my mind so that we can have as much *normal* as we can get for the next little while. There will come a time when normal will be a thing of the past. Remember, I've seen this before. I know how it works."

And I do. I saw something similar with my father. At nearly fourteen years old, I'd known that he wasn't well. I'd watched him wither with unexpected weight loss. I'd witnessed his unusual bouts of confusion. I'd seen him deteriorate over those few short months.

He'd done his best to hide the worst of it from me. He'd gone to work every day, made sure there was food on the table. He'd fought it so hard, refusing to give in until the very last. He'd even pulled himself out of bed to chase lightning bugs with me, begging me to come outside with him when I'd complained about being "too grown up" for it.

But he never gave up. Not for one second.

After my sister died, Momma grew distant, but not my father. He never neglected our time together. Daddy coaxed me outside to chase the lightning bugs right up until the day before he slipped into a coma. Taking that time with me, *making* that time *for* me when he had to have felt so awful, spoke volumes to me. His actions had whispered words of love and sacrifice that had reverberated through my life like the delicate ring of a sweet, beautiful bell. He never had to tell me that I was important to him, that he was fighting for me. Even then, I knew. His sacrifice was made clear in every breath he took, every step he made.

It just hadn't been enough.

I learned early on that Fate is a cruel, cruel bitch.

And that prayers are a waste of time.

"Lena, I…" Nate clears his throat. "Ar-are you sure you don't want to reconsider treatment? I talked to—"

Placing two fingers over his lips, I cut him off.

"I'm positive. I told you what Dr. Taffer said. She was diplomatic about it, but the message was still clear. There isn't any hope. Trying would just be pure hell. For *both* of us. And I don't want that for you, Nate. I know what that does to a person and you don't deserve that. Let's just enjoy our time as much as we can. While I still feel good. Can you do that for me?"

"I'd do *anything* for you. You know that." His answer is quiet, but strong. Steady and solid like hard wood. He would do anything for me. And I *do* know that.

"I know. It's one of the many reasons I love you."

There's a pause before he speaks. I know he's trying to rally, trying to put the somberness of reality on hold for a while.

Just a little while.

But it's so hard.

"Many reasons, huh?" His grin appears as Nate falls back on his sense of humor. That's his way. It always has been.

I can hear it in his voice—the mischief. But it's his tone that betrays what he's actually feeling. Beneath the lightness, I hear his exhaustion. He's still struggling to accept my decision and the battle is wearing him out.

I wish I could help him with acceptance, but I can't. The only thing I can do is ease his pain as much as I can in the meantime.

Even if that means pretending right along with him.

"Yep. There's a list," I reply teasingly.

I let my lips curl up into an evocative smile, resolving to steer our every conversation away from the subject as much as I possibly can. It's like an ugly black stain on this trip and I don't want to waste one minute of the rest of my life being unhappy or anxious. And I don't want Nate to either. I have to fight it because I want to give my husband some of his very best memories of me over the next few months. Moments and words and expressions that will one day override the horrible end when it comes for me, an end that he is bound to witness.

"A list? Does it begin with my engaging smile or my winning personality?" Nate is absently stroking his finger along the delicate skin beneath my chin.

"No, although both of those are *on* the list."

"No? Then what could be first? What could've caught the attention of the most beautiful woman I'd ever seen? Hmm, let's see. My sparkling green eyes?" His mouth is beginning to show the early signs of a genuine smile. I feel encouraged, my heart lightening noticeably. With a grin, I shake my head. "Lips that could charm the devil himself?"

"Nope," I deny, inching my way closer to him.

"Well, you hadn't seen me naked yet, so it couldn't be my—"

"No!" I hurry to say.

"Then what was it?"

I lift my hand and trail my fingertips over the contours of his face—the edge of his cheekbone, the hollow of his cheek, the dip of his chin. With Nate's eyes on mine, I skim his jaw and throat, brush his chest and belly, and then wrap around his waist to his tight butt. "Honestly? It was this ass," I confess with a squeeze of my fingers. "I'd never seen an ass this fine in all my years."

Nate succumbs to a cocky grin. "It *is* a mighty fine ass, I must say."

"That it is. Even after all this time."

"Wanna take it for a spin?" Nate flexes his hips, the muscle of his butt tensing under my hand. "I'm happy to oblige your every fantasy."

Desire ripples through me. As always, Nate can make me forget everything else. Our chemistry has been off the charts from our very first meeting and time has done little to diminish it. We haven't always made taking the time to enjoy it a priority, but the spark has always been there. Like a pilot light, ever flickering, always ready. Now, like never before, I appreciate my husband's ability to blot out everything but the sun.

I just never would've guessed I'd have so much I want to forget, that so much fear and uncertainty could surround my world when I'm outside the safety of his arms.

****

"Is this the best tea you've ever had or is it just me?"

"It's just you," Nate replies, smiling at me over his cup. "Because your company is even making *my* tea taste good."

"Then my company must be *very good,* O Ye Who Hates Tea." I grin and set down my cup so that I can pick up my scone. I bite into the dense treat, sending a spray of crumbs in every direction. They pepper onto my upheld hand, the table and even onto my lap.

As I chew, I take in the cake-speckled tablecloth and my now-dappled slacks. Sheepish, I glance up at Nate.

"Woops!"

"God you're messy," he teases in a playfully mocking tone, watching me as I ineffectively brush away the debris.

"That's what you love about me," I tell him around my full mouth. "I'm so classy." I pause to take a sip of my tea and wash down the sweet bread.

"Yep. Lena Grant, making a mess, talking with her mouth full. Bringing classy back to Stratford-upon-Avon." His smile is all mischief.

I chuckle, still dusting bits of scone from my lap. It seems like the more I brush, the deeper the bits burrow. "How do you know Shakespeare didn't like his women a little on the common side?"

"There's nothing common about you. And Shakespeare better damn well keep his hands to himself."

"Awww, still jealous. After all this time."

"Even of dead men," he adds.

"Even of dead men. How romantic."

Nate rolls his eyes and for some reason Nissa pops into my mind. Nissa and her suspicions.

I clear my throat. "This morning you mentioned you'd talked to someone. What were you about to say before I so rudely interrupted?"

"Messy, classy, rude as hell. The list goes on. It's no wonder I fell in love with you."

I smirk at Nate over the lip of my cup. "I'm quite the catch, don't you know?" Before we can get off topic, though, I prompt, "So? Who were you talking to?"

Nate's pause and the way he watches his fingers as they toy with the corner of his white linen napkin make me distinctly uncomfortable. My husband doesn't fidget.

Ever.

"Nate?"

The quiet intake of his breath can be heard even over the bustle of sightseers as they stroll up and down the street. In this moment, in this one single moment, doubt assails me and my pulse begins to dance in my veins, going from samba to salsa in half a second.

"Lheanne," he responds softly, hesitantly. "We met a couple of times at a bar not far from the office."

"Lheanne? Lheanne who?"

"Taffer. Lheanne Taffer."

"My oncologist? *That* Lheanne Taffer?"

"Of course *that* Lheanne Taffer. Do you know more than one?"

I frown. "Why were you meeting her at a bar?"

Nate continues avoiding my eyes, still toying anxiously with his napkin. "I wanted to meet with her off the record."

"Off the record?" *Thud-ump, thud-ump, thud-ump.* "Why?"

Finally, Nate raises his eyes to mine. I feel a momentary stab of panic at the guilt shining from the emerald depths. "I wanted to talk to her about your treatment."

"But I'm not taking treatment."

"I know. You'd already made up your mind, but I guess I just wanted to know more about the options."

"There arc no options, Nate. You know that."

His breath hisses angrily through his vocal cords. "Maybe I..." he begins harshly. The muscle along his strong jaw tenses as he grinds his teeth together, a tell of the temper he's had for as long as I've known him. "Maybe I just wanted to know what your chances would be if you *did* take treatment. I wasn't there when you got all the details."

"Is that what this is about? About me getting the results while you were out of town?"

"No, it's not that."

"Because I was just sparing you, Nate. When I saw the scan, I knew. I already knew it was bad. There was no reason for you to have to sit there and listen to her explain it. I didn't want you to have to go through that."

"But maybe I needed it. Maybe I needed to hear it. Maybe I wouldn't have even considered asking you to take the treatment if—"

My heart skipping a few beats, I fumble when I ask, "Is-is that what you're asking me to do?"

Fear grips me, stretching my every nerve as taut as the strings on a guitar.

He closes his eyes and shakes his head once. "No. No. I could never be so selfish. I just thought... I just... I wanted to know if there was *any* hope. *Anything* that could be done. Things she hadn't told you or things you weren't willing to discuss with her. Or with me" Nate sits back and scrubs a hand over his face. "I guess that was just *me* hoping, hoping you'd missed something, hoping that I'd get different answers. I was just...hoping."

I sit silently across the table from my husband, twisting my hands in my lap. I knew he was hurting and I did everything I could to keep this from touching him. But the truth is, there's no way to protect him from what's happening to me. The only thing I *can* do, I'm already *trying* to do—make the very most of every day, every hour, every second we have left.

And hope that's enough.

Reaching across the table with one hand, I curl my fingers around my husband's. For the first time I can remember, they're cold. Cold as ice. For years, I've teased Nate about being my own personal heater. I can curl around him on the couch or in the bed, at the drive-in or in the pool, and he keeps me cozy. It seems his body temperature is always at least a hundred degrees hotter than mine. He's always warm. Every inch of him.

Until today.

His cool fingers chill me to the bone.

"This is the best thing. For both of us. I promise. Sometimes it comes down to quality over quantity."

Nate nods, his smile of acceptance tight and forced. "I know. Now, I know."

"This trip will probably be our last good times together. When the pain gets too much, there will be drugs and oxygen and hospice. But we have *this*. We have today. Now. Let's make this count. Let's love enough for the rest of my life," I suggest with a wry half-grin.

His next words stop my heart.

"No, let's love enough for the rest of *mine.*"

I don't reply.

I can't.

I only rub the back of Nate's strong hand with my thumb. I know at some point I'd have to have the "you'll find someone else and you have my blessing" conversation, but I also know he's not ready for that now.

Honestly, maybe I'm not either.

I want him to be happy. Of course I do. More than anything. He's my Nate. My soulmate. His happiness feels like *my* happiness. But the thought of him laughing with someone else, the idea of him loving another woman, the mental picture of him putting his hands on my replacement…

I can't bear the thought of that.

Not just yet.

He's mine.

And I'm his.

At least for a while longer.

Neither of us speaks as we finish our tea and scone. Enough has been said. Maybe too much. There's such a thing as too much truth, and I think we're at that point. For now anyway.

Neither of us can shield the other from the pain.

Neither of us can change the future.

Neither of us can make the other unknow what we now know.

Our only choice is to go forward, one step at a time, one day at a time, into the future. No matter how brief that future is.

Enjoying the scenery and each other's company, Nate and I say very little as we tour the birthplace of Shakespeare and then the home in which he retired. We say even less when we visit the Henley Street Antique Centre. Neither of us wants to buy things for a future that seems so empty.

But we touch.

Every chance he gets, Nate touches me, brushing a strand of hair behind my ear, grazing my neck with his lips, rubbing the curve of my back with his palm. And I eat it up. I absorb it like nourishment for my soul.

We walk so closely that we bump shoulders, and when we stop, we stand so closely that I could fall over and never hit the ground. Nate would catch me without even trying.

He is a pillar of fire at her side—the heat I've always been drawn to, the one person in the world I've never wanted to leave.

As we walk the streets, hand in hand, I look around me and let my imagination take flight. Compared with tourist destinations in the U.S., being here is like being thrown back in time. Many of the buildings appear to be simply restored, still boasting their Tudor faces, as if time forgot to pass them by. The cool air carries with it the scent of literary history, smelling of old books, as though the spirit of Shakespeare himself is opening and closing books all over the cloudy sky.

Or at least that's how it seems to me. But I *want* to be in a different time, a time when my husband and I are enjoying rather than escaping, when we are running toward something rather than away from it.

So I let whimsy take my mind to another place.

Glancing around, I can easily envision the women who pass us dressed differently. I can picture them made up in Elizabethan finery—brightly colored, heavily padded and bejeweled. And the men, I can imagine them laced up from head to toe, the ridiculous clothing of that time making even the smallest of movements a challenge.

I journey back with all my senses, back to a simpler time. Back to *before.* Even if it's just for a moment, for a moment that exists only in my imagination.

Because "before" *for me* means Before Diagnosis.

****

Later in the evening, Nate and I enjoy a quiet dinner at the Rooftop Restaurant and Bar above the Royal Shakespeare Theatre, overlooking the River Avon. Our conversation is soft and inconsequential, our gazes lingering and meaningful.

I manage to keep my contented smile intact even as I force food into a stomach that threatens to reject every bite. Silently, I pray prayers I don't really believe are going anywhere. But I pray them anyway.

Out of desperation.

Sheer desperation.

I ask that my nausea be a result of stress rather than the progression of my disease. Because if it's not…if it's progression…I won't last three months away from home. Our trip will be ruined.

So I pray.

I haven't suffered much with symptoms up to now and I hold fast to the hope that I *won't*.

Surely the universe can give us three short months.

Surely Nate and I can have that.

6

Lay Your Hands on Me

Lena

It seems odd and counterintuitive that sex would get better after a terminal diagnosis, but I have found that to be the strange truth. Lately, Nate and I make love more often and with more fervor than ever before, even during our youth.

Maybe it's the knowledge that our time together is limited. It's ironic really. Life got in the way before, but now that life is being taken away…

Or maybe it's my sudden lack of concern with my thicker thighs and fuller stomach.

Maybe it's simply that we are both more open about our love and our feelings and our desires than ever before. (I mean, there's no reason to hold back now.) Maybe that's it.

Or maybe it's just desperation. Because we are both desperate. I can feel it.

Still, I can't be sure what it is, but something is at work between us.

After we watched *Wendy & Peter Pan* at the Royal Shakespeare Theatre earlier, Nate tucks me into our rental car and spirits me back to London as though we are being chased. There is an air of urgency about him, one that I shared but don't understand. Or maybe I do. Three months is an eternity in some instances, but when it is some of the *last* months, it is but a heartbeat.

And then it will be over.

Back at the hotel, with his fingers wound tightly around mine, Nate pulls me into the elevator and then into his arms, kissing me with an abandon that would've embarrassed me at any other time in my life. After all, we aren't alone in the little car. But I don't care. I'm as eager to *be* kissed as he is to kiss.

At our floor, we break apart just long enough to rush from the elevator and to our room, Nate flinging open the door and then slamming it shut behind us. From that point on, it is a beautiful tangle of hungry moans, clinging lips, and seeking hands.

We finally make it to the bedroom. Our lips, our hands, our hearts can't seem to get close enough, warm enough, deep enough.

We just can't seem to get...enough.

Nate unbuttons my blouse, tugging the tails from the waistband of my slacks, and then pushing the slinky material from my shoulders. With a fevered mouth, he kisses a trail down the curve of my neck and across my clavicle, easing away my bra straps as though they were made of magic and he is a talented magician.

"Nate," I whisper, reveling in the feel of my husband's name on my lips, the sound of it in the room with us, in the air. It's like if I exhale it, I can then breathe it in all over again, take him inside me. Keep him with this body forever.

Fingers trembling with need, I pull my husband's shirt over his head. Shakily, I thread the button of his pants back through the hole, hasty to get my hand inside his trousers, anxious to palm his erection.

I wind my fingers around his thick length, stroking a groan from deep in his chest. The sound rumbles from him and into me, shooting through my body and landing squarely between my thighs.

Breathing heavily, Nate bends his head and takes one of my tingling nipples into his mouth, working it with his tongue until he drags a soft whimper from me. I dig the fingers of my free hand into his hair and clench my fist, something I know he loves.

"Shit!" he hisses, backing away from me to run a hand over his face, searching for his composure.

Nate's green eyes are smoky with passion, and he looks, for the most part, like a horny frat boy. Like *my* horny frat boy.

"I want to look at you before you drive me so crazy I can't see straight," my husband explains as he struggles to catch his breath.

"You *are* looking at me," I quip, a languid grin stretching over my face as I reach for him.

He holds me at bay, lacing his fingers with mine and then bringing our joined digits to his mouth. "No. *Really* look. I want to memorize you."

Carefully, as though he's worshipping not only my skin, but the connection we share, Nate kisses each of my knuckles. My heart pounds. It pounds with desire, yes, but it also pounds with a love so profound I can't describe it. I can only feel it. Revere it. Bask in it.

Treasure it.

Releasing my hands to my sides, Nate reaches down to tease one nipple, his gaze locked on mine and eating me up as he does so. Slowly, deliberately, his arms come up and around me to unclasp my bra. My breasts fall gently from the confines of the cups.

Lovingly, Nate strokes my skin, his touch as light as a summer rain, before he moves to my waist to unfasten my pants. He squats before me, nudging the material over the curve of my hips then letting it fall to pool around my ankles. My panties follow, Nate's warm palms skimming the outsides of my thighs as he traces the length of my legs.

When I stand before him in nothing but the wedge of lamplight coming through the open bedroom door, he steps back to admire what he so carefully revealed.

"You are the most incredible woman I've ever seen. As stunning outside as you are inside." He takes a step closer. "Do you know that I still fantasize about you?" Nate rakes the backs of his fingers over the tips of my heavy breasts. "About doing things to you? Hearing you say my name, feeling your body so tight around mine? Have I ever told you that?"

My mouth is dry, and I'm spellbound.

Heart swollen, body aching, I shake my head. "No."

For years, I've been self-conscious about my physique. Despite Nate's insistence that he loves my body, I've never been able to shake my insecurity. I know my husband loves me, but I've always been afraid that one day he would see my flaws more clearly than he would see the things he loves about me, that he would realize there are prettier, younger, thinner women out there. But he never has. And I hate that I've underestimated him all this time, hate that I've wasted so many years being so neurotic.

"I do. I've never met someone who could so thoroughly captivate me. Even after all these years. I'm not sure I ever really thought it was possible—to still want someone this much after so long—and yet... Here I am. Captivated."

When Nate lowers his mouth to mine, I taste the salt of the tears I can't contain. Nate leans away and looks down at me. "What's the matter, baby?"

With the pad of his thumb, he wipes away a single droplet before it can run down my cheek.

"You've always made me feel beautiful, even when I didn't think I was, but now…" I swallow at the growing tightness in my throat. "For months now, all I see when I look in the mirror is the monster living inside me, but not you. You don't see it. You still see *me*. Just me. You look at me the way you always have. Like I'm perfect. Like I'm *still* perfect."

Cupping my face, Nate leans his forehead against mine. "You *are* still perfect. No one will ever be so perfect in my eyes. Ever. I'll want you this much, *this way*, always. Always."

When his lips take mine, they are at once gentle and passionate, reverent and reckless. Nate never loses control, though. Not once does he hurt me, not even with the grip of his strong hands.

But he thrills me.

God, how he thrills me!

He lets me know with his body how very much I mean to his heart. He whispers his love into my ear, he moans it against my flesh, he strains with it between my legs.

And when our release finally comes, and Nate is buried deep within my body, I hold him to me with every ounce of strength I can muster. I draw him into me—his body, his seed, his love—and tuck away the memory of it, far into one corner of my mind, knowing that every breath and every heartbeat we share are some of the best of my life.

And some of the last.

7

Someday Just Might Be Tonight

Lena

Six weeks.

It's already been six whole weeks since we left the States. To me, it feels like the blink of an eye. London, Paris, Germany, Switzerland—I've explored them all with my favorite person by my side, and each location was just as amazing as I expected. While it could be my mindset, the kind rife with the determination to enjoy every millisecond Nate and I are afforded, I suspect that Europe is, all in all, just a great place, full of beauty and charm.

The only less-than-ideal moments begin on our first morning in Rome when I wake to a debilitating bout of nausea. Since being diagnosed, it has never been *this bad*. My heart fills with dread and disappointment.

Again, I pray. I pray that it is transient. Maybe even something I ate. Because I know that if it is related to the progression of my disease, it will officially end our vacation. I know I won't be able to go on like this for six more weeks. And *that* makes me feel *emotionally* sick.

"Are you sure you don't want me to call for some crackers or some juice? I think if you get something on your stomach it—"

With eyes still closed in an effort to keep from having to race to the bathroom again and heave up nothing more than bile, I reach out until I feel Nate's hands. I take his fingers, fingers taut with the helplessness I know he's feeling, and I quiet him.

"No, but thank you. It won't help. This is...this is just part of it." It's all I can do to keep my voice strong, without waver. I turn my face further into my pillow, hoping he won't be able to see the fine tremble of my chin. It's one of the many things about my body that has sprinted beyond my control—my emotions.

"I know, baby, but..." Nate kneels by the side of the bed, resting his mouth against our entwined hands. "I just thought we had more time. I thought for just these three months, we'd be enough ahead of it that you wouldn't feel this way. I just wanted to give you a few weeks of peace and freedom and happiness. Three months of perfection."

I crack an eye and find my husband's worried gaze on my face. "I know you did. I had hoped for the same thing, but the progression is unpredictable. Doctors can estimate and give educated guesses, but no one really knows. Maybe this will pass, though. Let's just wait and see. Give it a few days. We don't have to give up yet."

"I know," he sighs. "It just…I'm just… It makes me mad as hell. Can't we have this? Christ Almighty, can't we *just have this*?"

I'm surprised by his sudden burst of anger. Nate hasn't gotten angry even once since the diagnosis.

Maybe he's due.

Still, my response is calm. I don't need to add fuel to his fire. "I hope so. I'll do everything I can to make it work out for us, babe."

He visibly deflates. "That's not what I meant." Another sigh, another shake of his head. "I don't want you to be dragging yourself around Italy, Greece, and Prague feeling like shit just because you think this is what I want. I can still give you the royal treatment at home, where you're more comfortable. I just…I just wanted to give you this. Give you Europe."

"I know. And I love you for it."

At the mention of home, I feel a stab of wistfulness. I'd give anything to be in my own bed, surrounded by my own things. Everyone is like that when they're sick. But I would never tell Nate that. This trip is as much for him as it is for me. Maybe even more so.

I didn't need this. Not really. Soon, I'll be gone, floating in a void on some other plane where memories have no place. But Nate will remain. He will benefit the most from a big stash of wonderful memories, things to detract from the awful ones that we both know are coming. He'll need a million good things to overcome the bad because they are bound to be *very bad.*

So it is for Nate that I smile.

"As long as I'm with you, I'm happy. Let's just lounge around for a while today and see how I feel later. Maybe go get some authentic Italian food for dinner. How's that sound?"

The thought of greasy Italian food makes my stomach roil, but I hold my expression steady. For Nate. I'd walk through fire for him. Fighting through some nausea ought to be a walk in the park. And maybe, later, it will be. But right now... I'm miserable.

"Yeah. Sounds good," he consents quietly. Although he agrees with his words, I can see the uncertainty and concern in the pucker of his brow and in the dullness of his normally-sparkling emerald eyes. It makes me worry, and not for the first time, about how hard this is going to be for him.

We've loved each other forever, it seems, but a wondrous love like ours leaves both of us open to heartbreak like no other. Losing a loved one is never easy. I know that from experience. But losing your soulmate? I can't even wrap my head around that.

Although I would never have wished such pain on Nate, I have to wonder if it's happening this way because he can take it, and I couldn't. I can take the sickness, but I'm not sure if I could handle losing my husband. My Nate. If the roles were reversed, I'm not sure I could be so strong. I have no idea how I'd carry the load *during it all,* much less carry on afterward.

Afterward.

As I let my lids drift shut, I'm careful to keep my lips curved into a smile, even though I don't feel it. "Afterward" is almost as scary as the next few months. Afterward holds more questions, questions like *what do I do now* and *how do I go on.* Afterward holds more time, time to think and relive and remember. Afterward holds pain that will take months, maybe years to overcome.

Afterward will be pure hell.

I quell my chaotic, troublesome thoughts as Nate climbs over my legs to stretch out behind me in bed. With a gentleness that he might use to handle a robin's egg or a delicate flower, Nate pulls me into the curve of his body, wrapping himself around me like a shield. I know he wants to protect me from this—sickness, fear, despair, death—but he can't, and I know that's hard for him. So hard!

Nate has always been my hero, rushing to the rescue at the first sign of distress. His broad, broad shoulders have always been able to carry the heaviest of loads, but lately I've seen them sag when he thinks I'm not looking. My sickness is making my Nate sick. My illness is something he can't fight and he can't fix, and I see how that helplessness is making him suffer. I see it when his dazzling smile falters, and I see it when his sparkling eyes dim.

My husband can't take my hurt away, and it's eating him up on the inside. A disease of a different kind.

But no matter how deeply he's suffering, he always takes care of me.

Just like he is now.

Because he's *still* my hero. And he always will be.

"Sleep, baby. When you wake up, you'll feel better." He kisses my temple tenderly.

I know he injected as much conviction as he could into his words, but I know him too well. He's probably already picturing the beginning of the end. And beyond.

Just like I am.

****

Nate

I've never been a particularly spiritual person. I guess I'm more ambivalent about it than anything else. Lena, on the other hand, has had some deep-seated bitterness that she's never worked through, not since her father died all those years ago. That's why I'm surprised when she wakes up just before noon, sits straight up in the bed, and looks back at me with laughter shining in those beautiful light brown eyes of hers.

"I might have to start believing in miracles," she declares with a smile.

"And why is that?"

"I feel better. Like *completely* better. Thank you, God," she mutters before rolling over to give me a smacking kiss then announcing that she's headed to the shower.

"In case you want to join me," she adds, throwing a wink over her shoulder and wiggling that curvy little ass at me.

Of course, I would never turn down an invitation like that. *Definitely* not now, now when I need to have her close to me, when *I* need to be close to *her* more than ever.

But I also know better than to follow her right in. She'll need a minute of private time first. Lena's shy when it comes to things like that. And I've always respected her need for space.

As the seconds tick by, I listen to her hum, wondering over her elevated mood. As she slept, I counted her every deep, even breath and tried to imagine my life without her. I've never, not once, not even after being given the news about her terminal condition, been able to picture what my existence would be like without her in it. Most of the time, I don't even want to try. She is the love of my life. She always has been, and I have no doubt that she always will be.

Till death do us part.

Death might part our bodies, but it will never part our hearts, our souls. Our love. Love like ours doesn't die. It will live long after Lena leaves me. I'll never be free of it.

And I don't want to be.

I keep wondering if she's going to have "the talk" with me, the one where she tells me to find someone

M. LEIGHTON

else, to remarry, to be as happy as I can be. I dread it. God, how I dread it! And I've already rehearsed my answer. I'm going to be honest with her. She deserves that much. I'm going to tell her that I have no interest in finding someone else, or even looking. I feel like it would be unfair to every other woman on the planet to be compared to Lena. And that's what would happen. I would hold them all up against the light of her memory, and they would pale in comparison, like the paper-thin sheers Lena has hanging over the windows in the sunroom. All I would be able to see when I look at any of them would be my wife.

There are a dozen reasons I dread "the talk" and will do everything in my power to put it off as long as possible. But on days like today, when she's gone from feeling so bad to feeling so much better, I dread it even more. When she's so happy and seemingly healthy, it's like having my old Lena back. Lena B.D., the one from Before Diagnosis. Seeing her this way—bright eyes, shining smile—makes it that much harder to think about life after her. Without her. I just can't bear to discuss it. Because I know deep in my heart that there *won't be* life after her.

No life of any consequence anyway.

"You coming?" Lena's muffled voice calls from within the bathroom.

Shaking off my melancholy, I head in her direction. She will never have to ask me twice.

****

Lena

For the rest of my life, as short as it will likely be, I will think of our first real evening in Rome as one of the most romantic nights of my entire life.

It began with a shower for two. Nate insisted that I recline against the cool marble shower wall while he shampooed my hair, shaved my legs, and washed me from head to toe. It was the washing that ended up getting out of hand. Functional became worshipful, laughs became moans, and caresses became kindling to a fire that seemed ever-ready to burn out of control.

Nate made love to me in the warm spray of the water, kissing me for long minutes as if he was memorizing the interior of my mouth, a moist topographical map to his own personal heaven. When I rested limply in his arms, caught between his chest and the shower wall, my beautiful husband held me up as he started all over, washing me with his free hand. By the time we got out, my skin was tingly and sensitive and attractively flushed, if I do say so myself.

Nate hasn't stopped smiling. He said he loves that he can still affect me that way. And who am I to argue? I do, too!

I know it won't last forever, that I won't always feel like making love with my husband. That's why I want to enjoy him *now*. As much as I can.

From the first time Nate put his hands on me, on my naked skin, he's had this ability to transport me to a place where nothing else exists. Just him and me and the extraordinary love we share. Even now, with so much sadness closing in on us, he can still whisk me away to that paradise. With a glance, with a kiss. With a touch.

And I'll let him.

As often as he wants to, I'll let him.

While he's still mine, and I'm still his.

Once I'm dressed in a black silk tank dress and stilettos (stilettos that set us back another couple of hours when my robust husband saw them), Nate escorts me out of our hotel and down the street. We stroll leisurely along *via Condotti*, dipping into Cartier and Gucci, then into La Perla, where Nate stops at a breathtakingly delicate silk organza nightgown.

"Do you like this?" he asks, fingering the material.

"I'm a woman. I have eyes. This is La Perla. So yes, I like it." My smile is light, my voice playful. I'm careful to keep it just so. No matter what.

"Sos this is good stuff?"

"Good stuff?" I snort. "Did you look at the price tag? This is *exquisite* stuff."

"*You* are exquisite stuff. And I'm going to buy this for you."

"If you want to see me in lingerie, just ask. I have all of that slutty stuff Nissa packed me." I grin at the thought. Nissa's tastes are...diverse. In her closet, you can find anything from a French maid costume to assless chaps and from cut-off denim to Prada.

"I don't want to see you in Nissa's things. I want to see you in *your things*," he explains, raising my fingers to his lips.

His eyes drag me in, pull me under. Like drowning in liquid emeralds. They're warm and loving and welcoming.

I would've argued in virtually any other circumstance, but I know it would be pointless. Ours is the vacation of a lifetime. It will not be repeated. To Nate, that meant spare no expense.

And he is sparing no expense.

Besides that, the way he's looking at me makes my stomach hot and fluttery. That alone is worth it to me—to see that look in my husband's eyes.

He selects the gown, and then we continue browsing. As we make our way to the register, I pause at an obscenely beautiful Maharani slip. Unfortunately, it has an equally obscene price. I move on, but Nate doesn't.

Without a moment's hesitation, he grabs my size from the rack and folds it over his arm. He didn't even glance at the price tag. I stare at him, mouth agape, for several seconds before I shake my head and follow quietly along behind him.

I make a mental note. From this point on, I know better than to pause to look at *anything* I'm not prepared to leave the store with. I have no doubt he'll purchase everything I give a second glance.

Finally, packages in tow, we leave La Perla and make our way farther down the street. We are quiet, and Nate's hand is at the small of my back, his warmth seeping into me and skittering up my spine. Up ahead, I can see the famed Spanish Steps. They're a sight in and of themselves, but with the sun beginning its descent behind them, they're positively breathtaking. I think to myself that this place, this night, with my husband by my side, the world couldn't be more perfect.

As though Nate can sense the direction of my thoughts, he reaches down to lace his fingers through mine, giving them a light squeeze. When I glace over at him, he winks, something he's done for all the years we've been together, and the moment feels *right*. So, so *right*.

Our destination is a restaurant at the top of the stunning stairs. Together, we take each step, one at a time, moving in a fluid ascent that feels more like floating than walking. Once, I catch my toe and lose my footing, stumbling, but Nate keeps me steady, the tips of his fingers clinging to mine until he can grip them more firmly. Even to climb some stairs, he won't let me go.

That's why I know he never will.

Not ever.

Once we are in the elevator, I rest my head on his shoulder, and he pulls me in tight against him.

The doors open silently to *Imago*, a restaurant that is, itself, a sensual experience. Mouthwatering aromas tantalize our nostrils the instant we walk inside. Then we're led to a table that overlooks Rome from the top of the Steps, a view so magnificent it could thrill even the most cynical eye. But if that hadn't been enough to wow me and overwhelm my senses, the delightful meal would've been. The food was spectacular from start to finish.

All in all, the entire affair is an Italian masterpiece. Even the walk back to the hotel seems like something from a dream. The air, the night, the company—I can't think of anything more perfect.

Until we get back to our room, and Nate insists that I model my La Perla gown for him. Within thirty seconds of stepping out of the bathroom, Nate is in front of me, carefully peeling the expensive material from my naked body and carrying me swiftly to the bed. I have only a few seconds to think of the gown lying crumpled on the floor before I can think of nothing except the hands and lips and words of the man I love.

Over an hour later, as I lie, sated, in Nate's arms, I think back on Rome. From the moment I'd begun feeling better to this very second, the whole day has been utterly flawless. It is by far our best day in Europe so far, despite its rocky beginning.

Unfortunately, I soon discover that *every morning* is destined to begin in the same way—with me so nauseated I can hardly move without vomiting. For hours each day, I lie in bed, curled on my side, sick to my stomach, wondering what new horror is taking hold in my body. Yet, every afternoon, I suddenly feel human again. Like the flip of a switch. Like magic.

It isn't until the fourth day that I begin to see a pattern. It's almost miraculous the way I start to feel better, as though my body suddenly passes a finish line I can't see. Or like a switch has flipped, from on to off.

Like a switch.

That's when my mind begins to wander in a totally different direction.

One not of death, but of life.

Late on our fourth morning, my thoughts racing in circles around themselves, I push myself into a sitting position and turn to find Nate. He's settled in a chair across the room, reading the news from his iPad, never far from me.

My pulse patters wildly in my throat. Could it be? Could. It. Be?

I clear my throat. "I think I might call down and see if they have any spa openings. Would that be okay with you?"

Nate looks up from his tablet and pins me with his perceptive stare. I do my best to hide my growing suspicion behind a casual expression.

"Of course. Anything you want to do. You know that."

"Great," I say, throwing back the covers and sliding out of bed. "I thought maybe we could drive to Vatican City later, once I'm all dolled up."

Nate tips his head to one side and casts me a derisive look. "It doesn't take a team of people to make you beautiful. You wake up that way."

"I love you for thinking so, but I figure I should look my best. I mean, we *will* be walking beneath some of the most gorgeous artwork known to mankind."

"Like it has a chance in hell of competing with you," Nate scoffs.

I can't help grinning. "Wow! You're really workin' this flattery angle lately. Anything I should know about?"

"Nope," Nate denies, unfolding his big body from the chair to come and stand beside me at the closet. He wraps his arms around me and laces his fingers together at my lower back. "Is there something wrong with me telling my wife every day for the rest of her life that she's the most beautiful woman in the world?"

"No. Especially when her life isn't going to be all that long."

I regret my flippant answer immediately. I see the sadness, the grief flood Nate's eyes, turning them a darker, grassy green.

"Please don't," he pleads simply, pain evident in the clogged sound of his voice.

From that very first day when I told him that I'm dying, Nate has been strong for me, kept his bravest face in place. But sometimes at night, when I wake in the wee hours and can't go back to sleep, I see him get up and go into the bathroom. In the quiet of our bedroom, I hear his soft sobs. They seep out from under the closed door like a fog. It thickens the air and makes it hard for me to breathe.

That broke me, hearing those sobs. Broke me in places I wasn't even aware I could break, to know how much this was hurting Nate. How much it *would* hurt him, and for how long.

But when he faces me now, he's the same tough Nate I met and married all those years ago. Solid. Unbreakable.

Honestly, I can't imagine anything in the world cracking his resolve to be rock-steady for me. As much as he can, he will hide his grief. He will bear it alone, just to spare me. No matter how much I wish it otherwise, no matter how much *I* try to spare *him*, he won't give in. That's simply the way he is.

Thankfully, the spa is able to work me in for a massage and a facial. I dress quickly and rush to the elevator, hurrying down to the waiting area. I've only been seated for a minute or two when the attendant comes to collect me. She smiles when I stand at the call of my name.

"What brings you to Rome, Mrs. Grant," she asks, making polite small talk as we make our way back into the bowels of the spa. "Business or pleasure?"

"Pleasure. I'm here with my husband."

"Ahhh. That must be why your skin is glowing *before* your facial," she says in her heavily accented voice.

My pace falters at the girl's unwitting use of such a meaningful expression. It is in this moment, *this very moment*, that the reality of my suspicion, of my situation, hits me.

And it rocks me to my core.

What if…

What if, what if, what if?

"Are you all right, Mrs. Grant?" the young woman asks as she pauses to wait for me, concern etched on her face.

"I-I'm fine," I huff. My heart is thudding so hard, I wonder that the girl can't see the beat of it through my shirt.

My first thought is that I should cancel my appointment and go straight back up to the room and tell Nate of my suspicion. In fact, maybe I should have told him as soon as the thought even crossed my mind.

But then I quickly discard the notion. It would be unforgiveable to put something like this in Nate's head without confirmation. I could never do that to him. Not until I know. For sure. I have to be *certain*, which means I need a pregnancy test. Without Nate to help me, though, without a partner in crime, how will I be able to sneak from the hotel and find my way to a drug store? In a town I am completely unfamiliar with and one where I don't speak the language?

Mind speeding through options, I realize that I have only one. The only one I can think of, anyway.

The concierge.

"Would you like me to call the hospital? Mrs. Grant?"

"No!" I blurt emphatically. I force myself to calm before I repeat, more reasonably, "No. No, thank you. Uh, but I *do* need to speak to the concierge briefly. Would you mind if I step out for just a moment to—"

"No, please. Wait here. I can take care of that for you. I will call him right away. Let me show you to your room. You can wait there for a few minutes, yes? More comfortably."

And in private. Where I can melt down if I need to.

I nod enthusiastically. "Yes, that would be lovely. Thank you."

"This is best. You should sit down."

I take note of the way the attendant is now watching me, like she's expecting me to drop to the floor any minute. I don't doubt that my face is colorless. I feel as though all the blood in my body is gurgling behind my chest wall, a turbulent sea of anxiety and excitement threatening to break the dam of my ribs. If it does, I'll bleed to death.

When I'm left alone with my chaotic thoughts, the questions come.

Is it possible for a person's biggest dream to come in the midst of their worst nightmare? Can life be so tragic and yet so beautiful, all at the same time?

I know that answer to those questions.

I know from vast experience that dream and nightmare can coexist, one wrapping around the other until they become indistinguishable. A blur of black and white, light and dark. Heaven and hell.

I saw it with my father, through his sickness and subsequent death, I saw it with my mother, who had completely checked out on me after Daddy's death, and I saw it with a multitude of patients, to whom I've had to deliver news of every kind. The good and the bad. The bitter and the sweet. I know all too well that life is both tragic and beautiful *most of the time*, at least in some small way.

But this... Could this be? Or is this nothing more than the last act of a desperate mind? A waterfall fantasy conjured from the dry earth of despair?

There is only one way to know for sure. And the concierge *has to* help me find out.

My consciousness tilts and twirls with questions and theories, puzzling pieces and unchanging facts. A tempest rages within the confines of my skull, whipping around. Circling, circling. But as I mull and think, the picture becomes clearer. Or at least I think it does.

I sit numbly on the edge of the plush white chair in the dressing room, staring at the serene paintings that adorn the creamy walls. As I await the concierge, I agonize over every second that passes. Each one seems like an hour, and my patience grows increasingly thin. When the knock at the door finally comes, I pounce, nearly pulling the knob off in my haste to twist it.

A short, thin man with ebony hair, olive skin, and wise blue eyes stands in the hall. He is the picture of poise—chin up, spine straight, feet together, hands clasped behind his back. I passingly estimate him to be in his early forties, old enough to be able to understand my distress, surely.

"Hello? Yes, are you the concierge? Please tell me you're the concierge. I'm Lena Grant. Were you called here for Lena Grant? I need to speak with the concierge. Please tell me *you're* the concierge."

I'm vaguely aware of repeating myself. I'm also vaguely aware that my words are like brightly colored blocks, tumbling out of my mouth and falling clumsily to the floor. But what I'm *most* aware of is my frantic need.

The man seems unaffected by my rapid speech. He only smiles and nods once. "Enzo Sabbadin, at your service. How may I help you today, Mrs. Grant?"

"I need something from a local pharmacy. Is there a way you could help me with this?"

"I can."

As delicately as I can, I explain what I want, smiling and describing it as a surprise for my husband.

Boy, won't he be surprised?

The concierge assures me of his discretion and promises to have the package delivered before I leave the spa. I hand him one hundred Euros and thank him again before he leaves.

"I hope congratulations are in order, Mrs. Grant," he says, bowing his head and pivoting on his heel.

Congratulations.

If this is true, if I *am* pregnant, that's what everyone who doesn't know us will say. *Congratulations.* Everyone who doesn't know I'm sick will congratulate us. They'll smile and shake our hands. Some will tell stories of their own children, some might ask if we've picked out names or if we know the sex yet. Everyone will have something nice to say.

Because none of them know.

None of them know I'm dying.

It's long after Enzo is out of sight that I finally mutter a weak "Thank you" as if he will be able to hear me. Then, dazedly, I close the door on the empty hallway and return to my solitude.

To my thoughts.

Robotically, I begin removing my clothes. When I turn to hang my shirt on one of the white velvet hangers provided, I catch sight of myself in the full-length mirror affixed to a graceful mahogany stand in the corner. I finish undressing and then approach my reflection slowly, almost skittishly.

For weeks, I've looked at my body as a traitor, unable to see past the intruder, the *killer* that's growing inside me. I feel disgust and despair, anger and bitterness, but never pleasure. Never happiness.

Not anymore.

Not until now.

Now when I look at my stomach, fluttering my fingers over the little bulge that has been there for at least five years, I feel an excited wonder about what *else* might be growing within me. What *good thing* I might be nurturing.

In a future that, just a day ago, had zero possibilities, I've managed to find one. And as it gives rise to purpose and optimism and *energy*, I can't help wondering if this is what kept Daddy going.

Me.

His child.

8

Backdoor to Heaven

Lena

I can't relax for my massage *or* my facial. All I can think about is how long it will take for the concierge's person to get back from the pharmacy and what the test will reveal when I take it.

What my spa time *does* achieve, however, is to give me enough time to think about my condition in conjunction with a pregnancy. An unthinkable combination, but I have to think about it.

Is it even possible to *get* pregnant? And if so, is it *advisable?* Will I, will *my body* and the disease I fight pose a risk to the baby? Will my condition impair me physically before I can deliver? And if so, will it affect a growing fetus?

All of those unanswered questions bring me back to the present. To the next step.

What will that be? What *should* that be?

Obviously, if the test is positive, I'll have to see an obstetrician. And a whole slew of other specialists, I imagine. Or will it even come to that? Will this tiny life be nothing more than a blip on the radar of existence? A life rapidly extinguished by the monster I'll have to carry alongside it?

If that was to be the case, how cruel would it be to involve Nate? To get his hopes up, to give him what we've always wanted and then take it away just as quickly?

By staying with me, he's already signed up for heartbreak. Could I, in good conscience, risk giving him *even more*? Would I be better off waiting, waiting until I'm a little further along? When the odds might be better? Shouldn't I wait until I get back to the States and talk to some doctors? Wouldn't that be the best course of action?

I think it is. In my heart, I *know* it is. If I can spare Nate, I will. I must. But already the guilt of keeping something like that from him weighs heavily on me. Even the contemplation of such a thing makes me anxious. But I *have to* contemplate it. I *have to* consider my husband. He's a good man. The best man. I might not be able to save him from the pain of my awful death, but I can certainly save him *additional* pain if that's how it will end—in another loss. Another death.

To this day, I can still see his face—the hopelessness, the betrayal, the hurt and the sadness—when I told him about my diagnosis. I don't want to see my amazing husband look that way ever again. *I can't* see him look that way ever again. I just can't.

My anxiety rises to fever pitch.

I need help. Guidance.

I need to talk to someone, but my "someone" is usually Nate. He's my "someone" in every situation. But he can't be my someone in this one, and the only other person I'm close to—Nissa—doesn't even know I'm sick.

That leaves me with no one. Not really.

A face pops into my mind. It's the face of a woman near my own age, one who looks strikingly similar to the reflection I see when I look in the mirror. I've heard all my life that I look just like her.

My mother.

She's the only other person I can think of. But she's unacceptable for a dozen or more reasons.

I was very young when I learned to hate being compared to my mother. I was young when I learned to hate her, too. Well, *almost* hate her. In any case, Patricia Holmes is *not* someone I've ever wanted to be like. Yet she's the only other person I can think of that I could turn to.

But my mother isn't really an option.

Not really.

The facial is over, and I'm no closer to finding an answer, a direction. It seems that taking the test is the only *certain* step forward that I can settle on. The result of that test will either bring to life or obliterate all of the complications and considerations my mind is currently plagued by. Until then, all I can do is worry. And that's not getting me anywhere.

I figure it's best not to borrow trouble. I have plenty of my own already. That's why I try my best to put it out of my mind until I have results.

Then, everything will shift.

One way or the other.

I'm putting my clothes back on when a knock sounds on my dressing room door. My heart leaps in my chest. I hurry to get my shirt over my head, tripping over one of my shoes on my mad dash to the door. I fumble awkwardly to fling it open.

A young woman with long auburn hair and sharp brown eyes stands smiling on the other side of it.

"Mrs. Grant?" Her posture is very similar to that of the concierge. The same stiff spine, the same bland expression. Oddly, I wonder if it's an Italian thing or a hotel thing.

"Yes. Did Enzo send you?"

"Yes, ma'am." She smiles wider and produces a white paper-wrapped package from behind her back.

With shaking fingers, I take the rectangle. I stare down at it, almost hypnotized by a mixture of dread and excitement, until the girl clears her throat and shakes me from my thrall.

"Will that be all, ma'am?"

"Oh, yes. Thank you."

The young woman is turning to leave when my manners finally return. "Miss?" At my voice, the girl stops instantly and pivots to face me. *Like beautiful, pleasant soldiers*, I think to myself.

I reach behind for my purse and take out some Euros, folding them twice before pressing them into the thin hand of the person I feel like has delivered to me either *really good* or *really bad* news. "Thank you again."

Once more, I'm given a calm, polite smile and a nod before the young lady disappears down the hall. The click of the door latch sliding into place is the last thing I hear for several long minutes.

I make my way slowly across the room, back to the plush white chair, hardly aware of the cool wood against my bare feet. Every nerve in my body is focused on my fingertips and what they're holding, like the box is the Holy Grail and I have to but drink of it to see my dream come true.

But that dream will come at a price. An astronomical one. And it could end as a nightmare.

Gingerly, I sit on the edge of the chair, paying no attention to the way the cushion gives beneath my weight or to the way the room smells of lavender. I simply sit so that I don't fall.

Now that the moment is at hand, I freeze. I cradle the package, much like I might cradle the baby I suspect might be growing inside me, and I wait.

I wait, and I ponder.

I ponder, and I question.

"Why now? We've tried for so long and...nothing," I explain to the empty room, unaware of how my voice bounces softly off the walls and falls lifelessly to the floor. "Why now?"

There was a time when Nate and I would lie in bed at night, nursing our hopes of conceiving a child like a woman might nurse a baby at her breast. We've been disappointed more times than I can count, the ghosts of dozens of negative pregnancy tests haunting every bathroom in our home. This was the year, magical number forty, that would've been our final year of trying. We'd agreed that if I wasn't pregnant by forty, we'd look into adoption. I knew we'd try until forty-one, though. I'd already given myself those few extra months.

But that was *before*.

B.D.

Before Diagnosis.

I'm startled from my musings by the muted tap of something falling faintly onto the white package held in my trembling fingers. The delicate patter draws me back to the moment at hand. Only then am I aware of the tears streaming down my cheeks, creeks of grief for the life that my husband and I will never have. The life, the family, the happiness. No matter what the test says, no matter how my body is able to perform, there is no future for me.

Not for me.

But there could be for Nate. And for our child. I could give him that. I could give him something to ease the pain, someone to share his life with. I could give him a part of me to hold close when he thinks of me, when he's reminded of all the years we've been robbed of.

That's something, isn't it?

Maybe that's *more than* something.

Maybe that's *everything.*

Slowly, I rise and walk stiffly to the tiny adjoining bathroom. Maybe there are miracles after all. Maybe there is one for me. For Nate.

I close the door behind me and turn the lock. No one will bother me, I know; I just need that extra measure of privacy, of solitude for this. The moment feels sacred, and I have to protect it from the world, my burgeoning hope as fragile as a butterfly's wing.

I slide my finger under the tape that holds the plain white paper over the box, and I fold back each flap with reverence, almost expecting it to shine when I reveal the treasure within. Although the writing is in Italian, I've taken enough of these types of tests to know exactly what it says. Or at least what the intent is.

The glue makes a hollow popping sound when it releases cardboard from cardboard on one end of the carton. I reach inside with numb fingers and remove the sealed stick that will tell me my fortune. Mechanically, I go through the motions, as I've done dozens of times before, only this time I feel a sense of providence.

Fate.

Kismet.

I can no longer want this for myself. My destiny has already been decided, sealed more tightly than the box I just opened. But I can want it for Nate.

And I do.

Oh, how I do!

Suddenly, I want it more desperately than I want anything else in the last months of my life. I want...no *need* to give my husband the gift of our love, personified.

A baby.

A child.

A piece of the two of us.

A piece of our love.

Living. Breathing. Carrying on.

I find that I'm talking quietly into the small room, my voice foreign even to my own ears. Words tumble from my lips and, for the first time in my life, I understand why my father prayed over me every night. Why he prayed only for me and never for himself. I was more important to him than his own body, his own life. And now I'm praying over the ones more important than *my life*—Nate and, perhaps, our unborn child.

9

Keep the Faith

Lena

Two pink lines.

If the diagnosis of cancer had thrown my life into a tailspin, which it had, these two pink lines have centered it. I can feel it.

They bring my every plan, my every purpose, my remaining energy into laser-sharp focus. In three minutes, my priority shifts from enjoying my last days and bowing out gracefully to *survival*. Or at least until I'm twenty-eight weeks along. And I need to do it without any drugs.

By that point in the pregnancy, the baby will be able to live outside the womb and, hopefully, without mechanical life support. The longer I can make it, the better our child's health will be, but the minimum is twenty-eight weeks.

That gives my baby a fighting chance.

A steely resolve fortifies my constitution as I wrap the pregnancy test stick in tissue and stuff it into my purse. When I open the door to exit the dressing room, I step out as an entirely new person. Or at least that's how it feels.

Three minutes changed everything.

I'm no longer making decisions for my own health. I'm making decisions for our baby's health, too. I have something bigger than myself to consider.

Now if I can just make it the rest of the way…

Although my heart stampedes behind my breastbone, and my hands shake like I'm detoxing, I find that I'm smiling brightly at everyone I pass. Life is no longer about the *end*, but about the *beginning*. Not for me, but for my child. I'm not just Lena Grant, wife, nurse practitioner, daughter, friend, and terminal patient anymore. I'm Lena Grant, mother. I'm a different woman than the one who left the presidential suite a couple of hours ago.

I manage to keep my composure all the way up to our room. It's when I unlock the door and walk in to find Nate standing in front of the television in nothing but a towel that I can't hold onto it anymore. As soon as he turns toward me, his jewel-like eyes passing softly over my face, the corners of his mouth turning up in a smile, I lift my hands, bury my face in them, and burst into tears.

I want to blurt that I'm carrying his baby. I want to see his mouth drop open in shock and pleasure. I want to feel his strong arms wrap around me in soul-deep happiness. I want to hear his voice become thick with emotion.

But I can't have any of that.

Not yet.

Not being privy to the secret I carry, Nate rushes to my side. Being my hero and protector, he's ready to disembowel the person who caused his sick wife to cry. "What's wrong, baby?" he asks, his fingers curling tenderly around my upper arms. "What happened? Did someone hurt you?"

All I can do is shake my head. And sob.

Nate winds his arms around me, holding me tight against his bare chest. His lips brush my hair as he speaks. "Then what's wrong? You're scaring me."

"I-I-I just love you s-so much," I stammer brokenly. And that is one hundred percent true.

At my words, I feel the muscles in his chest relax. He's no longer ready to go to battle; he's ready to comfort.

"I know. Because I love *you* that much. Maybe even more. I hope you know that." His voice cracks on the last as he struggles to control his own emotion.

"I do. I do," I assure him. "I wanted so much for our life. If I could have done it any other way, I would have. I would've given you everything."

"You already have. All I ever wanted was you."

I weep onto my husband's skin as he holds me. I weep for what will never be. I weep for what I hope *can be.* I weep for the secret I carry. I weep for the tiny life I might not be able to sustain. But most of all, I weep for the future, the future I will never see and the family I will never get to share with my husband. He will have to do it all alone.

Without me.

Forever.

But still, he will have our baby. Hopefully. He'll finally have the best pieces of both of us, all wrapped up in a little person he can watch grow and thrive, play and laugh.

If I can just make it that far…

When I collect myself enough to pull away from Nate, I drag my stinging eyes to his face. I reach up to cup his cheek, now smooth from a recent shaving, and I wonder what his expression will be like when I give him the news. If I could carry the baby until we get back to the States, I will tell him right after I see the obstetrician and my oncologist. I'll tell him when I know there is a chance that this could work. Then I will watch his mouth drop open, his eyes mist over, and I will see a pleasure erupt from his face, like the warm spray of a deeply hidden geyser.

But until then, I have to keep it together. For Nate. I will protect him as long as I can.

"What are you thinking?" he asks when I say nothing, just holding his cheek in the palm of my hand.

"That I can't wait to see Vatican City with you," I answer with a watery smile.

"You sure you feel up to driving over there? We can go another day if—"

"No. I want to go today." I'm firm on this. I'm prepared to pull out every stop, exhaust every resource to make our baby a reality.

That includes trying to believe in a God that my father briefly introduced me to so many years ago.

****

Vatican City.

If the outside of St. Peter's Basilica could be called breathtaking, the inside would be called magnificent.

Spectacular.

Glorious.

Every ornate carving, every beautiful brushstroke, every carefully selected detail is so superb that I could spend the entire day simply enjoying the splendor of it. Even the light, the way it pours through strategically placed glass in the ceiling of the dome, seems to shine in exactly the right way, the sun itself a part of the artistry.

Believed to be the house of the tomb of Saint Peter, one of Jesus' twelve apostles, the Basilica has long been considered one of the holiest locations in all the city, if not all the world. And while I would never have considered myself to be a religious person (at least not after the death of my father), *even I* am not immune to the piety of the place. In fact, I'm moved to tears by it more than once as we tour the hallowed halls.

Earlier, when we arrived at the base of the wide, graceful sweep of stairs that led to the Basilica, Nate, standing silently at my side, reached down and laced his fingers with mine. It wasn't a casual gesture, not as any onlooker would suspect. It was a slow twining of his fingers, his life, his hopes, and his fears, with mine. He was comforting and drawing comfort, supporting and receiving support. We are two halves of one whole, in it together until the bitter end, *whenever* that might be and *whatever* it might bring.

The moment we entered the church, I felt an overwhelming sense of relief and rightness. I could practically feel the prayers of countless generations humming through the air as one long, peaceful vibration. I stood quietly at the entrance, letting the tranquility of it wash over me. I needed something from this place; I just didn't know what. Healing from my disease? Absolution from my deceit? A miracle for my child? Something I couldn't name and didn't understand?

Maybe.

Maybe one of those.

Maybe all of them.

Neither Nate nor I spoke as we made our way to see some of the most revered sights on the planet — Bernini's Chair of St. Peter with its crown of golden angels, the long nave with its intricately arched ceiling, the *Pieta* by Michelangelo with its heartbreaking depiction of Mary holding the body of her dead son, Jesus.

The last spoke to me like no other. Life, now more than ever, had taken on a sacredness that I've never known before. Maybe it's that my own existence is drawing to a close. Maybe it's that I will struggle in my last days to give life to another. Or maybe it's that I'm contemplating life as it relates to the loss of it. I can't be sure, but the sight of a woman holding her dead child was nearly my undoing.

Every square inch of the church is bathed in beauty and grace. From the floor, intricately designed and polished to a high shine, to the walls, all adorned with ornate columns and sculptures, the Basilica is grand. Even the ceilings are decorated with gilt stucco and richly framed windows that allow natural light to pour in and illuminate every divine detail to perfection. It has to be one of the most awe-inspiring places on Earth.

Hours later, as we come back through the nave, we reach the area at the south transept cordoned off for those seeking to make confession. Nate squeezes my fingers and whispers, "Let me find the bathrooms before we head over to the Sistine Chapel, k?" He kisses my temple and starts off in the opposite direction. "Be back in a few."

I nod, perfectly content to just…be. I turn a slow circle, once more taking in the glorious sights laid out before me. I glance at every sculpture, absorb every sound, and commit every detail of Bernini's Baldachin, arching protectively over the altar, to memory before I make my way toward the velvet ropes that protect those who come to confess from the foot traffic of those who come only to look.

Impulsively, I walk around to a divide in the barrier and head to the first row of seats. I slide through the aisle to a chair in the middle. None of the others are occupied, which I find odd since there had been many people sitting here when we'd passed through the first time, earlier. I glance quickly left and right, at the confessionals sprinkled along each wall, to make sure I'm not going to be evicted. I feel as though I'm wearing my non-Catholic status like a robe, brazenly, for all to see.

When I'm certain I'm not offending anyone (there seems to be no one around to offend), I relax and focus on the painting inset into the wall at the end of the transept. It depicts a grown Jesus holding a child in His arms. I feel a stab of envy. And fear. And something I can't readily identify.

Tears mist my eyes as I take in the scene.

A gentle voice from near my right shoulder startles me.

"Are you enjoying your tour?"

My head whips around, and I see an older man, a *priest* standing beside me, two chairs down. He is dressed in the traditional holy vestments, black soutane with thirty-three buttons down the front. Upon his head is a shock of short, graying hair. His eyes are a brilliant blue, and his hands are clasped in front of him as though he has all the time in the world.

And he is taking a minute of it to speak to *me*.

I nod, recovering quickly. "Oh yes! Very much. It's an incredible place."

The priest's serene smile widens, and his head bobs once. "Very good." His voice is soft and lightly accented, and he has a placid quality that surrounds him like a calming cloud. I feel immediately at ease and wonder if all men of the cloth have such a soothing presence about them. "Are you here to give confession?" He raises a hand to indicate one of the many free-standing confessionals dotting the wall to my left.

"Oh, no. I'm not Catholic."

Blue eyes steadily search my face. The way he watches me would've made me squirm had it been anyone else, but today, with this man, I sit perfectly still and hold his gaze.

For some reason, I don't feel guilty or out of place. I don't feel ashamed or condemned. I don't feel wrong or unworthy. Somehow, I just feel...comforted by the way it seems he can see right through me, see right *into me* and not judge me for what I'm hiding.

"You might not be Catholic, but you are in need just the same."

It's an observation not a question. A statement of fact. Like he knows.

Like *he knows.*

"How—" I was going to ask *how* he knew, but I don't. I don't *need to.* Something deep within me *feels* the answer.

Something within me *knows.*

"Come. Let us seek the privacy of the confessional," he says, once more indicating the wooden booths behind us.

"Can we *do that* since I'm not a Catholic?"

"You don't have to be Catholic to confess your sins; you only have to be a sinner, as we all are. Or troubled and in need of guidance, as we all can be from time to time."

I don't question what makes me rise from my seat and turn to walk through the row toward the first confessional. I merely give in to the overwhelming need within me, the need to share my burden with another person.

Maybe there really *is* a God.

And maybe He really *does* listen to the soul.

I stop in front of the box. Despite its friendly label that declares it appropriate for those who spoke English, I'm still intimidated. The large wooden structure is stained a rich mahogany and, as with every other centimeter of the church, no detail has been spared. It's beautiful in an artistic as well as in a meaningful way.

I turn to ask the priest what I'm supposed to do next, but he's gone. I look around, wondering if I missed him going in another direction, but within a minute, I hear a muffled voice from somewhere inside the booth bid me to, "Come. Kneel."

I approach the opening. The interior is dark and smells of timber and varnish mingled with a subtle tang I can't quite describe. I imagine it is decades of misery and forgiveness carried on hot breath and held carefully within the grain of the wood. They linger here, like remembered promises.

After my eyes adjust, I can see where I'm supposed to kneel and where my elbows are supposed to go, placing me in the pose of someone praying. Once I'm in position, I clasp my hands and drop my forehead onto my interlocked fingers. "What do I do?" I murmur.

"Tell me what's on your heart," the priest's disembodied voice answers.

"Do I tell you that I've sinned?"

"Have you?"

"I-I don't know."

"We have all sinned. We do so daily. That's why confession is so important. We need forgiveness. We need it from our God, and we need it *for* ourselves."

To this, I say nothing. I don't know what *to* say.

But I feel.

I feel his words, and the truth of them, in a place I can't identify.

When I fall silent, the priest guides me further into the ritual, his tone comforting and conversational. "What brings you here? To Rome?"

I clear my throat and slowly begin to tell him my story, carefully opening that closet door so that the skis won't fall out.

"My husband brought me to Europe for three months. Sort of a once-in-a-lifetime trip."

"And what about this trip has you so troubled?" he asks, perceptive in ways I don't understand.

"We...I..." I consider how much I should tell this stranger, uncertain whether there is such a thing as "too much" in confession. But before I've done more than ponder my predicament, the closet door bursts open, and the skis—and every other hidden thing— come tumbling out in a rush of words that fall at his feet.

"Two months ago, I was diagnosed with stage four stomach cancer. You see, my husband and I had been trying to get pregnant for years. It was a very stressful time each month, waiting to see if it worked, mourning it for days when it didn't. I was anxious...*always anxious* it seemed, and my stomach was upset a lot. But any time I felt nauseous or bloated, I got excited, thinking it was pregnancy. I didn't really *look* for any other reason for the symptoms. I just always *wanted* it to be pregnancy, I guess. But I'm a nurse practitioner. Eventually, I climbed out of my hopeful shell long enough to notice that something was wrong. Very wrong."

My chin trembles, and I swallow hard so that my voice remains strong, so that it won't shake with the tears that have pooled in my eyes. I haven't cried about my cancer since the day I was told that it was stage four. It seemed pointless to spend the last part of my life crying over milk that had long since been spilled.

"By the time I was diagnosed, it had already spread to my liver and two of my lymph nodes. Being a nurse, I knew what that meant. Besides that, I've seen it before. With my father."

The priest says nothing. He merely gives me time and space and quiet. It is in that quiet that I reach for and give this holy man all that is in my heart.

"My dad died with stage four *esophageal* cancer. It's very similar to my condition, and it had spread to his liver and lymph system, too. I was a little girl at the time, so I didn't know much. And they hid things from me. But still, I knew. I could see that he was sick. Very sick. I could see what he was going through. That's how I know what's coming for me. I know it all too well."

My pause is short. Everything is rushing to the surface now, a tide beyond my control.

"My older sister had cancer, too. Childhood leukemia. So, you see, I've seen more than my fair share of what this disease can do. What it *will* do. I've watched it wreck families too many times, and I'm not going to let it wreck mine. That's why I refused treatment."

The priest is quiet, contemplative.

"And what did your husband have to say about that?"

I shrug. "Nate loves me. He would never ask me to do something I didn't want to do. Besides, he was part of the reason I made that choice. I watched cancer eat away at my father and my sister. I watched them fight it like there was hope and then lose the battle anyway. My mother watched it, too. Only she never recovered. *She* died in their battle, too. And I don't want that to happen to Nate."

"Your mother died as well?" he asks.

"No, not technically, but she might as well have. She more or less checked out of life after Dad died. She checked out of life, out of motherhood, out of participation in being *a human*. Seeing them die that way...it broke her. She just gave up. It didn't even matter to her that she had another child to raise. She stopped caring and trying, or even *pretending* to care or try. She just...stopped."

Before the priest can say anything, I continue, my lips curving into a darkly bitter smile.

"But I was lucky, I guess. Lucky that I was fourteen when he died. I was mostly grown and able to take care of myself, so when Mom quit doing it..." I shrug, even though the priest can't see it. "I did it for myself. For *both of us*, most of the time. I guess in some ways, *I* ended up raising *her* rather than the other way around. I wasn't able to grieve. I lost my dad, but Momma lost her soul. And I had no choice but to take up the slack. I held my mother while she cried. For hours sometimes, way up into the night. I gave her a bath when she wouldn't get out of bed to shower and the whole house smelled like sweaty feet. I nursed her as well as a grieving girl could nurse her mother and still try to keep her own life from falling apart. That's one thing I can sort of be thankful for, I suppose. Taking care of Momma is when I realized I had a pretty good knack for it—nursing. That awful time gave me a dream, a dream that I held onto when there was nothing else. I focused on going to college even when I had to learn to forge my mother's name so I could cash the Medicaid checks and buy necessities. I focused on getting out when I walked down to the corner market once a week to buy us food. I focused on college so I could get through high school, while I learned to cook and clean, while I did my homework and then did the laundry. College is why I didn't miss a single day of school. No matter how tired I was, I didn't miss a day. And I still took care of my mother, right up until I got the letter of acceptance to nursing school. Only then did *I* stop. That was the day I called Social Services and had them come to do an evaluation of her."

I link and unlink my fingers, fidgeting in the way I used to when I was a little girl. I haven't done it in years. But then again, I haven't rehashed the story about my mother in years either. The guilt over what I did is still fresh, as fresh as it was the day I made the call. And after all this time, the result of my actions still burns in my gut like a lifetime of swallowing battery acid.

"I was so bitter. I didn't want harm to come to her; I just wanted someone else to take care of her," I explain, the slow trickle of tears down my cheeks starting anew. It has been so long since I've cried over Momma, but I never stopped missing her, missing what could have been. What *should have been,* but never was. I felt grief, grief for the *other* parent I lost. I didn't lose her physically, but I lost her emotionally.

Sniffing, I continue.

"After a series of medical and psych evaluations, she was diagnosed with schizoaffective disorder and was sent to live in a mental institution. Until we came to Europe, I'd been to see her once a month *every month* since that day. I do it because she's my mother and I feel obligated, but some part of me..." I admit, my voice breaking, "...some part of me needs her to be my mother. A mother who cares. I need her to be Momma. I just *need her.*"

My emotions swirl through me, angrily whipping at my heart. My throat is thickening with my increasing desperation.

"I...I need to tell her that I'm dying, and that I'm pregnant. I need to tell her that I'm dying and I'm pregnant, and that I might not be able to *stay* pregnant *because* I'm dying. I need to tell her that. And then, I need for her to tell me what to do, because I just don't know anymore. I need to know how to make it through this, how to have *hope*. Because I've forgotten. I don't know *how* to hope anymore."

I sob quietly, covering my mouth with both of my hands and squeezing my eyes shut as tightly as I can, as if in doing so, I might be able to stop the pain, the hopelessness. After half a minute or so, when my throat has threatened to close up around my air, I take a deep breath and wipe my face. I wipe it *hard*, swiping at my skin as though I might scrub away the weakness I feel, too. I won't ever have my momma back, not the way I want, the way I need. The way I should. And I need to move past that harsh, cold fact. "But none of that will happen because she's never been my mother in the ways that count. That's why I need *someone else* to tell me it'll all be okay. I *need* that. Desperately. Can you tell me that? Can you *please* tell me it'll all be okay?" I plead. "Please help me find hope."

At that, I bow my head and let the tears run again, in earnest this time, without trying to staunch the flow. Maybe letting them out will exorcise some of my bitterness and anger and desolation. Maybe they'll cleanse what ails me. Or at least some of it.

I've never been so honest with a stranger. Hell, I don't think I've been this honest with *anyone* about my reasons for not taking treatment, about my fear and my lack of hope. I'm not even sure I've been able to admit it to myself. I wanted to be strong, even when I felt scared and weak and alone. But I'm not sure I can be strong *enough*.

Not for this.

When I manage to collect myself somewhat, I sniffle again and tilt my head back, garnering the last of my strength and courage to finish this confession.

I've confessed to the priest. I've confessed to myself. I've confessed through a throat that's as raw and scratchy as my battered and bleeding heart.

But I did it.

I did it.

"I think I declined treatment because I was afraid. I was afraid of what it would do to me to hope. I was afraid of what it would do to my husband. I didn't want to put him through that hell for nothing, so I didn't. I opted for no treatment so that we could live out my last days together, doing things we've always wanted to do. And for the first time in years, I never once considered a baby. In all this time, I haven't been able to get pregnant, I just didn't even think..." I pause, anger suddenly welling inside me. It bubbles up and bubbles over, pouring through me like a squall, escalating. Escalating.

I've always known Fate is a cruel bitch, but I wouldn't have guessed her capable of something like this.

Something so...punishing.

Turning my head, I stare into the blackness from whence the priest's voice had come before I began my breakdown. I pin his invisible presence with furious eyes.

Anger rolls and tumbles.

"Why is this happening now? *Why now* when there is no hope for me? *Why now* when I need hope more than ever? What am I supposed to do? How am I supposed to get through this? How can I tell my husband that I'm carrying a baby that might die before I do? How can I tell him that I might make his loss *even greater*? How can I tell him that his dream finally came true and I might be the one to steal that away from him? And there's nothing I can do about it. There's no way I can stop it. How am I supposed to deal with that? *What am I supposed to do*?" I wail in desperation.

Rage courses through me, a wildfire of crackling emotion. But like a wildfire succumbs to a heavy rain, my ire quickly succumbs to my anguish, the embers extinguished by tears that pour in watery rivulets down my cheeks.

I'm crying again. It seems I'm unable to stop the flood once I let it flow. My confession scraped off a scab, opened both old wounds and new, exposing my injuries to the elements. Leaving me more vulnerable than ever.

And so I cry.

Until I can't cry anymore, I cry.

And the priest lets me, saying nothing for what seems like hours. He holds his words for the moment when my well finally dries up and I can speak again. I'm more broken than I've ever been before.

Broken and dejected.

"How could God do this to me? To *us*? How can I have hope in a God who is capable of this? He's a *monster!*"

There's a long pause before I hear his voice, bathed in kindness and encouragement. "My child," he begins, "our God works in mysterious ways. It is He who has brought you the gift of this baby, and it is He who will see you through to the resolution, whatever that may be. You must only believe in that, believe in *Him*."

"But how can I? He's taken so much from me already. How can I believe in a God like that? Why should I believe in a God I have nothing in common with?"

"Because you do have much in common with Him. Much more than you think. Our God is a God of sacrifice. It is written throughout the ages, in His Word, in our lives. He knows your suffering. He knows what it is to love so deeply that He would give up His own life for that of His children. In fact, that is precisely what He did. He came to humanity in the flesh of a man, His son Jesus, and He was crucified so that we might have life. He knows the sacrifice of pain and death. He knows what it is like to be afraid and to feel alone. You must never forget that He has been where you are, where all of man has been. He knows your torment like no one else. But you must also believe that He loves you like no one else, as well. He would never allow tragedy without purpose, never give a gift without a plan. He will guide you in it if you but ask Him. He waits for you to bring this to Him. Give Him your sickness. Give Him your child. Give Him your choices, and He will make your way straight."

I feel as though the priest is spinning me in circles, talking to me in a secret code that I have no way of deciphering. I don't know what to say or what to ask, so I continue to kneel on knees that have long since gone numb, and I wait.

His next words are what bring it all together, what hit me right in the center of my chest.

"Take *hope* from here, my child. You lost it long ago, but God has brought you to this place to recover it. Maybe this is what He has been trying to give to you all along—hope. *His* hope. The hope that gives strength where there is only weakness. The hope that gives peace where there is only fear. The hope that offers a miracle where there is only despair. Perfect hope."

What he's suggesting sounds like surrender. He wants me to surrender control and worry and fear to God. Like I didn't surrender when my sister died. And when my father died. And when my mother all but left me. And when I was diagnosed with cancer. He's suggesting that I surrender this time. That I give up control and let someone else take over.

But how am I to do that?

"How do I get it? How do I feel hope again?"

"You accept it. Like you accept Him. It is that simple."

That simple.

And that difficult.

My phone chirps from inside my cross-body bag, causing me to jump. It reminds me that I'm not in

Vatican City alone. I'm here with my husband, and Nate will probably be frantic looking for me.

I have no idea how long I've been in the confessional. It feels like an eternity, but also like the blink of an eye.

A lifetime and a heartbeat.

Whichever it is, I feel sure Nate is worried.

I scramble to get to my phone. "I'm so sorry, Father, but I'm sure that's my husband. He won't know I'm in here. I need to go."

"I understand," he says softly. In my mind, I can almost see him nodding graciously, always kind. "May God bless you and guide your way, and may you find the hope that you are searching for."

"Thank you," I say, pushing out of the little cubicle inside which I've been kneeling. I pause, peering into the darkness, wishing I could see his piercing blue eyes, wishing I could see what's in them. "Thank you so much."

"Bless you, my child," are his only words before I feel his presence disappear.

10

Blaze of Glory

Lena

I float on a strange calm as I walk away from the confessional. I feel as though I sliced open my heart for that priest, as though I bled out on the floor for him and left many of my doubts and fears lying in the pool of my agony. I feel it the moment I exit the tiny room.

And evidently Nate notices it, too.

When I look up, he's standing at the edge of the transept, very close to where he left me, his fathomless eyes fixed on me as I approach.

"I'm sorry I didn't text you. I really...I wasn't planning on that," I assure him, hiking a thumb over my shoulder to indicate the time I spent in the sacred chamber.

M. LEIGHTON

"Yeah, I was a little surprised to see you in there."

"You saw me?"

"Well, when I couldn't find you and I didn't get a response to my text right away, I started looking. I recognized your shoes sticking out."

I glance down at my brightly colored Tieks and then smile back up at my husband. "I guess there's no losing me in these."

Nate grins. "No."

"Did you... Could you *hear* anything?"

He shakes his head once and repeats, "No."

"Oh. Okay." I try to hide my relief. I wouldn't want Nate to be burdened by my confession. And he would be. I know him.

"So...confession?"

I shrug. "Maybe it really is good for the soul."

"It sure looks like it. You seem...lighter."

I snort. "Did I lose weight in there, too? I should've tried it sooner."

"You know what I mean."

I search my husband's earnest green eyes and nod. "Yeah, I know what you mean. I *feel* lighter, too. Like maybe it'll all be okay."

Nate reaches for my fingers and brings them to his mouth. He holds them there for several long seconds, his lips pressed to my knuckles as he stares over them and into my eyes. I can't be sure what I see in his eyes, but I know what I feel in his gesture—relief. Maybe Nate needed someone to tell *him* that it's going to be okay, too.

I step closer to him, stretching up to cup his strong jaw in the palm of my other hand. "It will you know."

"It will what?"

"It'll all be okay."

He nods and continues watching me as though he's trying his hardest to believe me. Or maybe to find belief *in me.*

I inhale deeply and stand tall and certain before him, hoping that just this once *I* can be strong *for him.* He has no one to help him carry the load of my illness. Maybe this time *I* can be the comfort *he* needs.

"None of us are going to live forever, so we should live while we're alive, right? That's why we need to make the very most of this trip. Do it up big. Blaze of glory and all that."

My smile is intended to be carefree and full of life and fun, but it isn't enough to ease Nate's breaking heart. That much I can see.

"Blaze of glory," he whispers, kissing my knuckles again quickly before releasing them to pull me into his arms.

With his lips pressed to my temple, Nate holds me close. For a long time, he sways gently back and forth, taking as well as receiving comfort. I wonder if he's trying not to cry, but I'm not going to look and find out. Instead, I give him his privacy and don't move until he's ready.

When he finally withdraws from me, his eyes are dry and his smile is back in place. "So, where is this blaze of glory taking us next. Dinner?"

"Sounds good to me."

Nate slings his arm around my neck, keeping me close at his side as we walk away. I spare a quick glance over his shoulder to see if I catch a glimpse of the stranger priest, but the cordoned off area is once again empty.

****

It's well after midnight, Rome time, when I wake. The room is quiet, and Nate is snoring softly at my side. My first thought is of the life growing within me.

Of course, my drowsiness quickly fades.

I lie in bed for just over an hour, imagining what the future may or may not hold, before I become restless. Rather than risk waking Nate with my tossing and turning, I gently sit up and pull my legs from beneath the covers, sliding silently from the mattress until my feet hit the floor.

Grabbing my robe from the chair as I pass, I push my arms into the sleeves and wander through to the adjoining room. It's dark but for the silvery light filtering through the cracks in the draperies. I'm momentarily distracted by the geometric designs it makes on the floor.

Rome is a magical place. Even the moonlight seems more beautiful here.

I walk to the window and open the curtains. The majestic view of the Trinità dei Monti washes over me like a warm tide, as though the mere sight of it carries with it all the divinity of the church itself. Once more, I feel a sense of providence. This place, this time, these circumstances—they are all coming together precisely as they are supposed to. It's like a celestial orchestration that's playing out to a tune composed of moments and events and decisions.

And right now, it sounds wonderfully harmonious.

For me, someone accustomed to being in control of her life, it's a peculiar relief to relinquish command and let the remainder of my existence unfold as it is meant to. The only detail I need to worry about is surviving until my child can be born. The rest I can live with.

For however long I have left.

I reach down and place my hand over my stomach. It's amazing to me that something so impactful hasn't yet become discernible to the human eye or the human sense of touch. The tiny seed sprouting within me is so incredibly powerful that it has changed everything. And yet, it's still just a tiny seed.

So small yet so capable, capable of the greatest joy or the cruelest devastation.

Impulsively, I walk to my purse and remove my phone. I tiptoe across the floor and close the bedroom door, ensuring that I still hear Nate's snore before I walk away.

Crossing back to the window, I turn on my phone's camera, flick it to video, and switch the perspective until my face pops up on the screen. I position it in just such a way that the breathtaking towers at my back can be seen in the shot, and then I hit record.

There's a long pause before I start talking. For an instant. I wonder if I should've taken some time to think of what I'd like to say, but rather than stopping, I simply speak from the heart, smiling directly into the camera.

"Hello, my beautiful child. I just found out about you today. I don't know if I'll ever get to see you to tell you this in person, but I hope *you* get to see *this*. I want you to know that you made me so happy today. You changed *everything*. For the better. Already. I don't even know if you'll be a boy or a girl, but I feel complete today.

"I've wanted you for all of my life. All of it! I've dreamed of feeling you kick for the first time. I've dreamed of holding you in my arms for the first time. I've dreamed of what your face might look like—your smile, your hands, your little feet. You'll be perfect, I know. I know in my heart that you'll be the most perfect thing in the world. The best thing I've ever done. And I'll die happy if I can see you just *one time* before I go." I sniff, trying to hold back the tears that sting my eyes. "I love you. Today. Tomorrow. Always."

I hold my wavering smile for a few seconds and then hit the red button to stop the recording. Covering my mouth, I sink to my knees, cupping my belly with my free hand, and I pray.

For all I'm worth, I pray.

****

Nate

Waking to an empty bed is hard. When I roll over, the first thing I do is look for my wife, only she isn't there. The covers have been thrown back, and the sheets are rumpled yet cold. She hasn't been in bed for quite some time.

My first thought is that she's sick again, so I run to the bathroom. The door is open, and the interior is dark.

Empty.

At this point, I should be relieved not to have found her crouched in front of the toilet, heaving what's left inside her stomach. But I'm not.

Instead, I feel panic.

For an instant, my worst fear plays out in my mind.

What if something has happened and she's dead?

What if she suffered some rare complication and she woke up in the middle of the night, in distress, and died before I could help her?

What if she'd tried to wake me and couldn't?

What if she got out of bed and fell to the floor then passed away, all alone?

Jesus God!

My pulse throbs like a prized stallion at the track as I race to the adjoining room in search of my Lena.

Relief, bone-melting relief floods me when I spot her. My frantic gaze sweeps by the couch and stops. I see the familiar form of my wife, curled on her side, fast asleep.

I listen to the soft swish of her breathing and count to ten, calming my erratic heart rate. I remind myself that there is no reason to think that I'll one day wake to find her dead, unexpectedly. Cancer is, if anything, somewhat predictable when it comes to the end. At least it should be in a case like Lena's. I've read the reports. I've heard the stories. I know it's likely going to be slow and agonizing, and that it will end in a coma before she actually slips away.

But still…the thought of finding her already gone…of losing her sooner rather than later…

I squeeze my eyes shut, pushing the tightness in my chest and the worry in my head to the back of my consciousness. Ruthlessly, I cram those godforsaken skis back into the closet.

I can't let my emotions ruin what time we have left. I *won't* do that. Not to Lena. She deserves the very best of me—the strongest, the surest, the most confident— right up until she draws her last breath, and I'm damn sure going to give that to her. I'll put on a brave face, a happy face, *for her.* I'll never let her know that nearly every one of my thoughts are centered on losing her, on the gaping emptiness that will haunt me for the rest of my days.

I can't let her know that.

I can't let her know that I already know the panic that will move in to occupy my stomach. I can't let her know that I already know the overwhelming heartbreak I'll feel. I can't let her know that I already know that, one day, I'll die still feeling devastated and lost and alone.

Only half alive without her.

Despite having found her, safe and breathing and still with me, I can't shake the feeling of fear and dread that looms over me. It's like a shadow cast over my life, over every day of my existence, only it doesn't go away when the sun comes out.

It lingers.

Always lingers.

Glancing back over my shoulder, I look at the bed. It mocks me. Haunts me. Like the emptiness on the right side is a living thing, breathing cold air down the back of my neck. A predator hunting me, gaining speed.

Coming for me.

Coming to *take from me*.

A feeling of foreboding creeps over me, reminding me that there will soon come a day when that side of the bed will be empty forever. I have no idea how I'm going to face that I can hardly stand the thought of it now, much less the reality of it then.

Walking quietly over to where Lena sleeps, I squat down beside her, staring at the beautiful face, all dreamy and tranquil in repose. I memorize the arch of her brows, the scoop of her nose, the way her long eyelashes make crescents on the high blades of her cheekbones. I etch into my brain the texture of her skin, the smooth line of her jaw, and the shape of her mouth.

Those lips…

If I close my eyes, I can feel how they soften when I kiss them, I can practically *see* how they spread when she smiles.

I will never forget that. Forget her.

Any small detail.

My gaze moves down the graceful shoulders and the gently moving chest to the stomach she holds with one hand, even while she sleeps.   As much as I wish I could, I know I'll never be able to forget this either— her disease, her pain. What cancer is doing to the woman I love.

I bow my head, and my tears fall in absolute silence.

11

Gotta Have a Reason

Nate

Another six weeks later and I'm pushing open the door that leads from the garage into the kitchen and stepping back so that Lena can go in first. We are home.

I notice the way she pauses on the threshold and inhales deeply, her shoulders lifting and then dropping slowly as she savors the scent. Europe was wonderful, but I know she's glad to be back at our house, our sanctuary.

There's no place like home. *Our home.*

She turns and gives me a grin. "Home sweet home, baby." She stretches up on her tiptoes and kisses me, a quick peck of the lips. I'll miss that, more than she will ever know. The casual kisses, the second-nature touches, the intimate glances—I'll miss them all.

I'll miss *her*. Like I'd miss air if it was taken from me.

I swallow and muster a crooked smile for her. Always for her.

"Home is wherever *you* are, but I have to admit that I missed this place. The coffee isn't as good here, but..."

Lena laughs and elbows me in the ribs before she moves on through the door. "Take that back or I won't be making you *any* coffee, good *or* bad."

"I take it back," I supply amicably.

I stand, still technically in the garage, and watch my wife. Her gait is a little less energetic today.

Grief clutches my heart as I wait for her to move slowly into the living room. She flops down onto the couch and exhales loudly, letting her arms fall to the side and her head drop back.

She'd been so full of life on almost every one of our days in Europe, it's hard to see this. For me, the trip will always be bittersweet in more ways than I'd originally suspected. Having my old Lena back—the carefree, fun-loving, energetic one I met nineteen years ago—will make losing her, losing the woman I've always known her to be, that much harder. It's like watching her die twice. Once slowly, day by day, and the other...

I turn from the sight, my chest tight with barely controlled emotion. "I'll get the luggage," I mutter, hurrying back to the car. I don't know how I'm going to make it through this next part. I just know that I will.

For Lena, I will.

Always for Lena.

I would do anything for her.

****

Lena

Since I'm so tired, Nate offers to go to the grocery store to pick up some food and necessities. I'm more than happy to let him. Not only am I truly exhausted, but I also have an important phone call to make, and he can't be around when I do.

The instant Nate's car turns out of the driveway, I race to my phone and pull up the contact information for my gynecologist, who is also an obstetrician. I pray Dr. Stephens will be able to work me in at some point over the next couple of days. I already have an appointment with my oncologist next week, and I thought it would be a good idea to get input from both specialists as soon as possible. They'll have to work together, I'm sure. This will be a delicate dance if it can be pulled off. I need to have them both on board.

But I'm skeptical. Scheduling this close to Christmas will be tight, and seeing me on short notice might be an issue. It *is* already December twenty-first after all.

Although I hate to do it (and very rarely do), I pull the "I'm a nurse practitioner, and I need to speak with the doctor as soon as possible" card, and it works. I'm put on hold for three minutes, and the next person to come on the line is Dr. Stephens.

Using vague terms like "condition" and "illness" in explaining my situation to Dr. Stephens, who is familiar with our struggles to get pregnant, she's more than willing to work me in on December twenty-third. She might regret having done that when I tell her the details of what I'm looking at.

When I hang up the phone, I expel a breath it feels like I've been holding for weeks. Soon my questions will be answered, my mind will be eased, and I will have a certain path forward. Then I can get on with living the last days of my life. And hopefully giving life to another in the process.

Giving my life for another.

Giving my death *meaning*.

****

Two days later, I'm sitting in the waiting room at the obstetrician's office, fiddling with the strap of my purse. I can hardly sit still. I had to tell something far too close to a fib to Nate in order to get this time to myself. He isn't going to sit idly by and let me visit doctors without him anymore, so I had to work around him.

Not that I can blame him. I'm mature enough to admit that I should never have excluded him from the appointment where I got my official diagnosis. Nate needed to be a part of that, and I'd denied him, even though unintentionally. In retrospect, I can see the symptoms of denial written all over my decisions back then. I didn't *really* think I'd get bad news.

Certainly not *the worst* news.

My head snaps up when I hear my name being called. I stand, a bit unsteadily at first, take a deep breath, and plaster on a smile for the person who's taking me back.

"How have you been, Lena?"

Sherry is Dr. Stephens's primary nurse, and she's had trouble getting pregnant herself. We have a lot in common and have gotten along well from our very first meeting.

Sherry holds out a hand and indicates for me to step up onto the scale. I do so obediently. I haven't been back to see them since my diagnosis, so Sherry has no idea what's going on in my life.

She'll undoubtedly hear soon enough.

"I've had better days," I reply vaguely, conscious of the people surrounding us.

Sherry writes down my weight, but makes no comment of the three pounds I've unintentionally lost. I'm surprised by it, actually, because I thought I'd eaten well in Europe. I made a point to feed my body (and, therefore, my baby) well. Very well. Unfortunately, I can't control the fact that I feel full quicker. That's a result of the cancer, and yet another complication to pregnancy.

Maybe this whole thing is a pipe dream.

But just the idea that I might not be able to carry this child is a crushing blow to me. To my newfound hope.

My hand trembles when I take the urine specimen cup that Sherry holds out to me.

"Give me a specimen and leave it in the window, then I'll meet you in room number two."

I nod and turn into the bathroom, closing and locking the door behind me. I sit on the edge of the chair in the corner and drop my head down between my knees, letting the blood rush to my brain in hopes of fending off this sudden dizziness that I feel. Maybe I should've eaten more before I came this morning.

When I feel moderately better, I set about giving Sherry the specimen she'll need to confirm the pregnancy for their records. It's just a formality for the practice. *I* have no doubts about it at this point. I've missed two periods altogether, and my abdomen has begun to swell right above my pubic bone. That plus a whole slew of other symptoms assures me that I am, in fact, pregnant.

I cup my belly through my slacks and smile, letting the knowledge, the presence of the tiny life growing inside me warm me all the way down to my soul. I can't let fear of the unknown or doubt or probability get me down. I'm going to fight for the miracle, for this baby, even more than I'll fight for *my own* life. I just need to know how best I can go about doing that.

I slide the cup into the window built into the wall, wash my hands, and go to wait in room number two. When Dr. Stephens walks in, she's all smiles. I can't help but feel a bit sorry for her. As a nurse practitioner, I know how disheartening it is to find out that a patient you've come to know and like is suffering. Or, worse, dying. I know Dr. Stephens would be heartbroken for me when she finds out.

"Look who finally got pregnant," she says, setting aside her tablet and walking to the chair to hug me where I sit. "I'm so happy for you."

I bite back tears and a trembling lip. Yet when Dr. Stephens leans away, she still knows something is wrong.

"What is it, Lena?"

I gulp at the rock in my throat and make myself meet the doctor's eyes. "I was diagnosed with stage IV stomach cancer in August."

"Oh God," Dr. Stephens whispers, closing her eyes and dropping her head. There's a long, meaningful pause before she asks, "How long?"

"Ten months. Maybe a year. That's without treatment, of course, which I declined. I guess it's a good thing I did, or I wouldn't be here right now." I don't have to try to inject positivity into my tone. Despite the rest of the tragedy in my life, in the situation, I'm happy. So very happy about the baby.

At that, Dr. Stephens raises her head and pins me with her frown. "You-you're not going to try to carry this baby, are you?"

I inhale, straightening my spine. I expected one of two reactions. I was hoping for the other, but I understand this one more, from a medical standpoint.

"I am." When the doctor says nothing, my shoulders slump. "This is all I've wanted for as long as I can remember. This is a blessing in so many ways. And now I won't worry so much about Nate when I'm gone. He won't be alone. He won't give up. And that's a good thing, right? Please tell me this is a good thing."

I'm not asking for support. I'm asking for the odds to be in my favor, even in such a bad situation, because I *need* them to be. Badly. And I know Dr. Stephens knows that.

The obstetrician stares at me for long, tense seconds before the edges of her lips bend upward into a small smile. "It can be, I suppose, but Lena, you know the risks. I mean, having a child at forty comes with its own set of challenges, but you're sick. Very sick. And you're only going to get sicker."

"I know, but I just have to make it to twenty-eight weeks, right? Based on my last period, that's probably only nineteen or twenty more weeks from now. I just need to stay healthy enough to carry this baby until then and then he or she will have a real chance of survival, right? Right?" I ask again when my physician says nothing.

Finally, she relents with a resigned sigh. "Yes, that would be the minimum, of course. Provided that the rest of the pregnancy goes smoothly. But Lena, God!" she exclaims, rubbing the space between her eyebrows with two fingers. "This is going to be so tricky, and you are making a choice now that you can't make again later. If you decide right this minute that you want to have surgery and take treatment, you could still have a chance *to live*. But you have to do it *now*. You can't put it off, not for this long. So if you choose to carry this baby, you're sentencing yourself to a certain death."

I hold Dr. Stephens's concerned gray eyes. I hold them, and I let her see where my priorities lie. "I know. But this is what I want. More than anything. This baby…it makes my life *worth* something. He or she will do beautiful things in the world. A child will be my contribution to humanity. And to Nate. He needs this. He will need it *more* when I'm gone."

"So, you're firm? You've already made up your mind, it seems."

I nod. "Yes. I have. Unless I physically can't carry the baby, unless I lose it naturally," I croak, stumbling over words that feel like doom on my tongue, "then I will deliver this child, healthy and whole, before I die. I'm determined."

Dr. Stephens nods once and stands. "Then let's go get you on the ultrasound, see how far along you are."

****

Two hours later, I leave the obstetrician's office with a page full of lab orders I'm to confer with my oncologist about and an ultrasound. An ultrasound that confirms what I already knew, and confirms a gestational age I was already pretty confident of.

I slide the glossy square picture into my coat pocket after taking one last look. My hand rests over it protectively, my fingers stroking the cool, slick paper as though I'm actually touching some part of the baby growing inside me.

I finally have proof, proof of the existence of a dream.

I have a picture of my nine-week-old baby.

He or she looks to the world like a tiny baby-shaped kidney bean, but to me it's the shape of a miracle. Everything in my life is different now, has been since I took that pregnancy test in Rome, and will be for as long as *my life* will last. And in another thirty or forty minutes, my husband's life will be changed as well. Forever changed, for as long as he lives, which I hope will be a good, long time.

I walked into that office as a woman with a little newly-recovered hope. I walked out of that office as a woman with a lifetime of hope and a *reason*. A reason to live and fight and be strong and push through.

And I will do exactly that.

I will take one more chance on a God who has let me down before, and if He comes through for me this time, I'll gladly trust that my husband and our child will be okay in His divine hands.

Unlocking the door and sliding behind the wheel of my car, I sit for a moment, thinking about Dr. Stephens's last words.

"Talk to Dr. Taffer before you make up your mind, Lena. Promise me you'll at least pretend to listen to what she has to say."

I smiled and nodded, but Dr. Stephens knew there's nothing Dr. Taffer, my oncologist, will be able to say to change my mind. It's made up.

Once more, I take out the shiny black and white picture, the image of a future I thought had been stripped away from me, and I run my fingertips over the beginnings of a teeny profile. "I won't give up on you," I whisper, pressing my lips to the photo before stowing it away in my pocket again and heading home.

The garage door rising triggers an onslaught of emotion. Knowing what's coming, my chest tightens and my throat constricts. The conversation of a lifetime only moments away.

It will be as good as the conversation about my diagnosis was *bad*.

I'm excited.

I'm nervous.

And some part of me is a bit afraid of Nate's reaction.

Will he be upset with me for keeping this from him? Will he ever be able to understand my reasons for doing so? Will he welcome the baby as I have? Will he laugh, will he cry, will he stare numbly at me?

I have no idea.

So often over the last six weeks, I've imagined what he will do, what he will say, how he will react. I've pictured him ecstatic, walking with me through every day of my pregnancy, and then holding our child in his arms on the day of delivery.

Maybe that was all wishful thinking, but knowing Nate like I do, I think that's how it will be.

But still, I won't be able to rest easy—I *haven't been* able to rest easy—until I know. Until *he* knows.

Now that the time is at hand, I'm nearly sick with anticipation. I go straight into the house, search him out in his office, take him by the hand, and lead him to our bedroom.

Of course, Nate's smiling when I turn to face him, but not for the reason I was thinking he'd be smiling. *This* is the smile that says he's ready for sex. *This* is a lazy, sensual curl of his lips that's reflected in the smoke filling his eyes. *This* says he has no idea what's coming.

"Whatever this is about, you know I'm always your willing sex slave. Do your worst!" he teases, running his hands around my waist.

I laugh nervously, coiling my fingers around his muscular forearms. "Nate," I begin. I go no further when he goes completely still. His smile fades, and his features cloud with concern. He stills instantly, whether from my action or my tone.

"What is it?" His voice drips with trepidation. "What's wrong?"

I cast a jittery grin up at him, one meant to be reassuring. "Nothing. Just...just come and sit with me."

I back away from him, running my hand down his arm to his fingers, which I braid with my own. Tugging, I lead him to the settee that rests in front of the fireplace in our bedroom. I sit and urge him to do the same. He does so stiffly, apprehension evident in his every rigid muscle.

I realize the mistake I made in how I've approached this. The last time I took him aside for a "serious talk," I had to tell him I'm dying.

Purposely, I smile broadly so he can see it's nothing bad.

As I move my eyes over his handsome face, the face I've found even more appealing as the years have worn on, I see his Adam's apple bob as he swallows. My smile isn't working. He's trying hard to keep his anxiety from me. I love him all the more for that, but I feel horrifically guilty for causing it in the first place.

"I'm not going to mince words. All I ask is that you let me explain after I tell you this. Deal?"

"Deal."

I draw breath into my lungs, feeling supported by the air in my thorax, hoping it's enough to hold me upright if my strength fails me. "I'm pregnant."

In any other situation, the cascade of emotions that flit across Nate's features would've been comical. Only they aren't funny at the moment.

I simply watch them chase each other, one by one, over the topography of his face as he processes the bomb.

All I can do is wait.

When I'm certain he's passed through shock and is in clear understanding of what I said, I calmly continue.

"After the diagnosis, I wasn't thinking about birth control. I mean, we've had so much trouble getting pregnant, I'm not sure I'd have thought it necessary even if *I had* happened to consider it. But...I guess I should've.

"At first, I wasn't sure what was going on. Those mornings when I was sick in Rome, I thought it was the progression of the cancer, not...not...*this.*" Without thought, I reach for my abdomen. Nate's eyes fall to my hand, and he stares for a few seconds. I see his expression change, and that's when I know. I know for sure, for *a fact*, how my husband is going to react.

I feel his love swell like a tidal wave. I feel it stir the air as the whitecap whooshes toward me.

Before I can even continue, Nate is off the couch, kneeling before me with his hands pressed to my belly. He gazes at it as though if he stares hard enough, he might be able to see through my skin and muscle and tissue to the miniscule life growing within.

"Sweet God," he whispers, dropping his forehead onto my lap. I thread the fingers of one hand into his hair and cover my mouth with the other. I don't want my crying to steal this moment from him, so I remain absolutely still and silent until he raises his head and brings his misty eyes back to mine.

"Don't move," I tell him preemptively. I want to record this moment.

For me.

For Nate.

For our child.

Reaching into my pocket, I drag out my phone. I flick my finger over the small camera icon on the locked screen and then switch the perspective until it shows my own face. I've done it dozens of times over the last six weeks, unable to keep myself from speaking to our child, from recording my exuberance for him or her to watch one day.

I hit the video button.

I speak clearly and happily into the lens.

"Hello, my beautiful baby! We found out that you're real today. Our child. You're really *real*. I just told your daddy about you. He's so, so happy. I know you won't appreciate this until you're older, but I wanted you to see what he did when he found out he's going to be your father."

I turn the camera toward my lap, toward my husband, filling the screen with his breathtaking face. It's as luminous on the video as it is in real life.

"You're our miracle," he whispers, unable to hold back the shimmer of his voice as it quavers with emotion. He turns his attention back to me, his features full of all the love we've shared over the years, and he whispers, "Thank you."

Nate doesn't have to explain what he means.

I know.

As I turn off the video, my sweet husband comes to his knees. Tenderly, adoringly, he pulls me into his arms and buries his face in the curve of my neck.

It's in the quiet that I hear the softness of his tears, the beauty of his happiness.

12

Life is Beautiful

Lena

"Merry Christmas!"

That's the first thing I hear when I roll over onto my back. Before I can respond, Nate's hand is flattened out over my stomach, a tender gesture that he does more times each day than I can count.

I feel the rise of my nightgown and the falling away of the covers as my husband bends to press his lips to my belly.

"Merry Christmas, little one," he murmurs to our unborn child.

As it has so often in the last thirty-plus hours, my throat constricts. If I lived to be a thousand years old, I can't imagine ever being unaffected by his sweetness. I suppose whether God and I patch things up or not, I *have to* thank Him for Nate.

After pulling the covers back over me, Nate settles back onto the pillow beside me, bending his arm and resting his head on his fist. Then he proceeds to ask the first of many questions. "Why did you feel like you couldn't tell me when you found out? And *when did* you find out, by the way?"

He isn't angry; he's simply looking for answers. There is no place for anger in our relationship anymore. When I was worrying about how he'd react, I should've known that. Our time is limited. Nate won't waste a moment of it on something negative. He's as committed to "Blaze of Glory" as I am. But more than that, he's just an amazing *person*. *This* is just who Nate Grant is.

Caring.

Patient.

Wonderful.

"I didn't feel like I *couldn't* tell you. I just knew that it would change you as much as it did me, the instant you found out, and then if I wasn't able to carry it..." I sigh, closing my eyes against that possibility. "I couldn't do that to you. You're already losing me. I didn't want to give you a baby for a few days and then take that away, too."

"God, Lena," he mutters, leaning over to kiss my temple. "You carried this by yourself for all those weeks because *you* were worried about *me*."

It wasn't an accusation or a question, merely a statement. A statement of understanding. Because he would do the same thing for me.

"Yes. And I'd do it again if I thought it would spare you even one nanosecond of pain." I work to still my quaking chin, to calm my soul, but the dam is already cracked, already in danger of failing. "Nate, I…I worry about you being all alone. I worry about you *period*. And I know what you'll say if I tell you to find someone else and be happy again. I know I probably shouldn't even waste my time telling you those kinds of things. But I can't help worrying about it. About all of it. About all of *you*. So when I saw those two pink lines…I felt like my every unspoken prayer had been answered. Well, most of them anyway," I sniff on a bitter laugh. The healing I'd plead for felt almost like too much to ask on top of everything else. That's why I'll be content if I can just give him this baby. That will be enough.

It'll have to be.

Nate only nods. I know he isn't surprised. Not really. We know each other too well for that. He knows how much I love him. He knows to what lengths I will go to protect him. And I know he would do the same for me. It's who we are.

It's who we are *to each other*.

"Did you ever consider any other… alternatives?"

I know he knows the answer to that as well. I just can't decide if it's hope I hear in his voice or merely curiosity.

"Not for a single second. Why?" Nate shrugs, and I watch him carefully. When he doesn't answer, I prompt, "Nate, why do you ask?"

"I guess I just wondered if this might make you want to live a little more. Maybe try some treatment. We could try to get pregnant again later."

I turn onto my side and tug at the three-day stubble on my husband's chin. "It's not that I didn't want to live before the baby. I would stay with you forever if I could. But forever isn't possible anymore. And I'm just not willing to put you through the horrors of fighting a losing battle with a terminal cancer patient. I *wasn't* and I'm *still* not willing to do that. Nate, some things are worse than death. Even for those who aren't sick. For those who have to watch. For those who survive, but can never outlive the memories. And I won't do that to you. I love you too much."

He nods his understanding, but refuses to meet my eyes. "So, your mind is made up?"

"It hasn't changed," I clarify. "I choose *you* and your happiness and your life over trying to keep more of mine. The cost is too high, Nate. The cost is just too high."

The last thing I want is for Nate to think I love this child, or even the idea of this child, more than him.

"I just...it won't be the same without you," he explains, his voice not quite steady.

My heart splinters like a dry piece of driftwood under an unforgiving heel. "I know. I know, but it's the only way a part of me can stay. I'll be with you for the rest of your days now. In our child."

I scrunch down in the bed and press my cheek to Nate's chest, letting the tears flow between us, wetting both my skin and his.

His next words vibrate with emotion, and I bite my lip to keep my sobs inside. "I hope it's a girl. And she looks just like you. Because I can't bear the thought of my life without you, Lena. I…I don't know how—"

He stops abruptly, and I wind my arms around him and hold on tight. We draw comfort from each other, as much as can be had, and we mourn together over what will never be.

We lie this way, wrapped up in each other, for nearly an hour before either of us dares to move. But it's Nate who recovers first, always the resilient one.

"I guess we'd better get cracking if we're gonna get this tree up today."

"Tree? What tree?"

Nate slithers out of my arms, sits up, and then lobs a mischievous grin over his shoulder. "The Christmas tree, of course. You and I are going to do everything we can with the baby. And we're going to tape it all."

I sit up. "We are?" I'd planned to do videos for the baby so I can share with it all the things I won't have a lifetime to share, but this idea… I love this idea! Our child will be able to get a glimpse of what holidays and weekends and precious moments in life would've been like with two parents. And he or she will get to see how much it was loved by the mother who passed away.

"We are. We're going to decorate the Christmas tree and sing silly songs. We're going to document everything and make a mountain of shit I can use to embarrass that kid with later in life. It's what any responsible, loving parent would do, right?"

"Of course," I reply, not missing a beat, giving in to a grin that feels somehow like victory. A small victory, but a victory nonetheless. And I'll take all I can get at this point.

This is the Nate I love. This is the Nate I will always love, through death's door and far beyond. He will be full of enough life for both of us, and he will be more than enough parent and caregiver for our baby.

Not that I ever doubted him. I knew from the moment I suspected I was pregnant that my husband would be the best kind of father. Just like he is the best kind of husband. Nate doesn't know how to fail at anything. It isn't in his DNA.

This—this moment, this day, this *man*—assures me that I made the right decision in waiting to tell him. It didn't hurt anything, but had things gone a different way, it would've saved him enormous heartache. I suspected it all along, but I can see now that I was right. And I'm glad. The last thing I want to do is bring him *anything* except happiness.

The sun has long since set by the time we plop down onto the couch to enjoy the flickering lights of our handiwork.

"Go stand in front of the tree for a sec," Nate suggests, taking my phone from the table beside him.

Without question, I do as he asks. He turns on the camera and aims it at me, triggering the record button when he's happy with his view. "Welcome to your first

Christmas, Grant spawn," he begins happily. He's speaking to our child, but he's watching me on the screen. I can see his eyes. I can *feel* them, too. On me. Always one me. "This is your dad. It's Christmas day, and you're still a polka dot in your mom's belly." He smiles when I raise my hands to lovingly stroke my stomach. "I wanted you to see how beautiful she is, how beautiful *life* is with her. See how the lights sparkle a little brighter, how the tree stands up a little taller when she's around? That's all because of your mother. She makes everything around her better, and I hope you get all the very best parts of her. I love her. And we both love *you*. Merry Christmas."

Nate looks beyond the screen to the real me, not just my image. He meets my eyes and brings a smile to play around the edges of my mouth. He nods to me, indicating it's my turn to speak to the baby.

I clear my throat and smile wider.

"Hello, my gorgeous baby. I'd give anything to be able to hold you right now, to sit with you under the Christmas tree. Enjoy the lights and the fire. With your father by my side. But having you *at all* is the best Christmas gift I could ever ask for. I want you to know that you've made this year, this *very hard year*, the best of my life. You've made all this worth it. Kiss your daddy every day for me. And he will kiss you for me. I love you. I love you both. So much. Merry Christmas."

****

Nate

I tap the red button to stop the recording. As I lower the phone, I wonder if I'll ever be able to watch these films without feeling like the biggest part of me is missing.

And never coming back.

13

I'd Die for You

Lena

Despite the jovial holiday celebration Nate and I enjoyed, I'm uneasy. I know my husband well enough to know that he feels the same way. Beneath all the laughs and cute videos and tender moments, he's nervous. I can tell. I don't think either of us will feel comfortable about the pregnancy until I see Dr. Taffer again.

And today is that day.

Although I told Nate every word spoken between Dr. Stephens and me, he wants to go to my appointments with me. And I completely understand. I wouldn't have seen my obstetrician by myself had I not been trying to protect Nate until I had some answers.

Now, there's no way in the world I would exclude him, good news or bad. We are one hundred percent in this together.

On the drive to the oncologist's office, the car is filled with anxiety, and neither Nate nor I say much.

From a professional standpoint, I have a boatload of questions to ask, but from a personal standpoint, only one of them really matters. It's the same question I know Nate wants answered as well.

It's the one filling the car with the thickest of tension. *Can I carry this baby?*

That's the million dollar question, one only God Himself knows the answer to, but I'm willing to put enough faith in my doctors to at least ease my mind about it.

Dr. Stephens will be consulting Dr. Taffer, my oncologist, about me so they can manage the pregnancy together. I know, however, that considering the holidays and the short time period, it's highly unlikely they've exchanged calls, notes, or test results yet. If they had, I'd know. I would've gotten a call from Dr. Taffer. But since I haven't, I can only assume my visit today will be the first she's hearing about it.

Her expertise will be extremely important. Only my oncologist will know how the cancer will affect my body, which in turn will affect the *baby*. *That* is what I'm most concerned about. *That* is what I want her to tell me today—that this is manageable. That my baby can survive.

Nate takes my hand as we sit, side by side, in the chairs inside the small examination room at the cancer center. His grip is tight, tighter than usual. I know without a doubt that he isn't even aware of it. It's merely an outward sign of how frightened he is, how out of control he feels. I know that to be true because I feel exactly the same way.

Rallying the best that I can, I muster a stiff smile for Dr. Taffer when she walks in.

"So, how was Europe? How are you feeling?" the doctor asks right off the bat, patting the paper-covered examination table, a silent invitation for me to hop up there.

I remain seated. I know there is going to be a lot of discussion before an actual examination takes place, and I don't waste any time getting right to the point

"Europe was amazing. I was sick for a few weeks right in the middle, but it wasn't related to the cancer."

Lheanne Taffer's brow pleats for only a moment before it smooths out and she rolls on her stool to be closer to me. "No? What was it, the food?"

"No. I'm pregnant."

The only indication that Dr. Taffer even heard me is the two-second widening of her eyes before she brings her expression carefully under control. "Are you certain? Have you seen your obstetrician?"

"I have. She'll be sending you copies of everything. Probably giving you a call." My fingers tremble within Nate's. I feel the slight squeeze of his hand around mine, an offer of comfort, a quiet way of assuring me that it will all be okay.

"And?"

"I'm over nine weeks now. Nearly ten."

"So, it was confirmed via ultrasound?"

"Yes." I can't help my smile. The baby...it's all that matters. "Although she's obviously concerned, she's going to do her best to get me through this."

Dr. Taffer nods. "Is that what you want?"

"Yes." The word is firm, determined, unsinkable.

"And you're in agreement with this?" She pins Nate with a mildly accusing stare.

He nods. "I'm with her. Whatever she wants, if it's within my power to give it to her, I'm in."

The oncologist rolls a foot or two backward, clearing her throat, collecting her thoughts. "You realize that this will severely limit your care."

"I do."

"How much thought have you given this?"

"A lot."

"Have you considered taking treatment *now* and trying to get pregnant again later?"

"You and I both know what that treatment would do to my organs. I was having trouble getting pregnant *before* I was diagnosed with cancer. My chances will decrease dramatically after having surgery followed by what will probably be multiple rounds of chemo and radiation. And all that for a slim chance that I'd even survive two years. No, I haven't considered that option because it's *not an option*. At least not for me. This baby is a gift. A miracle. And I'm going to do everything I can to carry it."

There is a long, pregnant, unnerving silence before my doctor speaks.

"You know we won't be able to monitor the spread of the disease. Every effective test and drug that we would use is contraindicated during pregnancy. CT, PET Scan, MRI with contrast. And drugs... Every drug that I can think of is—"

"Yes, I know."

"And pain. We won't be able to treat your pain when it comes, Lena. And there *will* be pain."

I feel Nate's hand twitch. I haven't given him all the gory details that I've considered, but I *have* considered them. I know the consequences. I just didn't tell Nate about every single one of them. I couldn't be sure he'd have been so gung-ho about keeping the baby once he learned what my sacrifice would entail. Yet another reason I wanted to keep it from him as long as possible. So he wouldn't worry. So the fine points of my outlook wouldn't plague him.

But now he's going to hear it.

Every gory detail.

"I know there will be pain, but I'm willing to do whatever I have to, go through whatever I have to, suffer through whatever I have to in order to bring this child into the world."

"Lena, there are other risks that you might not have considered. The very nature of your condition will pose a threat to the health of the baby. The disease is in your lymph system. More spread is inevitable at this point."

"I realize that, but all I need is twenty-eight weeks. Total. And that's less than eighteen from now."

"The cancer itself will eventually cause wasting syndrome, which will impair nutrition to the baby. Have you considered that?"

"Yes, but I can get nutrition other ways."

"Bear in mind that you can't be put to sleep to insert a J peg."

"No, but I can have an NG tube. I know it's not ideal, but it's an option. And we can always supplement with parenteral nutrition if need be."

Dr. Taffer's lips thin. She's just beginning to see exactly how determined I am to carry this baby.

"If you've got all this figured out, why are you here? You don't need an oncologist. I treat cancer. You don't want treatment. There's nothing I can do to help you."

Her voice is harsh and sharp, and it cuts right through. My stomach twists in anxiety.

"Lheanne." I inject as much reason as I can into my voice. Lheanne Taffer and I have become friends, and I know that her sour statement is coming from a place of concern. Nothing more. She's too professional to speak to any other patient this way, I feel sure. "I still need your help. I need your expertise to help me head off complications before they happen. Like from my liver. We know the cancer has already spread there. How will that affect the baby? Can it be managed? I still need your help, just in a slightly different way. I don't need you to help me *live*. *Survive*. I need you to help me *carry this child*. As long as I possibly can."

Abandoning Nate's hand, I scoot to the edge of my chair, wiping tears that have begun to fall. "I would die for this baby. To give it life, I would gladly give mine. I'm asking you to help me hang on for as long as I can so I can do that. I want this baby. More than anything else, I want this baby. Please help me give this one last gift to my husband. Please."

At my confession, uttered on a desperate whisper, I hear Nate's sharp intake of breath. I glance his way just in time to see the shock, the devastation on his face before he releases my hand and drops his head low, toward his spread knees. I watch him as he stares at his fingers, fingers he steeples and flattens, steeples and flattens. He concentrates on them as though they hold the key to life. Or the key to his questions.

But that's not what he's looking for.

I know my Nate.

He's simply taking the time he needs to compose himself. For me. For my sake. He wasn't expecting this, and it's hitting him like a tanker truck loaded with explosive gas. And he doesn't want me to see the wreckage.

I reach down to place my hand over his. Because I know. Even when he tries to hide it from me, even when he tries to protect me, I know.

I know.

He stills except for the thumb of one hand which rubs back and forth over the sensitive outer edge of my palm. In the back of my mind, an invisible clock is counting the seconds as they tick by.

One one-thousand.

Two one-thousand.

Three one-thousand.

The clock has just reached a slow count of six when Nate bends to press his lips to my knuckles and then straightens in his chair, throwing one arm over my shoulders in a show of support. Of comfort. Of solidarity.

This is what he is to me.

This is what we are to each other.

Strength.

Commitment.

Unfailing love.

I turn my gaze to Lheanne. I see the subtle expressions as they shift over her face. Exasperation, sympathy, concern, and, finally, acquiescence.

When it comes, her submission, I welcome the sigh of her resignation.

"This is going to be tricky, you know that, right?"

I laugh outright, sniffing as I wipe my cheek, and scoot back in the chair to lean slightly against Nate's shoulder. Suddenly, I'm exhausted.

"That's exactly what Dr. Stephens said."

"Well, she was right. But tricky doesn't mean impossible. Women with severe liver disease have successful pregnancies. I can't manage the obstetrical part of your situation, but if this is what you want…I'll do my best to get you there from a disease management standpoint. And to keep you as comfortable as I can." Wheels start to turn behind Dr. Taffer's eyes. I recognize the look. "We should consult an internist, see what can safely be done from a pharmaceutical approach. And I know a holistic guy who has had some success with pain relief through acupuncture. I know he treats pregnant women. He might even be able to recommend some herbs to ease some other issues. I could give him a call. And we can look at some natural remedies for nausea. Ginger suckers are really good for that." She reels off a handful of other options and thoughts that have me sighing in relief.

Slowly, my optimism begins to return. When Dr. Taffer finishes listing the avenues we can explore, I take advantage of the pause that ensues. I have one more question to ask. It's the query I've been staring out over like a child staring out over the Grand Canyon. It's the uncrossable chasm, or at least it *could be*.

"So, bottom line. Do you see any reason why I wouldn't be able to carry this baby? As long as I'm diligent about keeping myself in the best health possible? I mean, as much as a terminal cancer patient can."

Dr. Taffer goes still and so does my heart. I feel it pause in my chest as though time and space and *life* are holding their breath, waiting for an answer. Teetering on the edge of implosion. Total annihilation.

"No, I don't see any reason right now that you won't be able to carry the baby. *Provided that* your disease doesn't progress too quickly. But in the grand scheme of things, there is little I can do to actually ensure that. You have to know that there are a million and one things that could happen, unpredictable things, things that we will have no way of treating. Or even diagnosing until they present a problem. If I can't monitor your disease progression and your health properly…" She holds up her hands in defeat.

"I know. And I'm not asking you for a miracle. Or even for a promise. I'm leaving that up to God."

Dr. Taffer raises her brows. In all our many talks since my diagnosis, never have I mentioned prayer or miracles or a higher power, something that a large portion of patients turn toward immediately when given such life-altering news.

Lheanne's lips twist wryly. "I hope His hands are more capable than mine."

"I hope so, too," I admit, clinging to the hope I found in Rome. "I hope so, too."

****

I feel more encouraged than I ever would've imagined by the time we leave Dr. Taffer's office. For the first time since I was basically given a death sentence, I feel like the rest of my life is going to mean something. I'm not just going to be giving my husband a lifetime of good memories while we wait for cancer to overcome my body; I'm going to be fighting for the survival of our child.

It isn't until we get into the car that Nate turns to me, distress written all over his face. In my excitement and relief, I momentarily neglected the fact that he's been delivered a nuclear bomb and has yet to say a word about it.

"You knew all of this and didn't tell me." His voice is mildly accusing.

"Knew all of what?" I ask, delaying the inevitable.

My heart pounds heavily. I feel the full force of his shock, of his alarm coming at me in a concussive wave.

"All of the reasons that this isn't a good idea."

"I don't know of *any reason* that this isn't a good idea."

"Lena, you're going to suffer. Horribly!" His words explode into the quiet interior of the car, reverberating off the windows and booming through me. His distress, his disbelief, his devastation is palpable, a low hum in the air that makes the hair on my arms stand at attention.

"I was going to suffer anyway, Nate," I remind him softly. I have to fight his fire with a calm, cool, rational breeze.

"You wouldn't take treatment because you didn't want me to have to go through that and you die anyway. But you're okay with *this*? With me watching you go through pure hell *for me*? To give this baby *to me*?"

"Yes, Nate. I'd do anything for you. Anything for this baby. Anything for *this family*. *I love you*. You're all I have. You're all I'll *ever* have, because my 'ever' is almost up. But when it is, and my time has come, you won't be alone. You'll have a child, a piece of us, to love and to hold. To me, that's worth whatever sacrifices I have to make. There is *nothing* I wouldn't do for you. Nothing."

"Lena, Jesus! How am I... How can I live with that? How can I live with *myself*, knowing that you did this *for me*?"

"You live *happy*. You live *whole*. You live for our child. And you live like someone who is loved. Beyond all doubt or reason or limit. Because that's how I love you."

He moans miserably, leaning his head back against the headrest and closing his eyes. "And until then? What am I supposed to do until then? Every day. Every godda—" He stops abruptly, clenching his teeth in impotent anger.

"You're supposed to love me. Like I love you. You're supposed to love me until I'm gone, and then you're supposed to love our baby until *you're* gone."

I see the deep rise and fall of his chest as he inhales and then lets out his breath. Seconds drip into minutes. The minutes slip into five. Then ten. Then fifteen.

I know my husband. I know this is hard for him. So very hard for him. And he won't come to a decision lightly. Or quickly. So when he finally lowers his head, so slowly that it seems he's having difficulty moving, I know he's made up his mind. But the grief in the green eyes that he brings to meet mine show me that he isn't quite there yet. And that he might not ever be.

Not completely.

So I reiterate, my hand reaching for his, like my heart is reaching for his across the space between us.

"Love me, Nate. All I need is for you to love me. That's all I've ever needed. That hasn't changed. That's *the only thing* you're supposed to do."

The seconds, they tick by endlessly. I begin to wonder if I'm asking too much, if I've finally reached the place where Nate can go no farther.

But I haven't. I know it the instant I see Nate's jaw firm with determination. I know it the instant I see the fighter fight back, fight *through*.

His Adam's apple bobbing as he swallows, my husband nods.

"If that's what you need of me, then you have it." His voice is solid. Resolute. "I'll love you. Every minute of every day of forever, I'll love you. I'll love you like I'm not afraid of losing you. And then I'll love our baby just as much. But know this, Lena Grant: There will never be another you. I'll die missing you, missing a piece of me. Nothing you can and nothing you could give me will change that."

A single tear slips from the corner of his eye and snakes its way down his clean-shaven cheek. It's the only actual tear I've ever *seen* him shed. It's the only outward indication of how much pain he's in. He can't stop it, can't control his anguish enough to prevent me from seeing this telltale sign of it.

And it breaks me.

"I wish things could be different," I murmur brokenly, reaching out to trap the droplet on the tip of my finger and bringing it to my lips. I kiss my fingertip, tasting the salt of his misery, taking it into my body, cherishing even these agonizing moments with the man I love more than my own flesh.

"I do, too, baby. I do, too."

We sit in the car, in the parking lot and stare into each other's eyes for what seems like hours before Nate turns away to start the engine.

I can't describe what passed between us in those poignant minutes; I can only say that we shared something profound, something that transcends words. Something that will, hopefully, transcend death.

14

Letter to a Friend

Lena

I knew I'd have to tell Nissa about my illness when we got back from Europe. I knew I wouldn't be able to put it off any longer. She's my best friend as well as my neighbor. Even if I'd *wanted* to hide my condition from her, which I didn't really intend to do, I couldn't. She would eventually begin to notice the changes. That didn't keep me from dreading the conversation for the last three months, though.

But now…now I'm more excited than apprehensive to talk to Nissa. Yes, I'll have to give her the bad news, but I'll have good news to share with her, too. News about the baby. And that makes me more eager to go and see her, to finally tell her what's really going on in my life.

Thankfully, the opportunity to tell my friend didn't arise unexpectedly. Nissa hasn't been over to visit since we got back and I told her before we left Europe that we'd need a day or two to recuperate once we got back to the States. She seemed fine with that, as though the request wasn't out of the ordinary. It probably helped that we'd emailed back and forth several times each week while Nate and I were in Europe. I sent her tons of pictures and told her of our adventures, so she wasn't champing at the bit to talk to me the instant we landed. But the time to tell her is finally at hand. Today is the day, and I'm cautiously, *nervously* excited.

As soon as I wake from my surprisingly deep sleep (between the disease and my pregnancy, I'm so exhausted all the time that I sleep like the dead), I go straight into the bathroom to brush my teeth. When I step into the kitchen, I see that Nate is already up and making himself some coffee.

"Goin' to Nissa's," I tell him as I push my arms into a light jacket and my feet into fuzzy slippers. "Wish me luck."

"Good luck," he says sleepily, yawning into his fist.

On my way by him to the door, I pause to give him a quick peck on the lips and a firm slap on the butt. It's too tempting not to touch that perfectly formed posterior of his.

"That's right," he says as I open the door. "Get you some of that fine ass."

I'm still grinning as I dart across the yard to Nissa's back door.

I raise my hand to rap my knuckles on the glass, but the door is yanked open before my skin can make contact. Nissa squeals once and jerks me into her arms.

"You're back! I'm gonna beat you for making me wait this long! What the hell?" she asks, leaning back to give me a mock-angry look.

I smile and remind her, "I *told you* we'd need a couple of days to recuperate, O Ye of the Short Memory." She shrugs, unconcerned, and I laugh. "Can I come in?"

Nissa rolls her eyes. "Can you come in? Whatever! What are you, a stranger? Of course, you can come in! Mi casa es su casa." She turns and walks off, heading to the coffee maker and taking a clean mug from one of the hooks above it.

I stop her before she can pour. "None for me." From the corner of my eye, I see the open-mouthed, shocked expression on my friend's face. I never refuse coffee.

Never.

"Okay, so I'm the last to know," Nissa finally says on a sigh.

My head flips up in surprise. "Pardon?"

"I'm obviously the last to know that we've been invaded by aliens. Or there's been a national disaster. Or you've converted to some weird religion that doesn't allow nature's finest beverage. *Something* is going on, and I'm *obviously* the last to know."

Again, I smile. "None of those things, but I *do* have something to talk to you about."

Nissa's face falls into a rarely-seen serious countenance. I can almost feel the unease radiating from her, like a soft touch that stretches across the span of the kitchen to lightly tickle my perceptive antennae.

I watch as my friend and neighbor methodically tops off her own coffee, adds another splash of cream and a sprinkle of sugar, and then turns toward the breakfast table. She resumes the chair she'd no doubt been seated in before I interrupted her.

After several long seconds and a sip of her hot-again coffee, Nissa raises her wary blue eyes to mine. "Okay, come and sit. Talk to me."

I do, taking the chair across from her. I set my hands on the table and entwine my fingers. "I have something to tell you. Well, two things actually. Then I have a favor to ask. A big one."

"Anything," Nissa says definitively. There is no hesitation, no reservation, no question. Because that's the kind of friend she is.

"You don't even know what I'm going to ask yet."

"Doesn't matter. I'll do it. Whatever it is."

"You should at least wait until you know what it is."

"It won't matter. I'd do anything for you. If it's within my power, you ask and it gets done. Period."

It strikes me, and not for the first time, how very fortunate I am to have a friend like Nissa. She's the thick-and-thin type, the loves-me-anyway type. She's the until-the-bitter-end type. The type that I will need in my life now more than ever.

And I won't ever be able to repay the kindness. I won't ever be able to do the same for her one day.

That's yet another tragedy about this situation.

"I love you. Have I ever told you that?"

"Not *nearly* enough," she says, trying for flippant but failing miserably. The apprehension in her eyes belies the nonchalance of her words. With a sigh that can be felt more than heard, Nissa reaches across the glass mosaic table and covers my hands with her own. "Tell me."

I find strange comfort in the fact that my best friend knows me so well. I don't have to tell Nissa that something is *wrong;* she just knows. Neither of us says as much, but her actions, her visage, her mannerism speaks as loudly as a bullhorn on a silent, starry night.

"I have cancer," I begin steadily. I pause only briefly, not wanting to get bogged down in the sorrow of my circumstance. I'd much rather lose myself in the hope of what's to come. "It's bad. Terminal. That's why Nate took me to Europe for three months. I didn't want to tell you before we left. That would be the suckiest best friend bomb *ever.*"

Like Nissa, I attempt flippancy.

Also like Nissa, I fail miserably.

Not only is Nissa *not* laughing, but she's retracted both of her hands and is now covering her mouth with them.

Instantly, her eyes fill with tears. They overflow her lashes and roll in a steady stream down over her knuckles. From there, they drip noiselessly onto the table top.

I continue before she can become any more distraught.

"The good news is that I'm pregnant."

Smiling, I stop there, giving my words time to sink in. I know my sweet friend will be completely astonished by this entire conversation, but after a day or so, she'll be the supportive person I've always known her to be.

"You-you're *pregnant?*" Nissa's jaw goes slack, her mouth hanging open in the shape of a hollow oval.

I nod.

"But Nate… What about the other woman? I know it was probably nothing, but don't you think you should—"

"He was meeting with my oncologist, Nissa. That's all it was. He told me."

"Oh." After a few seconds of digesting that information, she continues baldly. "Please don't tell me you're going to try to carry this baby."

My happiness falters as noticeably as my smile. I can feel it, the tremble of trying forcibly to keep it in place. "I am."

"Lena, what the hell are you thinking? You need *treatment!* This isn't the Middle Ages. Cancer isn't 100% incurable. There are hundreds if not thousands of medications and immune enhancers and all sorts of shit they could give you. *You're* the nurse here. I'm not telling you anything you don't already know."

"No, you're not. But Nissa, I've seen this before. I lived it with my sister and my father. There's a point when it's better to just live your life. Go for the quality rather than the quantity. Unfortunately, that's where I am."

"Well, if it wasn't, it will be *now*. You certainly can't take any treatment if you're pregnant."

Nissa gets up from the table and takes her coffee mug to the sink, angrily dumping the contents down the drain and rinsing the cup to stick in the dishwasher. When it is stowed away alongside the other dirty dishes, she sets her hands on either side of the sink and bends one knee, her hips shifting to one side in that way she has when she's getting frustrated with her kids. Like she's at her wits' end.

Only this time, she's frustrated *with me.*

I wonder briefly, sort of comically if Nissa is going to turn around and shake her finger at me.

Without facing me, Nissa asks, "What does Nate say about this?"

"He's supportive. He wants what I want."

"Somehow I doubt that."

"What's that supposed to mean?"

"I'm betting he'd much rather have *you* around for the next forty years than risk your life for a child you may or may not even be able to carry." Bitterness drenches her voice. I know she can't say the same thing about her own husband, which breaks my heart.

Still, I'm more than a little taken aback by Nissa's irritation. It hurts, more than I would've expected, to hear the disapproval in my closest confidant's voice, to feel the harsh slap of her condemnation when I'd expected nothing less than weepy support.

Fighting back tears, I stand and walk to the sink, turning to lean one hip against it so I can face my friend's pinched profile. I know her words, her actions come from a place of anguish, but that doesn't lessen the hurt to my battered heart.

"The odds were *not* in my favor, Nissa. No matter what I did. And I wasn't *planning* on getting pregnant. Right in the middle of dying is not exactly the best time to be trying to nurture a healthy baby. *But,*" I add with extra emphasis, "this child has already given me so much happiness and it's only been a few weeks. I feel like it has brought me back to a place I never thought I'd be. I have hope. *Hope,* Nissa. This cancer...it stole everything from me—my present, my future. Out in the distance, there was nothing for me but pain and sickness and death. But now, despite the pain and the sickness and the death, I could have a baby. In a child, I will be able to give my husband a tiny piece of me that he can keep for the rest of his life. And for as many days as I can make it after delivery, we will be able to be a *whole family.* That's all I've ever wanted. For us to have our own little family. Can't you please just be happy for me?"

Nissa whirls to face me, her face red with fury. "Be happy for you? Be happy that you came to tell me you're dying and that you're fine with doing nothing about it? What kind of a monster do you think I am?"

"I don't think you're a monster at all. That's why I need a favor. That's why I was going to ask you to help Nate. I was going to ask my best friend in the world to be present in my husband's life because I won't be. I *can't* be. I was going to ask her to help him with the baby, answer his questions, let him vent his frustrations because he won't have anyone else around. He'll be grieving, and he'll be overwhelmed, and the only thing I can do to help him is to give him the best friend I've ever had. *I* was going to lean on her if I ever had a baby. I was going to call her in the middle of the night for teething recipes and come to her door crying because I hadn't slept in days. I was going to proudly show her how I'd learned to change a diaper in thirty seconds or less, and I was going to take her to a spa day when the men had the kids. But now…since it won't be me, I had hoped my husband could do the same. That's what I was going to ask, but…"

I let my words trail off, my heart nearly exploding with sadness. Of all the reactions I might've anticipated from my long-time neighbor, my long-time friend, this was nowhere on the list.

Nowhere.

But I won't give up on Nissa coming around. I can't.

So with a trembling chin, I watch my friend. In silence, in patience, I watch her, and I wait.

Slowly, Nissa works through her ire. Twice she opens her mouth to speak, but ends up closing it both times, thinking better of it.

Once she sighs. Once she shakes her head. Once she presses her fingers to the bridge of her nose like her head is hurting. But ultimately, *finally*, after five or six minutes, she comes out on the other side of her emotions as the pal I've known for the better part of two decades.

Nissa buries her face in her hands and begins to weep. "Jesus Christ, Lena, I'm sorry."

I wrap my arms around my very best friend, and I hold her close, stroking Nissa's hair as she gives in to her distress. In my many years as a nurse, I've seen people react to bad news in all sorts of unpredictable ways, but they were, for the most part, strangers. I thought I knew Nissa better than to be surprised by her reaction, but news like this... No one can know how someone else will respond.

Also, I've never given her such horrific and wonderful news at the same time either. That might be too much for *anybody* to process without having a brief meltdown.

Nissa cries in earnest for a good five minutes. I hold her through it all, only gripping her tighter when her shoulders shake with deep sobs.

When finally Nissa pulls away, her face is puffy, her eyes are red, and her expression is one of overwhelming guilt and sadness.

"I'm so sorry. I just...I wasn't expecting that. Just the thought of losing you—" Her features crumple, and she starts to cry again. She's able to collect herself a little more quickly this time, though. "You know I'd do anything for you. I meant that. And for Nate. And for th-th-the baby." She sniffs and snorts again as she thinks of caring for my motherless child. "I'll support you in whatever you decide, but please don't shut me out. You're my best friend. Please let me spend this last time with you. Please. It's all I'll ever have."

At that, she breaks down again. Patiently, I wait for my friend's shock and grief to subside.

Eventually, it does. It dribbles off into an odd hiccupping-snuffling that I find curiously adorable. I love everything about my best friend, even her unexpected reactions and strange noises.

Grabbing a paper towel from the decorative wrought iron holder on the counter, Nissa blows her nose. I cringe, causing her to ask, "What, do I have a booger?"

I laugh outright. "No, you do not have a booger. I was just thinking how sore your nose will be tomorrow if you use a paper towel to blow it again."

"I'll switch to Kleenex eventually," she sniffs. "You sure I don't have a booger?" Nissa tips her head back for me to inspect.

"I'm *sure* you don't have a booger."

"It feels like I have a booger," she explains, wiping at her nose again. "And if I do, I'd blame you. One thousand percent your fault!" she shouts loudly to the empty kitchen, pointing an accusing finger at me.

"I'll take that. It's less than I deserve, I'm sure."

Nissa sighs audibly, one corner of her mouth curling up in a blend of humor and chagrin. "No. *I* deserve a kick in the boob for being such an asshole. Why did you let me act like that?"

Good-naturedly, I shrug. "Some kids react like that. Gotta let the tantrum run its course. See what a good mother I'm going to be?"

Nissa's eyes mist over. "You're going to be a *phenomenal* mother."

"For a little while anyway. I hope. I guess that could be the upside of dying when your child is still young. You don't get as many opportunities to screw up their life."

After a weak attempt at another smile, Nissa only nods in agreement. I imagine that her throat is thick and shaky with emotion.

"Also, Nate and I are making videos. All kinds of videos of anything and everything. I'd love for you to be in some of them."

"I'd adore that. And with me in its life, at least your baby will grow up with a good sense of style."

"That's definitely something you bring to the table. As long as, if it's a girl, you never pack *your* things in *her* suitcase for a trip. I'd like for you and Nate to be able to keep her off the pole as long as possible."

At that, Nissa laughs. "Are you saying I packed you stripper clothes?"

"I'm saying stripper clothes were modest compared to a few of the things you packed for me."

"But did Nate like them?"

"*Of course* Nate liked them! He *does* have eyes and a penis."

"Then what're you complaining about?"

We grin at each other, slipping easily back into the familiar comfort of our friendship. The rocky moment has passed, and now we will move on. As Nate and I have discovered, there is no place for anger now, when time is so drastically limited. We are unwilling to give it one second of such valuable space. Nissa, too, will realize that soon enough, if she hasn't already.

15

I'll Be There for You

Nate

For two months, things feel like a happier version of normal for Lena and me. It's easy to get lost in plans for the baby or details of the pregnancy and forget that my wife is dying and that no one knows how soon her condition will start to deteriorate. We *do* know, however, that once it starts to decline, there is nothing we can do to stop it.

The doctors are limited. *We* have limited them. We've tied their hands. They will only be able to treat Lena the best they can with medicines and therapies that won't harm the baby. She always seems okay with that, though. More than okay, actually. It's from her, from her calm certainty, that I've been drawing a lot of my strength lately.

I don't ever feel completely convinced that we've made the right choice. Then again, it was never really mine to make. Not totally, anyway.

Each day, we make at least one video for the baby, transferring them from phone to computer and then saving them to a flash drive for safekeeping. I admit that I'm almost obsessive about backing up those precious moments. Each time I download one and save it to the external drive, I watch it over and over a few times, falling more and more hopelessly in love with my wife as I do. I'm not sure how smart that is, signing up for even more pain when there's plenty to go around already, but it's out of my control.

Lena is irresistible.

Still, some small, overly-rational part of my brain thinks it might be wise to try to distance myself a little bit as time goes on, but I refuse to back away from Lena no matter how much grief it might save me in the end. I know perfectly well that loving her so much knowing that I will surely lose her will be the hardest thing I've ever have to deal with in my whole damn life. I also know, however, that I wouldn't trade these last days, weeks, months with her for all the gold (or comfort and painlessness) in the world. I'm content to throw myself wholly into our life, into our love, and into the growth of our baby until the very last day.

Until the end.

So I continue taping and downloading, taping and downloading, watching the videos over and over and over again on nights when I can't sleep, knowing that one day the short clips will be all that I have left of my wife besides our child and the memories I have stored away in my mind. None will be as clear as the videos, though. That's why I protect them fiercely.

One beautiful spring-like morning in early March, Lena and I are enjoying our morning ritual of coffee (decaf for Lena) with our breakfast of eggs and toast when the back door bursts open. I'd been reading the financial section of the paper, which I lower casually. I'm no longer surprised by Nissa's odd and early visits. Neither is Lena. She just throws up her hand and mutters "good morning" around her toast and continues to browse the Internet looking for baby things.

"Video up!" Nissa shouts as she comes sailing across the tile floor and plops a black, shag-cut wig on Lena's head. "She's Monica. I'm Rachel," she explains to me, as if that makes her plan clear to us.

It does not.

I only know that when she comes in and yells "Video up!" it's my cue to start filming. Beyond that, I never have a clue what Nissa is up to.

Obediently, I grab my phone, turn it toward my wife, and hit the record button. Nissa, also wearing a wig, hits play on her own phone, and the familiar guitar riff from the beginning of the *Friends* song fills the kitchen.

She takes Lena by the hand and pulls her to her feet, and the two begin to dance. When the lyrics start, both women sing along, stopping to clap at the appropriate times and then laughing when they do. I can't help smiling at their antics. It makes my chest tight with a bittersweet happiness to watch them.

Speaking just loud enough that my voice can be heard over the music, I tell our baby, "I think this is your mom's best friend's way of saying she loves her. You'll understand later, when I introduce you to the show *Friends*. When you're older," I add. "*Much* older."

Nostalgia warms me as I record and listen. Lena and I watched the comedy together in our early years together. After all this time, we still quote things to each another occasionally. Little insignificant bits from the show like "It's a moo point", "What kind of scary-ass clowns came to your birthday?", and "How you doin'?" which never fail to bring an answering smile. It's one of the million-and-one things we've shared in our life together that once seemed silly and inconsequential, but now seems painfully profound.

When the song is complete, the two hug and laugh before Nissa yanks the wig off Lena's head and vanishes, right back out the door she just burst through a few minutes ago. My guess is that she'll go straight home and cry. We all deal with our grief in silence and in private, in deference to Lena.

But we still have to do it.

Lena is still grinning when she walks over to me and drops down onto my lap, wrapping her arms around my neck. "You're my lobster," she says, rubbing her cold nose against mine.

"And you're my everything," I reply, my gut constricting at the trivial yet meaningful phrase. She *is* my lobster. She *is* my everything, and she always will be.

Even after she's gone.

I wish not for the first time that someone else were the videographer so we could capture moments such as these. I know there will come a time when these memories will start to fade, when I will forget what it feels like to hold her or what it feels like to look into her warm brown eyes, and the idea is crushing. I don't want to forget, but I know that as much as I try to commit every tiny detail to memory, they won't withstand the test of time with much clarity. At least not all of them. It's just not possible.

But if I had my way, I wouldn't forget one single second of the time I've spent with my wife.

Already I can tell that forgetting will be like losing Lena time and time again. And I have no idea how I'll bear it. I don't even know how I'm going to get through it *once*.

I sweep my hand, resting on Lena's hip, around to her growing belly, which I cup with my palm.

This is how I'll get through it, I think.

Her baby.

Our baby.

And that's all I'll have left of my Lena.

16

I Got the Girl

Lena

A legion of butterflies flutters in my stomach when Nate shifts the car into park outside the obstetrician's office. I take a deep, shaky breath and Nate reaches over to squeeze my hand.

"Try to stay calm. The last thing we need is for your blood pressure to be wacked out when you get up there."

He grins tolerantly at me.

"I know, but I'm just *so excited!*"

"I know, baby. I am, too."

"God, I hope she can tell this time."

On our previous visits, the doctor hasn't been able to sex the baby because he or she won't open its legs in just the right way. As much as I try not to be, I've been very disappointed, but evidently that's doing nothing to hamper my excitement *now*. I'm *allll* wound up!

"Maybe that sip of my coffee that I saw you sneak this morning will help."

I tuck my chin sheepishly. "You saw that?"

"I've got eyes everywhere," he states, going on to mimic the recognizable tune from *The Twilight Zone*.

"You must because I'm damn sneaky when I wanna be."

"You only *think* you're sneaky," he teases.

"I can be sneaky when I want to be."

"Like the time you tried to throw me a surprise party and forgot to tell everyone to park around the block? Or like the time you tried to kidnap me for our anniversary and called my line instead of my boss's for directions? Or like *every single Christmas* when I trip you up and get you to tell me what's under the tree?"

"Okay, fine! Sneaky isn't my strong suit, but I read on the Internet that a little bit of caffeine can get the baby excited and moving around. And if the baby is excited and moving around, we can see between its legs."

"I can tell you what the sex is if you really want to know."

Even though I suspect he's teasing, I can't help that my eyes round. "What do you mean? How would you know? Did she see something and tell you? Are you supposed to surprise me?"

"No, I just know what it is."

I'm more than a little deflated. "And how, pray tell, do you know that, Mr. All-seeing Eye?"

"Good old-fashioned reasoning."

"You've *reasoned out* what the sex of our baby is?" I'm skeptical at best, but curious enough to play along.

"Yep. It's a girl."

Despite the lack of soundness to this entire conversation, my heart swells at the thought of giving Nate a little girl. "And how did you *reason out* that it's a girl?"

"Well, if it was a boy, he wouldn't be able to hide his...appendage. After all, *I'm* the father and, well, have you *seen me* naked? I mean, come on! If they'd seen a third arm, they'd have known it was a boy. But they didn't. Therefore, it's a girl."

A bark of laughter bursts from between my lips. "My God! Men and their penises. You're like a tribe of psychos, released into the wild to go forth and multiply, aren't you?"

Nate see-saws his head. "Yeah, pretty much. But still, it's a girl, so you'd better settle on a name."

"*Me?*" I question as Nate exits the car. I wait until he opens my door before I continue. "*Me? What about you?* I've given you a thousand choices, and you never like *any* of them!"

Nate gently takes my hand, placing his other up near my armpit, and he helps me from the car. I'm anemic, they think because of micro bleeds associated with my growing tumor, and it further saps my energy despite the iron supplements I've been taking.

"I'm not worried. The perfect name will come to us. We've got time."

I feel Nate's pause as soon as the words leave his lips and drift through the air. *We've got time.* The one thing we both know that we *don't* have is time.

The words and the bleakness of our future settle around us like a cool, damp blanket. Sometimes it's so heavy, the future, that it makes even something as simple as walking a much more difficult task for me than it should be. But, as always, I put on a smile, aim it at my husband, and trudge on as if nothing is amiss.

I suspect that Nate is never fooled, but we're both content to pretend, to keep the wolf of depression and harsh reality at bay for a few more hours, days, hopefully weeks.

My enthusiasm returns, somewhat at least, by the time I'm stretched out on the table in the dimly-lit ultrasound room. Whether because of our relationship or because of my extremely high-risk status I don't know, but Dr. Stephens always performs the ultrasound herself. She always excuses the tech who performs them for everyone else. The special care makes me feel more comfortable, but it also makes me feel more fragile, like everyone around me is holding their breath, waiting for the moment when things will go sideways.

I try to put thoughts like that out of my head, but I can't stop them from creeping in. And when they do, they do their damage, no matter how quickly I can get them out. They've been steadily chipping away at my morale until sometimes I feel like all I do is worry, especially when it's quiet or I'm alone.

Nate, however...ever perceptive Nate, seems to know that I'm no longer fond of quiet *or* solitude. He makes a concerted effort to keep me entertained at all times these days, God bless him. Thankfully, he has invested wisely over the years and we're doing well financially, allowing for Nate to be with me twenty-four seven if need be. I don't necessarily *need* help that consistently, but I love having him around. And I think he just *wants* to be around, too.

This time is all we have left. Every second is precious.

Gratefully, I turn to find him in the dark room, reaching for his hand and entwining my fingers with his. "I love you," I whisper.

"I love you more," he answers. His smile is casual, but I can see the underlying tension. Although he never says as much, I think Nate is always concerned on ultrasound days. I suspect he worries that they'll find some sort of abnormality or not be able to find the heartbeat or something. He would deny that, of course, and he tries to hide it, but I watch him too closely. I'm too attuned to him to miss the slight change that occurs at this point every time we sit in this room, waiting for the doctor.

Today is no exception.

I flinch when the door suddenly swings open and a cheerful Dr. Stephens explodes through it. "Sorry for the delay, folks. Sometimes babies just don't want to wait to be delivered."

She is still in her green hospital scrubs rather than her normal dress clothes and long, white lab coat. Her shoulder-length brown hair is up in a ponytail with short tendrils curling damply around her face. She looks a bit...frazzled.

"Had to earn your keep today, eh?" Nate asks congenially.

"And then some! Phew!" she exclaims tiredly. But then she smiles, slaps her palms together, and rubs her hands vigorously. "How about we find out the sex of this baby today?"

I smile. Nate smiles. I squeeze his fingers. He squeezes mine back. I feel the slight tremor in his grip. He watches the screen and refuses to look into my eyes. And so we dance the dance of denial, the delicate ballet of pretense, until I, too, turn to watch the small monitor, waiting to see what our baby carries—or doesn't carry—between its legs.

As the doctor slides the probe around on my belly, spreading conducive jelly this way and that, she chats nonchalantly, asking me questions about my diet, my energy level, even my urine. Then, after a longish pause, she addresses another issue, one that she knows will be a sore spot for us.

"Have you given any more thought to an amniocentesis?"

My stomach clenches. I thought I'd made myself clear last time. I don't want to even *have* this discussion again.

"No. I haven't changed my mind."

"Lena, if there's a genetic abnormality—"

"That won't change anything," I interrupt somewhat tersely. "We want this baby. Period. We won't love it any less if it has some disability."

"But the test could prepare you for—"

"If there was no risk, I might consider it. *Might.* But there *is* a risk to having an amnio, and I already have enough risk stacked against me. I appreciate your concern, but I'm declining the test."

I know my tone brooks no argument, and the doctor simply nods, unwilling to press me any further.

Good!

"Well, I don't see any obvious abnormalities, but what I do see is…" The doctor pauses dramatically, running the probe over one spot and pushing up and into my belly. She clicks a button and then rolls a mouse, clicking again. Expertly, she wields the probe and works the computer until she turns to Nate and me, and with a smile announces, "I see no little boy parts. Mr. and Mrs. Grant, I'd like you to meet your daughter."

She enlarges a photo on the screen that shows our daughter lying in the perfect position for us to see the blank slate between her legs.

I gasp.

"It's a girl?" I whisper, trying to keep the quaver from my voice.

"It's a girl," Dr. Stephens confirms, her eyes crinkling at the corners as her grin widens. "And she's sucking her thumb." She minimizes the picture back down to its normal size, and I can clearly see the little arm with its tiny hand tucked up to her mouth.

"Our little girl is sucking her thumb," I say in awe, turning to glance back at Nate. He's watching the screen, mouth slightly ajar, eyes shining brightly in the eerie glow of the monitor, and I know he's moved beyond words. He merely nods. Only after a few more seconds of gazing in wonder at the digital image does Nate finally drag his eyes away and toward my face.

Between us, no words are spoken, but a wealth of sentiment is exchanged as we stare at one another. There have been moments in our life together when everything has changed. We've had so many of them in the last six months, it's hard to say which ones rank highest on the list.

Until today.

Today is something different, something special. And we both know it. This is real. This is happening. After all the trying and waiting and being disappointed, after finding out that I'm going to die and that our time together is drawing to a close, we're finally going to have a child.

Together.

The perfect mixture of each of us, a piece of both Nate and me that will live on long after we've passed. Nothing could be more important than that.

Nothing.

Dr. Stephens says something that neither Nate nor I hear and then gets up to leave. When the door closes and we are alone, Nate leans down and presses his forehead to mine.

"A girl. I prayed for a girl," he confesses on a shaky breath. "I hope she's the very picture of her mother."

His voice is thick with barely-contained emotion. "Please God, let her be just like her mother." He says the last with eyes closed and voice lowered, as if in actual prayer.

My heart lurches behind my ribs. It rips my insides apart to see my husband hurting. Even though he is, without question, deliriously happy about the baby, I know he's also devastated over the impending loss of his wife.

He's hurting. Badly. I can feel it.

I find it odd how happiness and agony so often travel in tandem, almost as though the one is made stronger by the other. The greater our happiness over the baby, the greater our agony over being unable to make a life together as a whole, *as a family*. As one grows, the other grows in direct proportion.

Exponentially.

It will always be this way, I know. For her as long as I live and, for Nate, as long as he does. But I also know there is no light without the darkness, no rainbow without the rain. I know without a doubt that it is the presence of my pain that makes the pleasure of this moment so much more meaningful. In the face of death, life takes on a new level of preciousness. And I have only a short amount of time to appreciate it before mine will be over.

Shortly after Dr. Stephens returns, we are released. I ask Nate to wait for me in the waiting room. All the pressing around Dr. Stephens did to get good pictures of the baby has stimulated my bladder.

It isn't until I'm in the bathroom, door locked and away from prying eyes, that I give into the urge to cry. Biting down on my lip, I slide down the wall until I'm nearly squatted on the floor. Silently, I weep, knowing the tears will do me no good, but needing to shed them anyway.

When the worst has passed, I get up and splash cold water onto my face. As I pat my skin dry, my hands slow to a stop, hovering in midair out in front of my damp forehead. That's the very moment that I know. That's the moment when I know who my daughter will be to me, and to Nate.

I take my phone from my pocket and flick on the video, positioning the screen in front of my face and pressing record.

"I found out who you are today," I begin, my smile still a bit soggy. "You're a baby girl. You're *my* baby girl. When I saw your tiny body on the sonogram, I felt like my whole world was complete." I have to turn away from the camera for a moment to collect myself before I finish the short message. "Your daddy and I have talked about names for a while, but now I know why we couldn't settle on one. We hadn't met you yet. But now we *have*, and we know who you are. You're Grace. *My* Grace. My precious, precious Grace. And I will love you long after I'm gone. My baby," I whisper. "My baby Grace."

When I stop the recording, my sobs begin anew. I fold over at the waist and let them have me. I can't hold them in anymore than I can hold in the mournful moans that echo through my chest like a coyote's howl, bouncing off steep canyon walls. I don't quiet until I hear a soft knock at the door followed by the concerned voice of Dr. Stephens's nurse.

"Lena, are you okay in there?"

Dragging in deep gulps of air, I compose myself the best I can, straightening my clothes and wiping my palms across my cheeks.

"Yes. I'll be out in just one minute."

Stillness greets me from the hall, and I set about putting myself back together before I dart from the bathroom and make my way quickly to the waiting room. I know when I see Nate's face that I must look a fright. I simply grab his hand and pull him along behind me toward the door.

He says nothing, and neither do I.

He knows.

He knows.

17

Bad Medicine

Nate

By the middle of March, Lena is twenty three weeks along. I think we've both begun to feel secure in her ability to carry the baby to the twenty-eight-week mark, and hopefully beyond. Her labs are holding up and the Chinese medicine man she's seeing routinely is really helping to keep her ailing body as fit and functional as it can be, all things considered. She's said more than once that she's beginning to think that God *really is* a God of miracles.

Every day, we put forth our best efforts to keep Lena and the baby healthy and to keep up our "Blaze of Glory" mentality. We make videos, separately, together and with Nissa occasionally, and I keep back ups for my back ups. My fear of losing them is still something that haunts me on a daily basis.

It's as I watch one of our January videos that I get an idea for something that might make my beautiful wife smile. I'm always on the lookout for things that will make every one of her last days bright and special.

I make a mental list of the things I'll need and then I text Nissa, enlisting her help. By evening I want to be ready to go on stage.

Gone are the days of being able to put things off. When I have an idea or something I want to do or say, I make a point of getting to them as quickly as possible. The ever-present, always-silent *tick, tick, tick* of a clock counting down is the rhythm to which I live my life now. Every day is a race against time and I know I have to make each minute mean something.

So after our dinner, a meal full of foods rich in nutrients and elements proven most beneficial to the immune system and liver function, I help my wife to the sofa, cover her legs with a blanket and tell her, "I'll be right back. I'm going to pick out a movie."

She smiles, never questioning me when I tell her what I'm doing.

Early on in our relationship, we discovered that we have many things in common, including a love for the same type of music. We grew up to hair bands and Lena still counts Bon Jovi as her all-time favorite group. She knows every song they've ever released by heart and she's always wanted to see them in concert. She had an opportunity when she was in high school, but an odd snow storm made it impossible for her to get there. Since then, we've never made catching a show a priority.

I wish we had. I wish *I'd* made it a priority.

As with so many things, though, we put it off thinking there would be plenty of time for that later.

Later.

Such a common word. So meaningless most of the time.

Only there aren't going to be too many more laters for us, so I have to "make hay while the sun shines" as my grandmother used to say. That's why, by seven PM, I'm tugging a wig into place and yanking on leather pants that are guaranteed to chafe my ass.

****

Lena

I'm resting my head against the curved neck pillow Nate bought me when the familiar tune of one of my favorite songs begins to play, quite loudly, from the house speakers. I raise my head and open my eyes just in time to see my crazy husband slide by the doorway in his sock feet. He's a blur of black leather pants, a ripped shirt and a dirty blond wig. And he's holding his old steel guitar.

My smile is wide and immediate. His "look" coupled with the music perfectly conveys who he's supposed to be.

Jon Bon Jovi.

Pushing myself into a sitting position, I watch the door for *my* Bon Jovi to reappear. When he does, he's pretending to pluck the strings of his guitar to the beat of the song. His face is screwed up in a rocker-intense way and I nearly laugh out loud at his antics.

Finally Nate makes his way into the room. And when the lyrics started, he begins to lip sync to *Bad Medicine.*

He pretend-serenades me with words of his addiction to my love, curling his upper lip in just the right way and banging his head when the music demands it. As I take in my husband's "mighty fine ass," stretching out the black leather to perfection, his still-chiseled abs, highlighted by the tears in his shirt, and his always-handsome face, I think to myself that this concert *has to be* even better than the real thing.

Nate is my real thing. He has been from the moment I met him. From out first kiss, standing outside the apartment I was renting right after I finished school. The night was cool and the air was damp, and Nate was my fire. I knew then that I was lost. That I would always feel lost without him.

And now I know that if I were able to live another hundred years, I would always feel the same way. He completes me. He's my other half. My soulmate. The other piece to the puzzle of my heart.

When the song ends, I throw back the blanket, intending to use what little is left of my daily energy supply to show my husband just how much I love him. But before I can haul my awkward body into a standing position, the notes to another song begin to play.

I recognize it immediately. My heart goes from racing with the thrill of my husband's performance to a painful thump, beating along with the tune of a bittersweet love song.

I settle back against the cushions to wait for what promises to be an unforgettably heartbreaking performance.

Nate crosses the room to me, tugging the wig from his head and kneeling in front of me. When the lyrics of *Always* should've begun, I don't hear Bon Jovi. I hear only the deep, scratchy voice of my husband as he sings each verse for me.

It's all for me.

The pledge each word is meant to be takes on a whole new meaning as I stare into Nate's green, green eyes. They shine with a love unlike anything I've ever known. Surely he must see the same thing when he looks at me. Surely he can see it. Surely he can see my heart in my eyes. It's there. It beats only for him. And it will until it beats no more.

As the music begins to crescendo, Nate's eyes fill with tears, tears I know mirror my own. As he sings to me of what he'd do for me, of the price he'd willingly pay, I take his face in my hands and I kiss him, silencing his pain the only way I know how—by taking it with my own.

I devour his words, swallowing them whole and making them a part of my soul. I ravage his mouth, memorizing the curve of his lips and the texture of his tongue. I consume his love, feeding on it like fuel to a starving engine.

Gently, but with an urgency neither of us deny and neither of us wants to, Nate pulls me to the floor and tears my clothes from my, bearing me, body and soul, to his hungry eyes and hungrier hands. We make love in that way that people who don't have time or might get caught do—with utter desperation.

And when we lay spent in each other's arms, Nate sings the rest of the song to me as my tears pepper the skin of his chest.

****

I wake with a start, confused for a moment by my surroundings. I recognize the entertainment center, but it's sideways and why am I on the living room floor?

Then it all comes back to me in a rush and I smile, turning until I can see the face of my husband, who rests quietly behind me, probably listening to me breathe.

"I would say we should've taped that, but..." I laugh lightly, thinking of our ravenous lovemaking. That's not something our daughter will *ever* be old enough to see, nor will she want to.

"Uh, I *did* tape it."

I sit up and swivel to face him fully. He's wearing a lazy grin that makes me want to start all over again with taking his clothes off, piece by piece. "What do you mean you *did* tape it?"

"You had your eyes closed, but I came in and set my phone up on the table so I could watch your reaction later."

"Well, you'll get to see more than my reaction."

Of course, I'm not worried. There might have been a time when I'd have balked or been concerned with who might be able to hack in and see something like that, but those days are over. The few things I let take up valuable space in my life nowadays are either horrific worries or love.

There is no room for anything else.

18

Let's Make It, Baby

Lena

Spring comes early, something that both Nate and I embrace with unusual appreciation. It feels as though the heavens have bestowed yet another gift upon us, the weather clearing and warming so much so that I'm able to go outside and sit on our screened porch for a few hours each day.

Although the nausea and bloating haven't increased, for which we are both exceedingly grateful, my energy has become nearly nonexistent. The signs of my disease still aren't overly apparent in any other way, but in *this manner*, I know. I know what's happening to me. This is more than just pregnancy-related fatigue. This is my body constantly fighting an invading foe.

And losing.

Still, when I wake each day, I'm glad I'm carrying my baby yet another step toward the goal. Bringing Helena Grace, a name which Nate insisted upon, into the world is the driving force in my life. Everything I eat, every step I take, every exhausting trip to the obstetrician, the oncologist, the herbalist, the internist, the chiropractor, it's all done with one singular objective in mind—keeping the baby healthy.

I force myself to cram as many tasteless yet nutritious foods into my mouth as I can tolerate without throwing them back up. I walk when I don't feel like it, drink water when I'm not thirsty, and get acupuncture once a week for pain I don't feel.

Yet.

And it's all working. The baby is growing and thriving, all my labs are (mostly) normal, and I've not only convinced myself, but Nate as well that I can do this. Everything is going along smoothly, as I hoped it would, and my faith is restored a little more each day.

Until one sunny afternoon in late March when a contraction hits. Nate and I are concluding our daily walk when the spasm takes hold. It steals my breath and causes my heart to pound with fear.

"It's just Braxton-Hicks, I'm sure," I tell my husband, fighting off a sense of panic as I try to convince myself of the same thing.

Slowly, we make our way back to the house where Nate escorts me to the bedroom. "You need to rest. You're done for the day, young lady." He's attempting light and breezy, but I can see the terror in his eyes.

"Let me use the bathroom first, and then I'll lie down."

It's in the bathroom that I see the blood.

That's when I realize that I might be in trouble.

I'm only twenty-six weeks along. It's too early to have the baby. I want to, no I *need to* make it to twenty-eight weeks. At least the baby will have a fighting chance then.

Please God, please God, please God, I pray as I right my clothes and shuffle back out to the bed.

"Nate, I don't want you to worry, but I'm spotting. I'm going to call Dr. Stephens and see what she wants me to do," I inform him calmly, taking my phone from my pocket and initiating the call. I will my hand to stop trembling. Nate needs my peace, not my panic.

Considering my overall condition, Dr. Stephens doesn't bother with having me monitor my contractions and my bleeding; as soon as she hears "bleeding," she orders me to go immediately to the Labor and Delivery department of the hospital. I'm not surprised. It's what I would do for someone in this position.

As tranquilly as I can, I ask Nate, "Would you grab my overnight bag from the closet? The one that has all my hospital stuff in it?"

I planned ahead for an emergency trip to the hospital, of course. My circumstances are too shaky not to. I knew, right from the beginning, the likelihood that I'd get through this pregnancy, while battling cancer, without at least one unexpected trip to the hospital was extremely low. And so here I am, making my first trip.

M. LEIGHTON

I pray that I'll be home soon, still carrying our child.

Although he makes no comment, I can tell by his jerky, abrupt movements that Nate is in a state of alarm. But still, he does as I ask and takes the bag from the closet. "I'll run this to the car. Be right back."

I can't see him, but I assume he actually *does* run my bag to the car. I'd wager that the instant he was out of my sight, Nate flew through the house to the kitchen, snatched his keys from the dish on the counter, and bolted out the door and practically threw the bag in the back seat. The little mental video clip makes me smile despite my heavy, wary heart. I knew he would return to me all calm and cool and composed. No doubt he expended just enough of his excess energy and fright in that mad dash to the car to keep me from seeing it.

But I know.

As with so many other things in our life, I just know.

Moments later, winded no doubt from his speeding pulse from his quick jaunt to the car, Nate reenters the bedroom and walks purposefully toward me. He bends to hook one arm through mine and the other behind my back so he can help me to my feet. I let him, partly because I know that helping me gives him a sense of control in a situation where he has none, but also because it's needed and appreciated. The scare of the bleeding has sapped what little vigor I had left.

Knees wobble and abdominals shake as I stand. I feel the power of Nate's hold increase ever so slightly. Not enough to hurt or bruise me, but enough that I sense the added support.

"It'll be okay," I tell him on a pant, smiling serenely. I don't feel serene, but I'm determined to be the strength that my husband needs, just as he is constantly being the strength that I need.

Nate holds me in place when I would've taken a step forward. I glance quizzically up into his face.

"I love you. No matter what." My stomach draws into a knot that he feels the need to tell me this *now*, as though he's expecting the worst.

"I know, baby. It'll be okay," I repeat, drinking down the emotion that fizzes at the back of my throat, trying desperately to take comfort from my own reassurances.

The ride to the hospital is a blur. I try to pretend that I'm not bracing myself for another contraction or for blood to gush from between my legs and terrify us both. Neither of those things has happened by the time we reach the hospital, however, which is a good sign.

Nate parks under the awning in the drop-off lane and runs inside to get a wheelchair, for which I'm immensely grateful. Back at the car, he helps me from the passenger seat into the wheelchair, and then ferries me inside to check in. Then I'm very kindly ushered to a room where a nurse is waiting by the bed, gown in hand.

"Hi, Lena! I'm Tiffany. Let's get you changed," she says politely. I nod, ambling to the bed. "Sir, if you'll go back out to the front desk, they have some paperwork for you to fill out."

Nate frowns. I can tell that my husband isn't too keen on the idea of leaving me for more than twenty seconds at a time. He goes along, however, but not before he crosses the room and kisses me, promising to return in just a few minutes.

"First time daddy?" Tiffany asks when Nate is out of earshot.

"Yes. How can you tell?"

"They all have that overprotective streak the first time. Our second, third, and fourth timers usually wait in the lounge."

I smile, but say nothing. No matter how many children we might've had, I can't picture my Nate being comfortable in the lounge while I'm in a room experiencing God knows what.

Expertly, Tiffany helps me out of my clothes and into a gown, then into bed. She hooks me up to the baby monitor that straps across my belly and then to a blood pressure cuff as well. Once both monitors are tracking as they should, the nurse begins her questioning. Although I know Dr. Stephens called ahead to give orders, I also know that this is an unavoidable part of the process. Paperwork, paperwork, paperwork.

How many weeks are you? Any previous miscarriages? When did the bleeding start? How heavy has it been? Have you had contractions? How long and how far apart? Any complications with the pregnancy? Any underlying medical conditions we should know about? Are you allergic to any medications? Do you have a list of current medications?

It's like the prenatal Spanish Inquisition. I know the doctor called ahead, but a good nurse wants the information herself. And being a nurse myself, I know the reason behind every question. That doesn't help to ease my mind, though. Nothing short of the doctor checking me and assuring me that everything is fine with the baby will do that.

Within an hour, just as Nate is stepping out to get some water, Dr. Stephens arrives. Rather than going on to the cafeteria, he merely adjusts his trajectory and moves to a corner of the room where he's out of the way.

I smile. He's settling in to stay. My husband won't let anything or anyone keep him from me.

The doctor asks a few of the same questions I already answered once, but I'm happy to do so again. All I'd pretty much gotten out on the phone was that I was bleeding. Besides, I want her to have the full picture and from *me*, not the secondhand word of the nurse.

"Since you haven't bled very much, let me go ahead and check your cervix and then we'll get an ultrasound, okay?"

I nod, scoot down on the bed, and brace myself for the exam. Although Dr. Stephens is a woman with small hands, she isn't very gentle when she performs a cervical check. I've been on the receiving end of them too many times over the last weeks to believe that it will be any different today.

But I'm wrong.

Maybe it's because I was already bleeding and a cervical examination could actually *cause* bleeding, or maybe it's because she feels the need to be more delicate so as not to rock an already partially unstable boat. Or maybe it's neither of those things. Whatever Dr. Stephens's rationale, I'm appreciative.

I exhale in relief when the doctor finishes.

"You're not dilated," she announces, peeling off her slightly bloody glove, "and you're not bleeding very much. Blood pressure is good. The baby's heart rate is good. When was the last time you had sex?"

Despite my training as a nurse, it's still a question that causes me to blush, especially considering that my husband is less than three feet away, propped in the corner, watching me. "Two nights ago."

Dr. Stephens nods as she digests the information. "Okay, let's see what the ultrasound shows." With that, she leaves the room. Only then do I relax against the pillow.

Nate crosses the room to my side, brushing hair from my cheek with the backs of his fingers. "Did I hurt you?" he asks, guilt in his voice and worry on his face.

"You absolutely did *not* hurt me, Nate. This has nothing to do with you."

"Then why did she ask about sex?"

"The cervix bleeds very easily during pregnancy. It doesn't take much to cause spotting. I always spot after she examines me and that's just with a couple of *fingers*."

The concern doesn't disappear from his handsome face, but he tries to pretend otherwise. "And we both know I'm packing more than a couple of fingers' worth."

His grin is lopsided and cocky and full of all the mischief I fell in love with nineteen years ago.

"Yeah, you are, baby," I purr supportively, teasingly. "More like a damn *weapon*."

Nate's lopsided grin inspires an answering one of my own.

God, how I love him!

I love how solid he is, how hard he tries to protect me, even from his own doubts and fears. I love how he can always find a bright side, even in the darkest times. And I love how his sense of humor has never failed us, just like it didn't today.

"I hope you're not going to try to get it registered."

His eyebrows shoot up. "You think I could?" Before I can retort, he begins nodding, chasing that silly thought. "Maybe they'd take pictures. Send them to Guinness and declare me 'The Most Dangerous Penis Alive.'"

"No, that sounds like you're calling yourself a penis. Do you want people to start calling you 'dick'?"

After giving it a few seconds thought, Nate's smile widens. "Not unless they call me *Mr. Dick*. You know, out of respect for The Most Dangerous Penis Alive."

Of course he isn't serious, but I go along with him anyway. "I think the last thing that you and every other man alive need is to revere your penises any more than you already do."

"Oh, come on. Admit it. You love my penis." When I roll my eyes, Nate tickles the underside of my chin with his fingertip. "*Commme onnn.* You can say it. 'I adore your penis, Nate. It's the prettiest penis in the whole wide world, Nate. Thank you for loving me with The Most Dangerous Penis Alive, Nate.'" A thump near the door has both of us stopping to listen.

I gasp.

Nate's eyes widen guiltily.

I'm sure he's hoping as much as I am that no one was listening to our odd conversation.

After thirty seconds have passed and we are still very much alone, Nate finally whispers, "Maybe we should keep The Most Dangerous Penis Alive between us. The world might not be ready for it yet."

"I think that's best," I reply, my words hushed and conspiratorial, too. "I'm not sure *I'm* ready for it yet."

We stare at one another for about fifteen seconds before we both give in to our laughter. We giggle and snort like two teenagers, and it feels good. It feels good to laugh, maybe even more so because we are covered by a dark cloud of uncertainty. But we are together, and that makes all the difference.

We are like two young lovers huddled beneath an umbrella in a rainstorm. We find shelter from the elements, warmth in each other's arms, and solace in otherwise unforgiving circumstances. It's us against the world.

Us against time.

As our merriment wanes, I lie staring up into Nate's eyes, and he into mine. "I love you more than anything," I declare softly. It's nothing he doesn't already know, but I'm more frequently impressed with the need to tell him these days.

"And *I* love *you*. We'll get through this," he pledges, bending to kiss my forehead, leaving his lips pressed to my skin for longer than the simple touch requires. "All three of us."

I exhale a breath I wasn't aware of holding. Maybe I just needed for him to tell me everything will be okay. Maybe I just needed for him to *feel* like everything will be okay. Whatever the reason, the tension in my muscles relaxes, and I sink further into the mattress.

Eventually, a tech comes to take me for an ultrasound. Then, when I arrive back in my room, it's only a matter of minutes before Dr. Stephens walks in to give me the results.

"Looks like placenta previa," she announces. "But it's nothing that I believe you need to stay here to treat, nothing that severe. Bed rest. Stay off your feet as much as you can. No exercise. No sex." She says the last with a playful amount of emphasis as she turns a warning eye toward Nate. "I can talk to Mr. Li. He's made house calls before. I'm confident he'll work with you at home so you don't have to come out so frequently." Mr. Li is the Chinese medicine man I've been seeing for herbal remedies and acupuncture.

The doctor goes on to give me a follow-up appointment date and a few other common sense instructions like no baths or douches, nothing in the vagina. No straining, be careful of falls, that sort of thing. Basically, I'm to treat my body as though it's made of glass. I don't think that will be a problem. Nate is already doing it for the most part. And, honestly, I don't care what I have to agree to; I'll do whatever I have to do to keep the baby safe.

"But everything is okay? I mean, the baby is going to be okay?"

Dr. Stephens smiles. "I don't see why she won't be. Just take it easy. You're almost there."

At that point, for the first time since I saw the blood, I fully relax.

****

"You don't have to carry me, Nate. I can walk into the house, for Pete's sake." I resist when Nate sweeps me off my feet after I step out of the car in the garage.

"I *like* carrying you," he assures me, swinging us both around as he pushes the car door shut. "It always reminds me of feeding the stingrays in Grand Cayman. Remember that?"

My head is on his shoulder, but I can hear the smile in his voice. "How could I forget? *Someone* talked me into feeding them, even though I was afraid of getting squid juice on me and getting a stingray hickey. But still, I was dumb enough to do it."

"The part *I* talked you into went fine. They warned you not to wipe your hands on any body parts. How was I supposed to know you'd brushed your leg after you fed them?"

"I didn't *mean* to do it. It was just sort of habit, I guess. I mean, we were in the water. I just didn't think about it."

"Until a big female stingray came up to suck the smell off."

"Yeah, I sure thought about it *then!*"

I smile at the memory. I'd gone completely motionless with panic when the stingray swam to my leg and turned its vacuum-like mouth on my skin. It wasn't really painful; it was more terrifying than anything. At least to me it was. I screamed and tried to get away, but my progress was very slow in the chest-deep saltwater. That had probably only aggravated the situation. But sweet Nate, he'd been so distressed by *my* upset that, once we got back to shore, he'd carried me all the way to the bus stop and then on to the cruise ship and then the rest of the way to our room when we arrived back at the boat. I wasn't actually *hurt*, but he was taking no chances.

After that, we'd made the most of the comical situation, and Nate had offered at every turn to strip me down and wash my leg. "You know, to make sure it doesn't get infected," he explained with his sexy, suggestive smile. The skin wasn't even broken, but I always relented anyway, loving how intimate our trip became after that. We touched and laughed and kissed every few minutes for the rest of the voyage. Despite the hickey, there was no point at which I wasn't blissfully happy.

That was just before we got married. We were young and energetic, and life was a beautiful mystery that stretched out in front of us like those stunning sunsets on the ocean—to infinity. And beyond.

If someone had told us then where we'd be *now*, neither of us would've believed them. I suppose no one really expects their life to end early or abruptly or painfully. Many *fear it,* but few actually *expect it.*

Nate gets me safely inside, and it isn't until he deposits me in our spacious master bathroom that I feel the tears come. Even though my obstetrician gave me no reason to think that I might lose the baby over this, I feel a deep ache behind my ribs that won't quite go away. A sense of foreboding pounds at the door of my heart, echoing through my muscles in a fine tremor that ends at my fingertips.

All alone, I shake like my bones are tectonic plates, rubbing together and threatening an earthquake.

When I finally calm, I move to the large dimpled ottoman and sit down, taking my phone from my pocket. With trembling fingers, I set it to video. I take another succession of deep, steadying breaths and wrestle back the sobs that refuse to vacate my throat.

Eventually it works.

A smile into the camera is a totally different story, though.

It takes me two tries before I can get one to stick, but when I do, I take full advantage of the moment and promptly slide my thumb over the record button.

"Hi, little Grace. It's your momma." As I speak, I rub my rounded belly as though I might actually comfort my child by doing so. Or that maybe my child can comfort *me.*

"I know today was scary, but I...I don't want you to be frightened. If *for any reason* you don't make it here to us in this world, I'll find you in the next. You won't be alone. I promise. If you wake up in heaven, watch for me. I'll be there soon. I'll find you. Then I'll be able to hold you in my arms. I'll rock you and...and s-sing to you. And we'll spend all of eternity together. So don't be afraid, little Grace. I will always be with you. Always. Just look for me. In heaven, in the dark, in the sound of the waves, in the lightning bugs. Wherever you go, I'll be there with you. I love you, sweet baby girl. In this life and the next. Always."

With strength reserved for my husband and my child, I hold my smile until I stop the recording. The instant the light goes dark, however, I drop my face into my waiting open hands, and I cry quiet tears of fear and helplessness. Of happiness and relief. I don't know what I'm supposed to feel, so I feel everything— the positive and the negative, the good and the bad. The hopeful and the hopeless.

I have no idea what the future holds, even though I'm afraid that I might, but I have a nebulous chill in my bones that whispers of death. Whether mine or my baby's I can't possibly know, but either way, the road ahead seems bleak.

I weep in utter silence. My sobs make no sound. Their noise is smothered by the agony that chokes me. The only vibration that tickles the delicate bones inside my ears is the sound of time.

Galloping away.

19

The Hardest Part is the Night

Nate

Over the course of the following weeks, Lena's health begins to slowly decline. It's as though the dark cloud that has been hovering silently in the distance sweeps in and bursts, pouring rain of reality and finality over her. Over me.

Over us.

It started on the morning following the placenta previa diagnosis and has run steadily downhill each day since. Lena fights it, of course. She still refuses to give up on our baby, but her vigor lessens with every week that slips by.

She battles depression. It seems almost like poisonous black strings have attached themselves to her heart. I can almost see them coiling and wrapping and knotting, pulling tighter and tighter every day, dragging her down, down, down.

Nissa has been trying to help with that. She comes over once a day to either read to Lena or watch a movie with her, usually something from their youth, something they sing and laugh to like *Grease* or *Flash Gordon*, which I find particularly amusing.

She combats confusion as well. She told me once a few days ago that it feels as though she's awakening from a dream, awakening to a life she doesn't recognize. Sometimes she's as confused about *when* she is as she is about *where* she is.

I first noticed that in relation to Nissa. She was at the house the other day. She'd been reading to Lena when Lena interrupted her.

"How are things with you and Mark? I'm sorry I haven't asked in so long."

Nissa reached across the couch to lay her hand on Lena's. "It's not like you've got a lot on your plate or anything." I saw the wink she shot my wife, and my wife's answering smile, sad though it was.

"Well? How are things?"

"Not great. No better, no worse, I guess. I just wonder sometimes how long we can go on this way. I mean, we might as well just be roommates. And babysitters. Well, that's mostly just me."

"I'm so sorry, babe."

Nissa shrugged. "It'll come to a head one of these days. I'm not too eager to push it until the kids are a little older. I have no idea what I'd do if he left me right now."

Lena nodded, her expression rife with sympathy, and the two sat in silence for a few minutes. Slowly, Lena's eyes began to get heavy, and she dozed off. Nissa watched her from the couch. I watched her from the island in the kitchen. I wondered if she hurt as much as I did to see my beautiful, vivacious Lena this way. Because it was damn sure breaking my heart.

She only napped for about ten minutes. When she woke, she smiled over at Nissa as if she hadn't been asleep and asked, "So, how are things with you and Mark?"

To Nissa's credit, she handled it well. Didn't miss a beat with her response. "He's an asshole, but I'm not surprised. He's always been an asshole."

The two laughed, but I died a little inside.

For a few days, Lena wouldn't talk about it. Tried to hide her slips. But I could see it. Even without the overt example of that conversation with Nissa, I could see it. I'm as aware of every subtle nuance of my wife as I am of my own body.

I know how she struggles, just as I know her reasons for not wanting to talk about it, to acknowledge it. She's trying to protect me. And I'm trying to protect her.

That doesn't change the facts, though.

The facts are that Lena's disease is progressing. And there is absolutely nothing we can do about it. For me, that means that I'm destined to watch the love of my life slip away from me in the most excruciating way imaginable—little by little, day by day, and with no recourse whatsoever.

I keep a watchful eye on Lena at all times. Periods when I feel like she isn't really *with me* are getting more and more frequent. Nights seem to be the worst. For that reason, I never let myself fall into a very deep sleep. My fear is that she will get up in the dark and I won't hear her. And I'm afraid that if she does, something bad will happen. She'll hurt herself or need my help. I'm terrified that I won't be there for her, so I sleep with one eye open at all times.

Tonight, Lena fell asleep on the sofa. She skipped supper altogether, which isn't like her. Even so, I was hesitant to wake her. I'm okay with letting it go *this one time*, but if it becomes a habit, I'll have to consult the doctors. Lena *has to eat*. For her, for the baby, she has to. I hope this won't be a trend, but I know if it is, I'll have no choice but to involve the doctor.

I want Lena to do well on her own for as long as she can. I know that's what *she* wants, too. What she *needs*. Besides that, I've read enough about terminal cases such as Lena's to know there is a point of no return when it comes to their ability to sustain their own life. Having to be fed through a tube is one of those points, and I'm in no hurry for my wife to arrive there.

I carried her to bed and tucked her in around eleven, and I've been drifting between wakefulness and sleep ever since. The moment Lena's weight shifts off the bed, I'm wide awake.

I bolt upright.

"You okay?" I ask.

"Fine, fine," she answers, her voice sounding clear and lucid. "Just going in here to get some orders."

Orders?

I slide out of bed to follow her. My eyes quickly adjust to the darkness, so I have no trouble seeing her as she makes her way down the hall. I also have no trouble seeing her when she stops, glances down at her arms, licks her finger, and begins flipping through papers that aren't really there. I watch her as she closely studies something, running her finger down the imaginary page. I wonder what she's seeing. And why. Obviously it's work-related, which doesn't surprise me. She's been a nurse practitioner for most of her adult life. She's as comfortable in her white lab coat as she is in her pajamas.

"Elevated ammonia levels," she mutters before tucking the nonexistent papers against her chest and resuming her walk down the hall.

I trail her into the kitchen where Lena pulls out a stool at the island and sits on the edge like I've seen her do at work so many times. It seems a habit that many medical personnel adopt—to perch right on the edge of those black vinyl stools that can be found in every emergency room in the country. The ones that roll. Maybe it's so they can get up quickly. Or maybe it's because the stools themselves aren't very stable. I don't know the why of it; I only know I've seen many of them do it.

Lena sets her unseen papers on the granite in front of her and flips through the pages again. She examines them for a couple of minutes, flipping back and forth as though she's looking for something specific. Finally, she reaches out into space and grabs at the air. She grasps with her fingers, appearing to take something from several invisible slots and adding them to her pile. I assume she's compiling the orders she said she was going after, probably getting them from the tower of black cubbies I've seen stacked on one corner of her desk, the kind that keep stacks of papers organized.

She has no idea that she's in our kitchen or that I'm standing behind her. She's present in a world that only she can see and hear and touch.

A lump forms in my throat. It feels roughly the size of my first car, an old Buick that had a rusted fender and mismatched tires. I swallow several times, but it doesn't lessen the ball of grief lodged there. It's painful to watch, seeing my wife in such a weakened, fragile state, but watch her I will.

I won't leave her. Not now. Not ever.

So I lean against the wall in the kitchen and keep an eye on my Lena as she fills out papers that only exist in her imagination. She works diligently on them for five or six minutes, writing with a pen only she can feel, before she picks up a banana from the fruit bowl on the counter and holds it to her ear as if it were a phone.

"I need you to put in orders for the patient in room six. Ultrasound of the liver, a liver function panel, and I'd like a repeat CBC done as well. I think it might be a good idea to get a PT/INR, too. As soon as possible, please. Thank you."

Before she hangs up the banana phone, she holds it out and stares at it. She laughs softly and lays it aside, but makes no comment. I wonder if she finally realized that it isn't a phone at all.

Lena resumes her "work," stacking her papers over and over and over before laying them neatly on the counter and folding her hands over them. I wait to see what she will do, but she seems content to just sit where she is, in the dark, in the quiet, lost in another world. Eventually, she begins to murmur, to work out the details of her patient's case in the muddled halls of her mind.

"Right upper quadrant pain, loss of appetite, increased fatigue, confusion" she ticks off as though she's putting puzzle pieces into place. "I bet it's the liver."

I know little about medicine, but between spending nearly half of my life living with a nurse and attending numerous appointments with Lena over the past months, I've picked up enough to know what some of this means. She's treating someone with some sort of liver dysfunction, and I can't help wondering if her own fears, fears of how the cancer has progressed in her liver, are playing out in her mind. Is it possible that some part of her is cataloging her symptoms and working out her own condition?

Suddenly, Lena's murmuring ceases. When she remains quiet for several minutes, I give up my position against the wall and speak softly as I cross to her. "Hey, babe. Wha'cha doin'?"

Lena turns toward me, a breathtaking smile spreading across her face. It makes me pause. I feel like I've been hit with a gale-force gust of wind. It rocks me all the way down to the bottom of my soul, that smile. I've seen it hundreds of times throughout our years together. It's the smile I fell in love with, the smile that says she's happy to see me, the smile that says she's happy *period*.

It's the smile I haven't seen in a while.

Since the diagnosis, all she's been able to do is pretend at perfect happiness, but it's just that—pretend. I can see it now, plain as day, when I compare *this* smile to the ones I've seen since she was declared terminal. She's done her best to hide her heartache from me, but I know.

And down deep, she's withering.

"What a nice surprise!" she exclaims, tilting her face up to mine for a kiss. I oblige her. Gladly.

These days, I feel like I can't touch her enough, can't get close enough, can't *stay* close enough. Like if I blink, I'll open my eyes and she'll be gone, having disappeared without a trace. I'm afraid of missing something. *Anything.*

This is all we have left.

I brush the back of my index finger down her satiny cheek as I think of something to say. I'm momentarily dumbstruck. Her beauty, her goodness, a goodness that shines through the pores of her porcelain skin, is staggering. It always has been. I've often wondered throughout the years how I got so lucky.

Now I know.

I'm only going to get to keep her for half of my life, not nearly long enough. The price of loving her is that I will lose her. That I will love her forever, even after she's gone and I remain.

"You hungry?" I ask.

I don't know what else to say that might play into whatever is going on inside her head. I've always heard it isn't wise to orient someone to the present if they are somewhere else *mentally*. I have no idea if that applies to Lena, but I'm not willing to risk it, so I just go along with her delusion.

"Starving," she says, linking her fingers behind my neck and leaning in. I kiss her again, happy for anything that might still the tremble I feel beginning in my bottom lip. It's getting harder and harder to bury this agony that I'm drowning in.

I swallow before I speak again, clearing the bulge of emotion currently tampering with my vocal cords. I don't want my wife to be able to pick up on my dismay. I wouldn't have a clue how to answer any questions she might have, and I certainly don't want to cause her any additional stress.

So I hide it.

As I've made a point to do all this time.

For the sake of my beautiful Lena, I hide my own pain from her and try my best to act normal. I don't want her to know that I'm dying in a different way, the kind of dying that will leave my body alive but the rest of me a pile of dead and broken pieces that have no way of healing.

"Let me make you some eggs," I offer.

"Eggs sound wonderful."

Reluctantly, I pull away and walk around the island to turn on the soft light over the stove. It will give me just enough of a glow to cook by.

"How was your day?" I ask nonchalantly as I take a skillet from the cabinet, get the eggs and butter from the fridge, and set about making my ailing mate some scrambled eggs.

Lena sighs heavily. "Better now that you're here. I have a patient that I think might be in liver failure or, worse, have liver cancer. She...she..."

Her words fade into the shadows as Lena falls silent behind me. I turn to look at her, and she has taken six apples from the fruit bowl and is in the process of lining them up on the countertop.

"She what?" I prompt.

Lena jumps, turning vacant eyes toward me. "What?"

"You were telling me about a patient you think might have something going on with her liver."

"Hang on. I just need to get these sorted. Give me a minute." She directs her attention once more to the apples before her. She lines them up from left to right and then lines them up top to bottom, making sure that each apple is touching the ones on either side of it.

As I scramble her eggs, I keep an eye on Lena. She never offers to move or speak again, though. She just keeps straightening and restraightening those apples, lost once more to the world in which I don't exist.

Lost to me.

The backs of my eyeballs sting as I recall something I read about the natural occurrences that transpire during the last weeks of life, as different organs begin to fail. The article, one I'd found on a hospice site, mentioned that patients often straighten odd things as their time on Earth comes to a close. It's a subconscious effort to get the affairs of their life in order before they die.

Before death.

I have to turn away from Lena and squeeze my eyes shut against the surge of anguish that washes through me.

I'm going to lose her.

I'm going to lose my wife. My soul mate. My partner in crime. The very air I breathe. I'm going to lose her, and there is nothing I can do about it.

For as long as we've known her condition is terminal, on some level I've refused to think that there is really *no hope* for her, that there is really *nothing* that can be done. I believed that, because she's young and healthy, her body would last longer, fight harder and they'd be able to find a way to make her better. I didn't *purposely* mislead myself, but now I recognize that's precisely what I've done—deceived myself.

Somehow, I managed to convince a part of my mind, *of my heart* of that inaccuracy, and now the reality of the situation—that my wife's body is failing her, that she is now steadily making her way toward the end—stabs me in the stomach like the horns of a bull, a bull that has been taunted and is now hell-bent on destruction.

That bull of truth gores me.

Through and through.

I slide the skillet off the burner and take a step back, bracing my arms against the edge of the stove and letting my head drop down between them. I stand motionless for a handful of seconds trying to collect myself.

It takes everything I have in me to control the devastation that's wrecking my heart. It takes every bit of my concentration, and even then, it's another minute or so before I actually achieve an acceptable degree of equilibrium. Only when I'm once more composed enough to let Lena see my face do I turn toward her again.

Then I'm shaken again. To my core, I'm shaken. The sight of her…

Jesus H. Christ!

Lena is still lining up apples, still getting her life in order. And it still feels like she's ripping my soul out of my chest rather than organizing our fruit.

"Eggs are on," I say as brightly as I can, smiling when Lena's eyes flip up to me. Her brow wrinkles as though she has no idea where she is or why I'm here with her.

"Eggs?"

"Yep. You didn't get dinner. You need to eat."

"Oh right, right. I'm starved," she says again, as if the previous ten minutes hadn't just elapsed.

I plate her eggs and walk them to the island on legs that feel like a newborn colt's—shaky and uncertain. When I set the saucer down, it clanks and rattles. My hand is anything but steady.

I grab a fork from the drawer and hand it to her. Then, quietly, reverently, I stand in front of the love of my entire existence and watch her scoop eggs into her mouth and laugh at something I can't hear.

I watch her, and I mourn her, already agonizing over the battle she faces, the battle I'll have to watch her fight.

The battle she's going to lose.

And I'm already dreading what the rest of my life is going to be like without her.

****

The confusion worsens over time. There is nothing the doctors can do because any medication they could give to help flush the ammonia from Lena's system, a build-up caused by her deteriorating liver function, is hazardous to the baby. This is part of the disease, I've been told, and is prognostic in and of itself.

It doesn't bode well.

Lena doesn't have much more time left.

My strong, amazing wife has already made it past the twenty-eight weeks she was aiming for. On days when she's coherent and awake, she's extremely happy about that fact.

I'm happy that she's happy, and that she's lucid.

I've learned to take advantage of those periods, to say what needs to be said, to enjoy every moment as if it were the last, because in truth, each one could be.

During the good times, we continue making our videos. They've gotten shorter and shorter, though.

Less and less animated. Now, they're more or less little thoughts that Lena wants to pass on to her daughter, disjointed words of wisdom sprinkled with the occasional anecdote.

I treasure them just as much as I do the ones that make perfect sense, but they're harder to watch. It's as though I can see my wife fading right before my eyes. She's a pale, ghost-like version of the vibrant woman who'd begun making the videos, and each second of film is like a stake to my heart.

Today, I'm aiming my phone at her, nodding for her to begin. When she does, my stomach crunches up into an unbearable knot of grief.

"Laugh often and love deep, little Grace," she says, her eyes seeming to look *through* the camera lens as if she can already see her daughter's face somewhere on the other side of it. "Fill your jar. As long as your jar is full, your life will never be empty. And every chance you get, put your face in the sun, and show the wind how to fly. Be fearless, my baby girl. Be fearless."

Usually she ends each video with a smile, a bright one that belies what's going on in her life, in her body. But this time, her voice cracks, and her brow pleats as she struggles not to show her true emotion. I wait for several seconds, wait for her to recover and either continue or end it, but she never does. She just sits quietly on the couch with her head bowed. Through the screen of my camera, I watch her. I catch the steady rise and fall of her chest and realize she's drifted off to sleep.

She does that more and more often these days—just falls asleep. Nods off unexpectedly. She's beginning to sleep more than she's awake.

I wonder how long it will be before she just doesn't wake up at all.

I know eventually that will happen. She'll slip into a coma and never wake up.

That is my last thought every single time she dozes off—*Will I ever get to see your beautiful eyes again?*

I press the record button to turn off the video. Slowly, I rise to my feet and walk silently from the room. Only I'm around the corner and out of sight do I sink to the floor, running my fingers into my hair and giving in to the sensation of defeat.

I save all the fight I have left for my wife. I keep my chin up for her. Anything to keep her going.

But when she can't see me, I crumble.

****

The following week, when Lena is thirty-one weeks along, the pain begins. The first thing I noticed was her grabbing her right side and wincing, gasping and holding her breath for a few seconds.

"You okay?" I asked initially.

Each time she's done it, I've watched my wife gather her courage, the fight she refuses to let go of, and smile.

I watch her put on her own mask.

"Yep. Just a little twinge."

Over time, the "little twinges" have come more and more frequently and lasted longer and longer. Mr. Li is coming twice per week now, doing everything he can to ease her discomfort. Different herbs and teas and powders. More acupuncture and aromatherapy and guided imagery. Nothing seems to help very much, though. Lena just grits her teeth and gets through the pain, smiling at me once they've passed as if nothing is wrong.

Even in her sickness, even in her pain, she's constantly trying to comfort me, to make me think everything is okay, that *she* is okay. But I can see right through her efforts. Of course, I can. I know her.

I *know* her.

I can see the odd pallor of her skin, the circles under her eyes, the dazed expression she carries more often than not. I can plainly see that she is *not* okay.

There are times when I want to scream at her to show me how she *really* feels, to stop hiding it from me. Some part of me gets angry about it because *sometimes* it feels like she's trying to protect me because she thinks I can't handle it, that I'm not strong enough. But the *rational* part of my brain always slows my roll, reminding me that this is just who Lena is. She's nurturing, loving, protective. This is her way of loving me the best way she can.

The only way she knows how.

That's why I squash those stubborn bursts of anger. There's no room for ego or pride or selfishness anymore. There's just not.

As it turns out, the pains in her side were only the beginning, the beginning of worse things to come. Little by little, Lena's ability to eat is becoming compromised.

At first, I learned to blend nutritious shakes for her to eat, anything to offset the whole foods she was no longer able to swallow. I added the herbs that Dr. Li recommended to help with her pain and with her liver function, and for a while it seemed to work. Her weight didn't suffer, and her labs, all but a few, looked good, so I kept that up.

For the most part, she's *existed* on those shakes for two weeks. It wasn't hard for me to see when the tides were taking another turn for the worse, though. Lena began to get choked trying to swallow drinks of the shakes. She also began to get tired more and more quickly.

But now I *know* things are going downhill. No suspecting or guessing or supposing. I *know*.

She just weighed in for her weekly appointment with the obstetrician, and my fears are now confirmed—Lena is losing weight.

"I think it's time to think about getting her some supplemental nutrition," Dr. Stephens says, her face wreathed in sadness. When she speaks, she addresses me. Lena has all but stopped participating in the doctor's visits. These days, she spends the majority of her time in a world that doesn't include us, doing odd things that make sense only to her. Today, she's busy lining up pens on the small desk that's attached to the wall in the corner of this tiny exam room.

Over and over, she tidies the pens, as if nothing in the world is more important. "And we need to consider options for delivery if…well, if her level of confusion continues to increase and a vaginal delivery becomes problematic at any time."

"C-section is fine. Whatever is best for Lena and the baby." I hear a man's voice bounce off the walls in the claustrophobic room, but it doesn't sound like mine. I don't even recognize the hollow monotone.

From behind me, I hear a voice, I hear words that cause my heart to stutter in my chest, like it's threatening to stop.

"Goodnight, stars. Goodnight, moon. Goodnight, lightning bugs. Come again soon."

I glance around at Lena and find her staring down at her belly. She's rubbing in big circles, and in her other hand is a miniature jar of some sort, something she evidently found at the desk.

Lena cradles it in one hand and her stomach in the other, her voice gentle and kind as she repeats the rhyme to our unborn child. "Don't go to bed with dirty feet or an empty jar. Say your prayers every night, and never stop chasing the lightning bugs."

Grief gushes under the door, out from the vents, through every tiny crack in walls. It fills the room to overflowing, promises to suffocate me. For a moment, I feel like I can't breathe, like air has simply ceased to flow into and out from my lungs.

I gulp at the dense, heavy atmosphere. Still I can't take it in.

"Excuse me," I mutter gruffly on a gasp, practically leaping from my chair. I lunge for the door and lurch out into the hall.

Fumbling my way along the ever-narrowing hallway, I grab the first handle I come to and nearly fall into an empty exam room. Slamming the door behind me, I slump to my knees and let my chin drop to my chest where I give in to the urge to panic.

My muscles shake from head to toe as I kneel here, picturing my wife in the next room, reciting her father's nursery rhyme to our baby. All I can think is that there is a tremendous likelihood that our child, that our sweet child for whom my wife is giving her life, will never get to hear Lena say those words. Grace will probably never get to see the way her mother's features soften as she rhythmically recounts the short tale. She'll never get to feel the tender touch of those slim fingers on her face. She'll never be held by the arms that love her most.

The tragedy of it is consuming me faster than I can recover and today…today I just can't fight it.

So I don't.

On my knees, I let sorrow have its way. I let my face crumble and my eyes tear. I let my fists clench and my chest heave. I let my heart break and my soul scream. I let it go until I'm too weak to move.

Only then do I breathe.

Only then *can I* breathe.

Taking deep, calming swallows of air, I inhale and exhale slowly. A picture comes to mind, one of my wife in the next room, confusion written on her stunning face as she wonders where I went. And why I haven't come back.

I can't bear the thought that she might, even for a single heartbeat, think I've left her. It's *that* thought, *that* image that brings me to my feet and sends me back the way I came, back to the one who has brought me the most pleasure of my life.

And, now, the most pain.

20

Stick to Your Guns

Nate

A loud crash followed by a dull thump wakes me. I'm on my feet and out the bedroom door before my brain has time to fully process the fear that's gripping me.

"Lena?" I call.

No answer.

Frantic and bewildered, I search first the kitchen and then the living room, berating myself as I go. How did I fall into such a deep sleep that I didn't hear her get up? How did I let myself relax so completely?

I know the answer—exhaustion. I haven't slept soundly in weeks. That, coupled with constant worry, has finally caught up with me.

When I put Lena in bed last night and crawled in beside her, she'd turned to snuggle into my side like she used to do. "I love you," she'd murmured right before she fell back into her coma-like rest. My heart had been so full of adoration and agony, I thought I'd never be able to sleep.

But I did.

I must've dozed right off and stayed that way through her exit from the room.

"Christ Almighty!" I breathe when I spot my wife lying on her side on the brick paver patio. She's visibly struggling to help herself up, but very ineffectively. She's reaching for something to hold onto, but her fingers grasp at thin, vacant night air.

Rushing to her side, I take her gently under her arms and ease her into a sitting position. "Are you okay?"

My eyes rake her from head to toe, pausing at the pale cotton material between her legs to look for signs of bleeding. I exhale in relief when I see none.

Lena laughs, a high-pitched sound like a little girl. "I slipped in the wet grass," she explains, patting the bricks beside her. "But I almost got it. Look!" She's pointing up into the dark sky, gesturing toward something only she can see. "Get it, Daddy! Get it before it gets away."

That's when I realize what she's seeing—lightning bugs. In her mind, she's a child again, chasing fireflies with her father.

Her reality drifts further and further from mine with every passing day, it seems. I'm losing her hour by hour, millimeter by millimeter, breath by breath. I know it won't be very long before she leaves my world and never comes back.

Another crack in my heart widens into a gaping chasm, leaking a little more of my hope and strength and *soul* into the cool predawn air.

I reposition myself and bend to scoop Lean into my arms. Her gaze remains trained on the insects I can't see, her face bright and full of wonder. Despite her sunken cheeks and the blue-black smudges still visible beneath her eyes, she's strikingly beautiful in her thrall. Enough to make me catch my breath.

Still.

Always.

That's why I pivot toward the lounger, the one with the cream-colored blanket thrown over the raised back, and sit. I pull Lena against my chest and reach behind me for the fuzzy cover, dragging it over both of us to ward off the slight chill. She tugs it up to her chin and nestles her head into the curve of my neck then lets out a long sigh like she couldn't be happier. I brush my lips over blonde hair cast silver by the moonlight, and I hold my wife until she falls back to sleep.

****

The following day, I drive Lena to the hospital for the placement of a nasogastric tube through which she can be fed supplemental nutrition. The oncologist suspects that her decreasing ability to swallow means that the tumor has spread up into the bottom portion of her esophagus. Dr. Taffer wants to get the NG tube in as soon as possible, before the cancer grows even more and prevents her from passing the tube beyond it.

I'm not sure if it's a good thing or not, but Lena is especially coherent today.

As she rests on the stretcher, awaiting her doctor, she turns her soft brown eyes up to mine. "This will be a good thing, Nate." Her smile says she's trying to convince herself as much as she's trying to convince me. "You'll see."

"Anything that keeps you with me longer is a good thing."

Somewhere along the way, we made the silent agreement to drop the pretense of her survival. Now we speak about more time in terms of weeks and days, not months. Definitely not years.

I figure Lena has worked it out because of her worsening symptoms. She seems to be aware of that even when she isn't lucid for extended periods of time. I worked it out from all of the looks I've been getting from the doctors and nurses. On their faces, they wear sadness and a form of pity that rips through my heart like a poison-tipped arrow. They know the end is coming. It's coming fast, faster than I think I can handle sometimes.

"They'll show you how to use it for when I can't," Lena assures me. Her words are matter of fact, but there's a hollowness to them, an emptiness that tears at my insides.

It's a strange and awful thing to discuss dying this way.

****

Much to my relief, having the feeding tube placed has made a noticeable difference. I've been diligent about feeding her exactly as prescribed. I keep the fridge overflowing with organic fruits and vegetables that I blend into highly nutritious shakes to give to her via the tube three times a day. I also give her the blue-green supplement twice a day and flush the tube with plenty of water before and after use each time. Not only is Lena livelier and wakeful, her overall appearance doesn't seem so...sickly. Her skin has pinked up, her mind seems to focus more readily, even her eyes seem brighter. And for better or worse, the improvement gives me a small burst of hope.

If we can just get through the delivery, maybe she can start treatment. Maybe there will be something *they can do. Maybe it won't be too late.*

"You didn't realize this was going to be a full-time job, did you?" Lena teases me. We are smooshed together on the patio lounger, basking in the late May sunset.

"Why do you think I left the bank? I wasn't about to miss a single second with you, even if it does stain my shirts." And it does. The colorant that's used in the supplemental nutrition can be seen on every one of my lighter-hued shirts.

I grin every time I do laundry. I can't help thinking of all the occasions when Lena has come out from the washroom over the years, shaking her head, muttering about how messy I am. I can now see that she was right. I have no idea how I get that damn food everywhere, but I can't deny that I do. The evidence of it is right there on my clothes. That's why I started wearing my grilling apron when I deal with that stuff.

"I'll be curious to see who's messier, you or Grace."

I smile down into Lena's exquisite face, my eyes drifting over the gentle curve of her brow, the pert tip of her nose, the lush bow of her mouth. I love hearing her talk of days when the three of us will be together. I hope against hope that there will be many of those.

My smile falters for a split second before I catch it, rescue it. I have to be even more careful these days. It's getting harder and harder to combat the surges of sadness. They hit me when I least expect them sometimes, but I'm still as determined as ever to hide them from my perceptive wife. "I can't wait to see you with her. You were born to be a mother."

Lena says nothing, only stares up into my face like I'm the sun in her sky. Finally, after a long silence, she speaks. "Nate?"

"Yeah, baby."

Tracing the collar of my shirt with the tip of her finger, Lena chews her lip nervously. "Do you think we could go see my mother?"

I tense. "Why would you want to do that?"

I feel her shrug against me. "I'd like to see her one last time."

My heart! Jesus!

It twists painfully behind my ribs, a sensation I'm becoming quite accustomed to. "I'm not sure that would be the wisest thing. I mean, you're supposed to be on bed-rest."

"But I haven't bled since I got back from the hospital." She pauses, concern crinkling her brow. "Have I?"

Another stab to my chest. Lena knows that she loses pieces of time. And she knows why. When she's lucid, she becomes aware of how sometimes whole days have passed that she can't remember. She knows what's going on. That's undoubtedly why she wants to see her mother. And why she had to ask if she's been bleeding.

"No," I confirm softly, my voice perceptibly choked. "No, you haven't bled any more."

"Then maybe we could make the trip?" Her whiskey eyes are hopeful.

"Let's check with both docs first." Lena nods, but is obviously deflated, so I add, "If not, then maybe I could bring her here. I'm sure they'd let her out for the day. With me. For this."

"Thank you, my love."

"Anything for you," I reply, caressing the silken arch of her cheekbone. And I mean it. Anything, anything at all for her.

I'm reminded of the way she organizes and tidies things when she's at her most confused. This effort to see her mother is probably part of her process of getting her life in order—making peace with the woman who gave up on her.

I resolve to make the reunion happen, by hook or crook. I want my wife to have whatever makes her happy, whatever will ease her heart and mind, even if that means her spending time with her mother.

We fall silent after that, each lost in thought as the setting sun bathes us in the golden glow of day's end. We watch as the sky fades from bright orange to deep, royal blue.

It's Lena's keen eye that catches the first glimmer of a different light.

"Nate!" She sits up so suddenly, it startles me.

"What? What's wrong?" Every muscle in my body is instantly straining beneath my skin, prepared for action.

"Go get a Mason jar! Quick!"

For a few seconds, it's *me* who is confused. But then, I notice her expression, open and excited, and follow her eyes to where she's looking. A single firefly is blinking off and on as it makes its way into our backyard. I probably never would've noticed it, but Lena spotted it right away.

"Okay, hang on," I tell Lena, trying to maneuver myself out from under her without unseating her. When I manage to untangle myself, I make my way quickly into the kitchen, flinging open cabinet doors, looking for a Mason jar, but having zero luck. That's when I hear her voice waft in from the patio. "Look in the pantry," she instructs.

I spin on my heel and head for the pantry, flicking on the light and spotting a single empty Mason jar on the top shelf in the corner. I think I remember Nissa bringing us homemade strawberry jam in it last year.

On my way back outside, I pause at the counter only long enough to use the tip of a steak knife to poke holes in the lid. With that done, I grab my phone from the charger and go back outside.

Lena is sitting upright in the lounger, her pregnant belly touching the chair between her spread thighs. She reminds me of a beautiful blonde Buddha.

Impulsively, I turn on my phone, raise it to find her on the screen, and snap a picture. I know without a doubt that I'll go back and look at it often. Something about her face is magic. Pure magic.

Then I look up and see our yard.

My mouth drops open.

There are lightning bugs everywhere. Dozens and dozens of them, flickering on and off in a haphazard display of their talent. It's as if they're showing off their brightly-lit bellies in a performance just for Lena.

I approach her with the jar. My first thought is she shouldn't be up running around the backyard in the dark. It seems that she's thinking the same thing when she turns to me and says, "Go catch a few, and I'll film you. I doubt I should be up darting around the yard."

To see this light in her eyes, on her face, and know that she can't even fully enjoy this simple ritual feels too much like fate sticking a dagger in and twisting it. Even the little things are too much for her now.

With a smile I hope is agreeable rather than as bittersweet as it feels, I nod, handing over my phone then uncapping the jar.

I walk out into the yard, the grass tickling my bare feet, and I begin corralling the tiny insects into the big-mouthed jar. Lena excitedly directs me from her place on the patio. "Get that one!" she says. "No, to your left. It's right there at your head."

We laugh as I spin at her guidance. I nearly lose my footing more than once as I whirl and turn, looking up into the night sky for the ones she wants me to catch.

Once I pivot toward her, my head sort of spins at the abrupt action, and I pause to get my equilibrium back. My eyes settle on Lena first, and the sight of her expression makes my stomach flip over. From this distance, in the softening light, she looks like the vibrant young woman I married all those years ago. To me, she's always been that woman, just growing into better versions of her as she's aged.

I stop to watch her, profoundly grateful that I'm getting to see her this way again. Just in case it's the last time.

Noticing me watching her, Lena lowers the phone. "What?"

"It's your turn," I explain, walking over to hand her the jar and take the phone from her fingers. "You just sit tight. I'll bring them to you."

It takes me a few minutes, but I manage to wrangle seven or eight winking bugs and sort of herd them toward my waiting wife. She sits on the end of the lounger, eyes wide, jar at the ready, and as soon as they're within reach, she starts collecting them. As though God Himself sent a slight breeze to blow them right into her expectant hand, Lena tenderly coerces each firefly into the jar until it's giving off enough light to illuminate a small room.

Her smile is nothing short of dreamy as she screws the lid on tight and holds up the bright jar to gaze inside it. She considers it from several angles before she glances down at my feet and then up at the camera.

"Look at your father's feet how dirty," she says, speaking to our unborn child now, to the eyes that will one day gaze adoringly at her mother's face as it fills the screen. Obligingly, I aim the phone down and bend my leg so that the green sole of my foot is visible. I laugh and so does Lena. "*That* is why you need to wash your feet before you go to bed. Never go to bed with dirty feet."

"I guess I know what I'll be doing next," I say into the camera before I turn it back on my wife. She's slumped a little now, fatigue written in the slope of her shoulders and the sag of her smile.

"And now it's time for bed. Goodnight, baby Grace," she whispers, rubbing her bulging belly. "I love you. Always."

Always.

The single word has a ring of finality to it, even though, by definition, it signifies no end at all. But there will be an end. I *hope* for longer, better. More. But in my gut...

Just like that, something sweet and meaningful melts into something sad and heartbreaking. Everything does, it seems. It's unavoidable. No matter how much we laugh or how many good days we have, it doesn't change anything. Not really. The end is still coming. It's always out there, hovering, like storm clouds on the horizon. But the storm is coming at us faster than we can outrun. Eventually, it will catch us and drown us.

And we both know it.

21

Born to Be My Baby

Nate

June third, Lena wakes up hurting. I hear her gasp. I roll over so quickly, I nearly fall out of bed. I find my wife propped up on one elbow, pressing her fingertips into her right side at the bottom edge of her ribs.

Her liver.

An arctic blast of torment blows through me like a cold, winter wind. She's been hurting more frequently and more intensely lately. Maybe it's that she seems a bit more oriented since her nutrition is better and now she's aware enough to feel *all* the pain. Or maybe it's simply that she's having more pain.

I don't like to think about either option.

Both mean that, for matters to get better, I'll lose my wife. Whether to a state of consciousness that doesn't involve me (via high doses of painkillers) or to death, I know I'll lose her if she's to be free of this pain.

Like so many things in this whole situation, there's no good answer, no perfect solution.

Only sorrow and heartache or empty devastation.

Within a few minutes, the discomfort that began in her right side, where it so often hurts, begins to radiate into her lower back. She can't find a comfortable position, can't get situated in bed, so I sweep her up into my arms and carry her into the living room, to her favorite chair, hoping that will help.

It's as I'm depositing her onto the thick cushions that I notice the wetness. I look down toward my feet and then behind me, down the hall the way we came, and see that we left a trail of droplets along our path.

I shift my glance to my wife, ready to comment about it, when I see her eyes are already round with a combination of both alarm and excitement. "I think my water broke."

From that statement on, all hell breaks loose. Everything is a mad dash to move quickly, yet think of everything for all the just-in-cases that might happen.

Lena is only four weeks from term. She's made it to week thirty-six of a pregnancy she wasn't sure she'd be able to carry *at all*.

Now the time is at hand. The baby is finally coming, and I find that I'm struggling to keep a cool head. Fear plagues me, a fear I've refused to acknowledge.

Secretly, I'm terrified that I will lose both Lena *and* Grace during this tricky delivery. Lena's not exactly the picture of good health and strength, and there are literally dozens of things that could go wrong. I try to focus on the positive and hold my misgivings at bay, but damn, is it hard!

For the millionth time, I shove all those thoughts back, back to a place where they can't hurt anybody. Just like cramming those damn skis into the hall closet.

Where they wait to crush me one day when I open the door.

****

Lena

I fight through the web of confusion that tangles my mind. I know I'm pregnant and I'm going into labor. I know I'm sick and my disease is likely progressing. But I also have the sense that other things, other times and places and people, are vying for my attention. I feel torn and find that I have to continually struggle to stay *here*.

Odd moments and images trickle in, spurring thoughts that threaten to whisk me away to another place in time. I'm aware of that when it happens. At least to a degree, but I'm helpless to stop it.

This time, it's scarier than usual. One minute I'm in the car with Nate on the way to the hospital and the next I'm being prepped for an emergency C-section.

Someone is getting ready to cut me open.

Hysteria rushes in. It scratches at my consciousness like a dog digging up old bones in dry dirt. My breath comes fast and hard.

"What's going on?" I cry. "What's happening? Is the baby okay?"

A scrubbed, capped, and masked nurse anesthetist bends to look into my face. All I can see is a smooth brow and wide gray eyes. "The baby has a nuchal cord, Mrs. Grant. That means that the umbilical cord is wrapped around your daughter's neck. You're being prepped for a caesarean. Can you take a deep breath for me?"

The woman's tone is professional yet cool. It brings no more comfort to me than the plain white ceiling above my head.

I need warmth.

I need familiarity.

I need answers.

I need *Nate.*

"My husband. Where's my husband? Where's the doctor? Why can't I feel my legs?" Questions tumble into my mind like marbles from a felt bag—unchecked and chaotic.

Clanking and rolling.

Roaring.

I pant frantically, my mouth as dry as cold air stinging my eyes. "Somebody tell me what the hell is going on!"

My mind tilts and jerks, searching desperately for solid ground, for words or moments or images to fill in the yawning gaps.

I find none.

Time...time has come and gone. It's dumped me into a present that I can't piece together. I have no idea how I got here, to this point. What has happened that I now require a caesarean?

Only moments ago I was at work in the E.R. where I pull shifts periodically to keep up my clinical skills. And before that, I was catching lightning bugs with Daddy. And before that...

Or was I?

Confusion mounts, and my anxiety intensifies.

"Lena, take a deep breath for me," the anesthetist instructs sternly.

I try to be compliant, try to take a deep breath, but I can't. My lungs refuse to cooperate. Rather than loosening, they squeeze tighter, shut, shut, shut.

Heart racing and throat constricting, terror surges through me.

"Please," I plead as the woman stretches a royal blue drape up in front of my face and clips it to the poles on either side of the table. "Please let me see my husband."

Seconds, minutes, hours later, I hear an achingly familiar voice croon, "I'm here, baby. I'm here."

Cool, strong fingers brush over my forehead, and I close my eyes.

Nate.

I feel him in every corner of my soul. Even before I pieced together that it was his voice I heard, I *felt* him. I recognize his touch on a cellular level.

Relief sweeps in and brings with it a rush of emotion of a different sort. Suddenly, I'm heartbroken, and I don't even remember why. What have I missed? What's happened?

"Nate, what's happening? I'm scared." Though my tears are hot, they leave icy tracks from my temples into my hair.

"Shhh." His voice soothes. "Don't be afraid. I'm right here, and I'm not going anywhere. You have an epidural. That's why you can't feel your legs. Dr. Stephens is taking Grace because her cord has wrapped around her neck. You'll both be fine. I promise. Don't worry, baby," he whispers, his lips at my ear.

When I look up at Nate, his upside down face only makes me feel further confused. Desperate to see him, desperate to see the familiar angles and planes of his face, I tilt my head until the image of him is mostly righted. Only then does the level of my alarm yield to the point where I can take a single deep, calming breath.

"Nate," I say simply.

The sound of his name in the quiet room, the feel of it on my tongue...it's everything. The moon and the stars, the sun and the wind.

My world.

He is my world.

"Don't cry, baby," he murmurs, his face blurring as he leans down to set his forehead against mine. "Don't cry."

I think I hear a catch in his voice, but I can't be sure. The slowing beat of my heart is thudding in my ears, in my head, making the world around me tremble unsteadily.

"Don't...don't let them..." Nate's face swims in front of my eyes. I try to blink to better focus, but the darkness, the silence is pulling me under.

"Lena, you can relax now," a voice I recognize as Dr. Stephens's hums. "In just a few minutes, you'll be meeting your daughter. Rest. Just rest."

I don't want to rest. I want to see Nate, to hear him and feel him, but sleep is relentless in its pursuit of me. And I'm too weak to fight.

"I love you, Lena Grant," is the last thing I hear before I drift off.

Nate.

****

Nate

I keep my eyes glued to my wife's resting face as I listen to the foreign sounds of an operating room during an operation. Despite the questions and concerns chasing one another around in my head, seeing my precious Lena sleeping so quietly calms me.

It seems like she hasn't rested well in a lifetime, even though I know it can't have been that long. But it feels like it. It feels as though the days since her diagnosis have crept by like years, but also that they've flown by at the speed of light.

I want desperately to rewind the clock, back to a place in time where there was solid ground, firm footing. I long for the days when our biggest worry was where to spend Christmas and what color to paint the sunroom we added on to the rear of the house. Any time before today, before *now*.

Now is the beginning of the end. Even more than the diagnosis had, this *feels* like the beginning of the end.

Once Grace is born, everything will change. I can't be sure how, but in my gut I know it will. Lena has fought to carry this baby. Will she give up now?

We've had a reprieve from following the progression of her disease. Will they find that she's beyond time and treatment now?

I have no way of knowing the answers to those questions, but in the darkest part of my mind, I think I already know.

I'm so lost in thought, lost in the silky-soft texture of my wife's hair that I've tuned out the goings on around me, but a sound, one single sound, brings me back. It's a shock to my insides, one I wasn't expecting.

It's the cry of a baby.

My baby.

Our baby.

Every hair on my arms stands up at attention when I lean around the makeshift curtain and see the doctor place a slimy, squirmy little purple-red bundle into the towel-draped arms of a waiting nurse. The nurses turn away, but not before I catch a glimpse of the most beautiful profile I've ever seen.

Aside from my wife's.

It's Grace's.

My child's.

Now completely spellbound, I watch the back of the nurse. My eyes don't leave her as she moves her arms, as she shifts this way and that, working on my daughter.

I watch and I wait, wait for the moment when I can see her again.

Suction slurps in the background. Voices ring alongside it, voices like Dr. Stephens as she asks for things like suture and staples and more light. A nurse's as she responds. All the while, I don't take my eyes off the place where the newest addition to my life is being held.

Then, as if she's moving in slow motion, the nurse picks up Grace and turns with her, smiling as she makes her way to me. My heart pounds so briskly, I feel like it might rip through my chest like in *Alien*. The beat grows harder and louder with each step the nurse takes.

And then she's passing me a small bundle.

With greedy hands, I reach for my baby. I take her into my arms, cradling her as I would cradle a wounded baby hummingbird. I feel as though I'm handling something so tiny and delicate. Something so precious that a deep breath could crush it into oblivion.

I stare down at the only skin visible from the tight folds of the blanket—a small, angelic face still pink from her gusty cries.

"Helena Grace," I breathe, part in awe, part in relief.

A love second only to that which I feel for my wife courses through me. For seven months, I've wondered how I'd feel about this baby, about this parting gift from the love of my life. Would I be able to love it like she'd want me to? Would I see it as a reason that my wife is gone? Would I resent it?

Now I know.

Now I know the answers to all those questions.

Yes, I will love my child as Lena would want me to. That's the only answer I need. The other questions seem ridiculous now.

As I stare down at the sweet little life in my arms, I know what the adoration of parent for child feels like. I know how it invades the hidden spaces and stretches them wide. I know how part of my heart has been lying dormant, hibernating, waiting to beat for a face such as this.

Grace makes some cute gurgling sounds, her face all screwed up like she might cry, but then she snuggles toward my chest, like she's snuggling in for a long, quiet nap.

Love and warmth pour through me.

I hold her close and gaze down at her, willing her to open her eyes. I don't know what to expect, only what I've been hoping for, what I've been praying for.

Then, as if she just wants to put my curiosity to rest, Grace lifts her lids and shows me that my prayers have been answered. Staring up at me from the tiny face of my little girl are my wife's eyes. Although they're an indeterminate color right now, I don't have to see the color to know that they'll be just like Lena's.

In this very moment, in this split second of a life measuring forty-two years thus far, I know I'm a goner.

If I hadn't known it before, it's clear the instant Grace looks up at me with eyes as familiar to me as my own. I know without a doubt that I *can* and *will* love this child enough for two parents.

"I love you already, baby girl," I croon, curling the little bundle toward my face so I can kiss the sparse, damp, blonde waves that top her head.

"Nate?"

The sweetest voice speaks my name. I don't have to turn and look at Lena's face to know what I'll find. Her heart will be in her eyes. I know it. I can almost feel the happiness, the fulfillment in them like a warm trade wind rolling off crystal-blue waters, filling all the recesses of my soul.

Overwhelming gratitude gathers around my vocal cords, choking off any words I might've said otherwise, drowning out the raw, bleeding love that's spewing from my heart. So rather than speaking, I move slowly toward my wife and lay my little bundle across her chest, pressing my cheek to Lena's as she cries.

"Thank you for her, Nate," she mutters, sobbing softly over our child. "She's perfect. She's my perfect little miracle."

I couldn't have said it better myself.

She is.

She is perfect, and she is a miracle.

As I take out my phone and start recording this moment, I wonder, with a heart never happier yet never more aggrieved, if Grace will be the only miracle the two of us will be fortunate enough to get.

22

Blind Love

Nate

Lena has dozed off and on since delivery. I saw Dr. Taffer talking to Dr. Stephens in the hall right after we were brought up to this room. And just a few minutes ago, a nurse brought Grace and helped Lena to feed her for the first time.

Someone might as well have had a knife, twisting it in my gut. That's exactly what it felt like to watch my beautiful wife put our beautiful child to her breast. There is no doubt in my mind that I will *never* see anything more breathtaking than the two of them together.

I'm *positive* I'll never forget Lena's expression either.

Her world is complete. This is all she's ever wanted–for us to be a family—and she got her wish. It's there in every loving line of her face—the awestruck gaze, the curved lips, the smooth brow. She's whole.

And *I'm* whole merely watching them.

The scene was absolutely perfect until Dr. Stephens came in to check on Lena. With her, she brought the first niggle of unease to my mind.

"Looks like momma and baby are getting acquainted," she says with a placid smile. "I'm glad she latched on quickly. I think it's important to breast-feed her for the first day or two. Get as much of that colostrum in her as you can before we put her on formula."

"Formula?" I ask.

Dr. Stephens turns her never-wavering smile toward me. "Yes. Considering some of the medications Lena will be taking, her breast milk won't be safe for the baby."

I say nothing.

Although my mind is spinning with questions, I don't want to ask them now. Not at a time such as this. To disrupt this precious moment, the time when Lena is first feeding and getting to know our child, seems tantamount to sacrilege. So I stand silently by the bedside, processing the doctor's words, my dread growing, until Dr. Stephens turns back toward Lena.

I watch my wife glance up at her obstetrician, her features more peaceful than I've ever known them to be, and she nods. She doesn't question, she doesn't argue. She simply agrees. Maybe she knows something I don't.

It's the consequent visit of Dr. Taffer, Lena's oncologist, that fills in some of those blanks.

"How are we doing?" Lheanne Taffer asks when she walks in, perching one hip on Lena's bed and angling her body so that she can see both Lena and me.

"Wonderful," Lena replies without hesitation.

"Glad to hear it. Looks like the little one made a grand entrance." She leans in to look down into Grace's face, her expression closed.

"She did. But she's here. That's the main thing."

After only a second's pause, Dr. Taffer turns all her attention to Lena. "Are you in pain?"

"No."

"While you're here, I'd like to order some testing so we can get a bead on where you are with the cancer before you're discharged. How does that sound?"

Lena takes her time in answering, something that makes all the muscles in my chest tense up. "Can we wait a few days? Let me enjoy her a little bit first?"

It's Dr. Taffer's turn to pause. I wonder what she's thinking. Is she debating whether to push the subject? Is she considering giving Lena some less-than-welcome news? Is she trying to soften a blow that I alone can't see? Is she, God forbid, thinking Lena doesn't have time to wait?

My lungs seize at the thought.

When the doctor finally responds, everything from her features to her body language is carefully neutral. "Of course, if that's what you'd prefer."

"It is."

The two women share a long, intense look before the oncologist stands. It's obvious she wants to say more, but isn't sure how and when to go about it. "Lena, you're *at least* going to need to start a couple of medications."

I can't hear Lena's sigh, but I see it lift her chest along with our child who rests on it. "Why? What's going on?"

"I was looking at your labs. Your ammonia levels are climbing. The stress of the pregnancy on your liver only aggravated an existing problem. We need to get that down. I suspect you're working on hepatic encephalopathy. Grade one at least. It's crucial that we get a handle on this, Lena. I know you've been having some confusion, too, and... Well, you know how it goes."

While Lena may know what the doctor is getting at, *I* do not.

"What are you saying?"

Dr. Taffer turns, tight-lipped and firm, to face me this time. "I'm saying that I think her disease has advanced considerably, and we need to know what we're dealing with so that we can get her on *some kind* of treatment as soon as possible, even if it's palliative."

Palliative.

In my extensive research, done when I couldn't sleep for worrying about my wife, I came across that word all too often in reference to Lena's condition.

Palliative.

Palliative care is for comfort only. It isn't used to treat anything except pain or other uncomfortable symptoms associated with terminal conditions. It isn't intended to heal or prolong or delay. It's the use of medication strictly for those who are dying. And who will be in a great deal of pain or discomfort from it.

Palliative.

And it's used when death is fairly imminent.

A wave of nausea rolls through my stomach. It comes on like a white-capped storm surge, curling over a sandy shore—quickly and unexpectedly. I want to yell at Lheanne Taffer, to tell her that this is supposed to be a happy day and she's supposed to give us hope, not...not...*this*. I want like hell to kick her out the door and erase everything she's said since she walked in.

But I don't.

I *can't* do either of those. My job is to keep my wife calm and uplifted. Throwing her oncologist out on her ass or getting myself forcibly removed by security would accomplish neither of those, so I swallow my complaints like the bitter, jagged pills they are.

Then I swallow again.

"So, you'd give her something to help the pain in her side? A-and the...confusion?" I ask. I hate talking about my wife as though she's not here, but I need to understand the options.

"Yes. *At least* those two things. We'll know more when we can get some testing done."

I wonder if I pale visibly as I consider what this means because Dr. Taffer reacts as though I did. I catch the quick succession of several emotions as they play over her face.

I can't help wondering if, in her haste to get my wife on some kind of treatment, the doctor forgot that Lena Grant is someone's wife and, now, someone's mother. I wonder if she didn't even consider the possibility that Lena would want to enjoy her family, uninterrupted, for a few days before she gets poked and prodded and possibly given *even worse* news.

Whether she had or hadn't considered these things, I'll never know. I only know the moment that she recognized those truths, she finally let some compassion in, and let it take the wheel.

Dr. Taffer explains to me that she'll be putting Lena on a pain patch that will give her continuous relief from the increasing pain in her side. It can be increased incrementally until she gets complete relief.

She also tells me about the Lactulose she'll prescribe, a drug which will help eliminate some of the excess ammonia from Lena's body, and hopefully, reduce the bouts of confusion.

When she's finished, Lheanne glances back over her shoulder at Lena, sadness stealing over her features. "The main thing is that she's able to enjoy as much of this as she can." With one hand, she gestures toward Lena and Grace. Grace has fallen asleep after getting her belly full, and Lena is holding her as she sleeps.

Impulsively, I take my phone from my pocket and snap another picture. I never want to forget the tender look of adoration on my sweet wife's face or the way our baby fits so perfectly in her arms and against her chest. It's a scene Michelangelo himself couldn't have adequately captured.

And one that will forever be etched on my heart.

"I hope you're doing a lot of that," the doctor says quietly, nodding at the phone before she moves back toward the bed. She lowers her voice to a whisper when she addresses Lena. "Congratulations, Lena. She's absolutely beautiful. Just like her mother."

Lena turns proud, shining eyes up to her physician. "Thank you."

Dr. Taffer nods to her then to me and makes her exit. Although she didn't give us worse news per se, it feels as though she did. There's an implied urgency that makes my soul shrivel as if the world has suddenly frozen over all around me.

I hope you're doing a lot of that.

I hear her words over and over again.

I make the determination right this minute to do it even more.

****

Grace is three days old when she's cleared for us to bring her home. She's a good baby, sweet-natured and agreeable, and I know that Lena and I feel the same way about her.

It's like seeing the sun for the first time.

Or, for me, maybe like seeing the sun for the *second* time. I've known a love like this before. But only once in my whole life. It's the love I have for my wife. I never thought I'd ever feel anything that could compare to it. But Grace... She snuggled her way into my heart right alongside Lena within thirty seconds of meeting her.

I'm as disappointed as Lena that she won't be able to continue breastfeeding our daughter, but we both know that it's for the best. Anything that can keep Lena comfortable and *present* for longer is, in my eyes, worth it.

The only problem is, the medication that Lena has been given to help lower her ammonia levels hasn't had as dramatic an effect as we were hoping. In my mind, it should've put Lena back to rights. Completely. Only it hasn't worked out that way, hasn't worked quite that *well*.

The first time she was given a dose in the hospital, the nurse who brought it mentioned that it *should* help *some*, qualifications that didn't inspire much confidence. And, as far as I could tell, it had *only* helped *some*. Lena still spends substantial quantities of time confused. She slept a lot in the hospital, but when she was awake, she was often disoriented.

At least the spells seem to be less dramatic now. Maybe that's how the medication is helping—maybe it lessens the length and severity of her bouts of confusion. I'd hoped for total eradication, though, and so far, I'm very disappointed.

On the plus side, Lena seems content and more at ease at home. And I still harbor a tiny spark of optimism that the effects of the medication will be cumulative and that familiar surroundings will help things along. But only time will tell. And I'm not certain how much of that we have left.

I try to put the dismal future out of my mind. It feels something like betrayal to dwell on it, like I'm cheating on the present if I spend one moment of it mourning what hasn't yet transpired. But it's hard. It's hard not to worry, not to watch my wife, sharply and constantly, as though she might disappear like a vapor if I look away for too long.

The mattress dips ever so slightly, and I come instantly awake. It's the middle of the night, but it only takes a few seconds for my eyes to adjust to the silvery moonlit room. All my senses come online with surprising rapidity these days, and all seem more acute than ever.

I listen closely for the cry of our child, but I hear nothing except for the muffled pad of my wife's feet as she crosses the thickly carpeted floor. I hold myself perfectly still and wait for Lena to leave the room before I get up to follow her.

I'm still not sleeping soundly. Not only am I listening for my wife, but I'm also listening for sounds of our daughter. I can't help wondering if I missed her cry, though, and if that's what roused Lena.

When she sleeps, she often sleeps so deeply that she won't even respond to the call of her name, but so far, she seems to hear even the most hushed whimpers of little Grace. A mother's sensitivity, maybe.

Quietly, I trail my wife down the hall to the baby's room. I stop in the doorway and lean one shoulder against the jamb. I can see perfectly—the padded rocker in the corner, the cheerful mobile hanging over the crib, the puffy quilted letters that spell out Grace on the wall. Despite the dim glow of the nightlight, the room is still fairly bright. The pale yellow paint helps, makes the walls look like French vanilla ice cream at night, soft and velvety.

Lena crosses slowly and silently to the white crib, bending to peer down over the padded rail. "Hi, beautiful," she coos tenderly, reaching in for her daughter. She lifts her out, expertly tucking Grace against her chest. "What's your name, little girl?"

When I hear the question, I tense. I have no way of knowing if it's just Lena's way of chatting with the baby or if she's so confused she can't remember her own child's name. Or that Grace is even *hers*.

These days, I can't assume anything. All evidence seems to be pointing in the wrong direction, to the worsening of her condition rather than the stabilizing of it. However, Lena's occasional bouts of prolonged lucidity—sometimes up to a few hours—are always just enough to allow the thin, fibrous roots of hope to take hold in me.

I know it's a mistake to let my guard down. To hope. I know the risks, know the consequences of false hope will be devastating, but sometimes, I just can't seem to help myself. It feels too good to cling to something positive, to think about a future with my wife and child.

It just feels good to hope. *Too good.*

Turning with Grace in her arms, Lena comes to an abrupt stop when she spots me lounging in the doorway. "Who is this?" she asks, tipping her chin toward the baby she cradles. "Did I forget that we are babysitting for someone?"

"That's Grace, baby. You had a C-section a few days ago. Isn't your stomach still sore?"

A faint frown pulls at the skin between Lena's eyes, and I know she's performing a self-assessment. I also know the instant it clicks into place. She smiles and tries to play it off. "Of course, I remember that, silly. My memory isn't getting *that* bad." She crosses the room to me and stretches up to kiss my cheek as she passes. "Go back to bed. I've got her."

"I'm already up. Why don't I keep you company?" I don't give her time to argue; I just fall in behind her and follow her into the den. I can't trust that she won't forget something vital and accidentally hurt herself or Grace.

As I tiredly pursue my wife through the house, my gut clenches with grief. This is all Lena wanted for so long, and now she isn't even able to really enjoy it. Such a cruel twist of fate.

As quickly as she slips into confusion, however, Lena often slips out of it just as rapidly. It's as she's preparing a bottle for Grace that I notice the shift.

"...won't be around to do it with you later, maybe tomorrow we'll get out the jar and catch some lightning bugs. I'll save up all my energy for it so I can carry you around the yard and catch the ones you want me to get. And *they* can be your nightlight, like they were *my* nightlight when I was a little girl. And Daddy can film the whole thing so you can watch it when you're older.

You can see how much your momma loved you and how she caught your very first lightning bugs for you. Does that sound like fun?" Lena glances up at me and grins. "In case you didn't hear that, she said, 'Hell yeah!'"

I smile, but in my heart is an unbearable ache. It happens more and more often of late. It seems the less I see of the real Lena, the more it hurts when I *do* see her. Those glimpses become increasingly bittersweet as time wears on. It's as though I'm losing my soul mate over and over, degree by degree, and it's tearing me apart.

"You take my breath away," I confess, my voice thick with emotion. And her answering smile *does*. For a few seconds, I literally can't breathe.

I wonder if I'll ever really be able to breathe again.

When Grace's bottle is ready, Lena and I head to the sofa. I sit and Lena scoots in beside me, snuggling into the curve of my body and resting her head on my shoulder as she feeds our little girl. She hums softly, craning her neck to look up at me every couple of minutes. It seems that she, too, is aware of how precious these moments are.

Slowly, the humming trails off, and Lena falls silent. Her relaxing hand pulls the nipple of the bottle from between sleeping Grace's lips. I reach out and take the bottle, letting it fall quietly to the floor so that I can have both hands free to hold my wife.

Winding my arms more tightly around Lena, I hold her to me as snugly as I can without waking her. I'm desperate to keep her close, to hold on as long as I can.

And not just tonight.

Some part of me knows that our window is closing and that I'm helpless to stop it. I can sense that Lena knows it, too. I suspect that's why she didn't want Dr. Taffer to run tests while she was in the hospital. She didn't want to know she only has days or weeks left. And I can understand that. I'm not sure I want to know either.

Slouching down enough that Lena can rest better against me and Grace against her, I try to put my haunting thoughts away and just enjoy the feel of my wife in my arms. I take a deep breath and let my eyes close. I focus on how soft her skin is under my fingertips, how her hair smells of flowers and cinnamon, and how the slight weight of her feels on my chest.

As I drift off, I'm only barely aware of the single tear that slips from between my lashes and slides slowly down my cheek.

23

Hush

Nate

The first streaks of dawn coming through the window wake me. My wife is still in my arms, and Grace is fast asleep in *hers*.

Even in her unconscious state, Lena holds our baby closely yet carefully. There's a tenderness in her secure grip that I think comes with becoming a mother, as if the instinct to protect and nurture changes even her muscle memory. That thought causes a convoy of other thoughts to file through my head, like ducks swimming in a straight row across an empty pond. That succession of thought is why, as much as I hate to move her, I shift and slide out from under my wife and little girl.

The first place I go is to the kitchen. I walk to the window to look out across the yard, toward the neighbor's house.

I'm glad to see Nissa's light on. I hate for anyone to suffer from insomnia, but I've always been secretly grateful that Nissa does. She's provided Lena with company and comfort in ways I never thought to. And she's awake *now*, which is fortuitous on a day such as this. I have plans, and I need Nissa's help.

Quickly, I shoot out the back door and bound across the yard to the next house over. I knock quietly, glancing back through the windows of my own house to make sure I don't see signs of movement.

Nissa opens the door and is visibly surprised to see me on her stoop rather than my wife. "I don't have long. Got a second?"

"Of course," she says, opening the door wider.

"Nah, I'll just stay here, thanks. I want to keep an eye on Lena and the baby."

"Okay." She crosses her arms over her chest, pulling her robe tighter around her against the slight chill in the early morning June air. "What's up?"

"I need to run out for a while today. Think you could come over and keep an eye on Lena until I get back?"

"Sure."

I work out the details with our neighbor and then race back over to my house. Carefully, I open and close the door then tiptoe silently through the kitchen to the living room. The two loves of my life are still fast asleep, one of them snoring softly. I stand in the doorway watching them for several long, bittersweet minutes. It's yet another scene I want to burn into my memory, knowing that one day it will be all I have left.

I snap a picture before I finally pull myself away from the sight, moving back toward the kitchen to start a pot of coffee and make more concrete plans for the day.

****

Lena

I know that something isn't right. I've been a nurse for almost two decades. I've worked in several specialties, mostly because in the beginning I didn't have a clue what my niche would be. But then I landed a full-time job at the cancer center. I loved it right off the bat and decided to make my work home there and take on some part-time critical care work to keep my clinical skills sharp.

I've seen a lot in my years, especially with cancer patients. It doesn't take me long to put the puzzle pieces together. When I'm awake and aware and notice that there are enormous chunks of time missing, then I add it together with the pain (which is thankfully under control) and some things Dr. Taffer said…I know.

I know.

My liver is failing. The cancer has spread to the point that it is dramatically affecting my hepatic function. I've seen it enough with my patients to know that progression to this point is beyond anything except palliative measures. I know the smart thing would be to call hospice. They can take care of things that will make the whole process easier, especially for Nate.

Nate.

A stinging knot forms behind my tonsils.

God, how I hate to leave him!

The thought of it, the *idea* of it feels suffocating.

Overwhelming.

Devastating.

I hate to go *at all*, but I hate even more that he'll be left with such awful memories of me.

Pain and sickness.

Disease and death.

Periods of time when I neither look like nor act like myself. Those will be what Nate remembers most for a while.

And it breaks my heart.

There's nothing I can do about that, though, short of taking my own life. And I'm not going to do that. Living with my suicide would be an even worse pain for Nate and Grace to bear.

Grace.

I smile just thinking her name.

My child.

My daughter.

My baby.

The living embodiment of the love my husband and I have for each other. I'd have given almost anything to be able to live long enough to see her grow up. Or even to see her walk and hear her first words. But I know in my gut that it isn't going to work out that way.

It isn't that I have no hope. It's that I simply have a certainty about things, about the outcome. I've seen it happen with dozens and dozens of terminal patients. They seem to have a supernatural sense about their death. Now I can understand it. I know I'm going to die, and there isn't a damn thing I can do about it.

Except face it.

Head-on.

Try to make it as easy for my loved ones as I possibly can. So that's what I intend to do.

While Grace is sleeping and Nate is gone, I go in search of my phone. I can't remember where I had it last.

I search the bedroom, the bathroom, the living room, and, finally, make my way into the kitchen.

I gasp when I see Nissa sitting at the island, sipping a cup of coffee, scrolling through something on her iPad.

"Hi," she says brightly when she hears my gasp.

"You scared me. I didn't expect to see you sitting there." I'd have to be blind and stupid to miss the look of sadness that flits across my best friend's face. And I'm neither. I can only guess at what it means, but I guess right. "How long have you been here?"

"A couple of hours," Nissa answers in a strangled voice.

"I'm guessing I've already seen you then?"

Nissa's eyes fill with tears, and she nods, silent.

I sigh deeply and come to sit on the stool beside my long-time confidante. I drape an arm over her shoulders and rest my head against Nissa's. I feel the tremor in my friend's muscles, and I know that she's holding back sobs.

"It won't be long now," I tell her.

I don't have to explain; Nissa knows what I'm referring to. She makes no sound as she begins to weep, but I can feel it. Nissa's upper body is shaking uncontrollably, heaving as grief gushes from her in great waves. They quake through me, too, where I sit beside her.

Never having been one to give empty words of solace, not even to my patients, I know now is not the time to start. It won't help anyone. Not really. I'm simply going to *stay*. I'm going to sit with my best friend in the world while she comes to terms with what lies ahead, while she exorcises the anguish. I only hope staying is enough.

"I'm sorry," Nissa finally says, sniffing loudly, her words cracked and broken.

"Don't be. I love you. I wish I could make this easier, but I can't."

"What the hell is wrong with you?" she asks in mock anger. "*I'm* supposed to be the one wanting to make things easier for *you*."

"I'm sure you want to. It's human nature to want to take away hurt from those we love. And you love me. I know that because I love you just as much."

Nissa's crying is renewed, so I pull her close and wait. Grieving is a process. One cry won't get it out. For some, it takes weeks or months of crying.

When Nissa seems to settle again, I continue. "Nate loves you, too. And Grace will. I want for you three to take care of each other. For me. Do it for *me*. I'll feel much better if I know that Nate won't be in this alone. And that my daughter will have a wonderful woman in her life. Promise me."

Nissa nods as she wipes at her eyes. "I promise."

Knowing what kind of reaction my announcement will incite, I wait for a couple of minutes before I tell Nissa my plans. And when I do, she starts to sniffle again, as I suspected she might. Hospice is a dirty word, a painful word. And they all know what it means. I don't have to explain it.

"I'm going to call hospice today. I want to do it before Nate gets back. It will kill him. I know it will, but it'll help him, too. More than he realizes."

"It'll help *you, too*," Nissa insists.

"It'll help me, too, yes." My own comfort is far down the list. I'm more worried about those I love. "Nissa, I...I..."

I'm not quite sure how to continue.

"What?" she prompts when I don't finish my sentence.

"I don't want you to stop coming around. No matter how hard it gets to watch, don't let Nate go through this alone. Please."

Tears bite sharply at my eyes, but I will myself not to cry. For me, the time for grieving is over. My fate is sealed. It's pointless to spend my last days mourning the future. Or what it might hold.

"I'll be here. Every day."

I nod and we sit in silence for a minute more before I reach for my phone. I smile as I hold it in my palm. The kitchen. I left it in the kitchen, probably when Nissa arrived earlier, which is something I have no recollection of.

My fingers tremble for a moment as an intense pang of regret lances through me. It's sharp and cutting, more like a jagged piece of metal than something smooth and well-honed.

It's regret, regret that I'm missing out on so much of these last days with my family.

Even though it's beyond my control, I have no idea what I'm saying or doing half of the time. I can't remember all the times I've held my child or kissed my husband. I can't remember if I've told them I love them today. I can only hope I've done it all.

A lot.

Gathering what little strength I can manage to garner these days, I flip through my phone's directory and find Dr. Taffer's contact information. I click on the number and leave word with her secretary that I'll be contacting hospice.

I've been on the ordering end of hospice care enough times to know that all my oncologist will have to do is forward some paperwork and a diagnosis and I'll be in.

My condition permits it.

My love for my husband dictates it.

My next call is to Wendy, the coordinator of my favorite hospice center. I listen as Wendy sniffs discreetly, as though she might be holding the receiver away from her mouth. She wouldn't want me to know she's crying for me as she puts in the last request I'll make of her.

The last hospice request of my life.

****

When I wake to Nate sitting on the edge of the bed, I'm not even aware that I'd been asleep. "Hi there, beautiful," he says, love permeating both his voice and his gentle smile.

"Well, hello, handsome," I reply, returning his smile despite the disorientation I feel. I have no idea what to expect from one moment to the next, and it's very disconcerting. I feel like I'm always playing catch-up, like I'm always a step or a moment or a day behind.

I'm always questioning things. What have I missed? How long have I slept? What have I been told that I no longer remember?

I search my memory for evidence of coming into the bedroom, of lying down, of drifting off to sleep, but I find nothing. Not a single reference point to which I might cling.

The last thing I remember is pretending not to notice Wendy's soft crying. And then...nothing.

Just a blank.

"I've got a surprise for you. Come see."

It's getting harder and harder to mount much enthusiasm for *anything* really. I'm just so tired all the time, I feel like I only have the energy to do the basics, like walk and breathe and hold a bottle to my baby's mouth. The change has been swift and sudden.

At least I think it has.

"Great," I exclaim with as much eagerness as I can muster. I don't argue when Nate helps me to sit and then to stand. I don't argue when he helps me down the hall, walking so close that I can literally lean on him. I don't argue because I know I need the support. My legs don't always want to cooperate anymore, and I feel dizzy fairly often.

Or at least I think I do.

As far as I can recall.

Guiding me slowly into the living room, Nate stops in the doorway, his arm slipping nearly unnoticed around my waist. Maybe he knows how tired I am. Maybe he thought I'd need the extra reinforcement when I saw the "surprise". Or maybe his arm has been there all along and I haven't even been aware of it.

I'm certain of very little these days.

Leaning harder against my husband, I catch my breath as my eyes take in the unfamiliar and unexpected sight before me. On the couch, in my home, looking as uncomfortable as I feel, is my mother. She's feeding Grace, a bottle propped expertly in her hand, with an unreadable expression on her face.

"Momma?" I mutter before I can stop myself.

My mother raises her head, bringing sad eyes almost the exact color brown as my own up to my face.

"This is why."

This is why.

Those are Patricia Holmes's only words, enigmatic as they are.

I watch as she begins to rock against the cushion at her back. One might think that she's rocking Grace, that it's merely a grandmother soothing her granddaughter, but I know better. I've seen my mother do this before when she's upset. I just can't figure out what's happened to upset her.

I know *I* couldn't have said anything to distress her. It seems I've been asleep for quite some time. But I have no way of knowing what transpired before I came into the room. Did Nate say something to her? Have they fought? Did my mother make some out-of-the-way comment about Grace?

I don't know.

What I *do* know, however, is that I don't want my mother holding my child if she's going to have a fit. Because, at this rate, that's what will come next.

Like a bolt of lightning snapped at my heels, I streak across the room. Obviously, Nate wasn't expecting it and he loses his hold on me. He lunges, grabbing at me, but only catches the tail of my shirt and the breeze I left behind.

I'm reaching for my daughter before my husband can stop me.

"'This is why?' What does that mean, Momma?" I ask, taking my baby girl into my arms and then smartly reaching for the bottle to continue feeding her. The instant Grace is no longer occupying her hands,

Momma begins to wring them, watching them as though she can't work out why they're suddenly empty.

I feel a stab of guilt over hurting my mom, but it's short-lived. I'm protecting my daughter. No woman should feel guilty about defending the well-being of her child. So I won't. I refuse.

Momma doesn't answer my question for several minutes. Everyone in the room—Nissa, Nate, me, even little Grace— seems to be holding their breath, waiting quietly for her to calm herself and reply. As the silence drags on, I can't help wondering if everybody else is as tense as me.

"This is why I didn't want you anymore," my mother finally explains. "I knew I'd lose you, too. And I just couldn't lose anybody else. Can't you see?" She begins to whimper, a pitiful sound that tugs at my heartstrings, despite the trouble we've had in the past. "I couldn't lose *anybody* else."

A streak of resentment runs through me, the aftershock of an earthquake that happened long, long ago. My mother had only been concerned with what *she* would lose, how *she* would feel. She obviously never took a minute to think about how her only remaining child might feel. She didn't bother to think about how it would affect *me*.

There is a noticeably frigid edge to my voice when I respond. Even *I* hear it.

"Oh, I can see, Momma. You forget that I was in the exact same boat. I'd lost my family, too. First Janet, then Daddy. But *I* lost even more because then I lost *you*.

They didn't have a choice when they left, but *you* did. *You did*, didn't you, Momma? I lost you because you gave up on me. You were all I had left, and you just...gave up. You might as well have left me, too."

I can taste the bitterness on my tongue like a mouthful of bile.

"I didn't leave you!" Momma defends.

"You didn't leave me physically, but you left in all the ways that mattered. You just checked out and left me to raise myself, to take care of myself. And to take care of you. I was a *child*! I'd lost *everything* and I couldn't even grieve. I didn't have time to. I had to go to school and cook and grocery shop and clean and take care of you. I didn't have the luxury of giving up."

I can see my mother's chest rising and falling rapidly. The room is silent but for the muted pant of her breathing, no one else daring enough to interrupt our emotional face-off. Mother and daughter, we simply stare at one another until she breaks the taut stillness.

"And now you've brought me here to get back at me. Is that it?"

My mouth drops open. "Is that what you think of me? That I would subject you to this *horror* just to get revenge? After all these years?"

"Then *whyyy?*" she wails pitifully, rocking faster, bouncing off the cushion like she's propelled, only to slam back against it, over and over and over.

Suddenly, as though someone has opened up an invisible cavern beneath my feet to sap it silently from my body, my small store of energy dissipates, leaving me to waver on legs made of warm rubber. Before I can fold, however, my sturdier half, my *better* half materializes behind me.

Nate.

He is never far.

Long fingers wrap gently around my upper arms, providing me with much-needed support. I feel the hot solidity of my husband's broad, muscular chest at my back and, for just a moment, I lean into him. As always, he's my rock, my ever-present rock in my time of need.

When he starts to bend, I know to sweep me off my feet and carry me to calmer waters, I stop him by turning to place our daughter into his strong, capable arms. I meet his eyes, my determined brown colliding with his worried green, and nod before I pivot.

When I face my mother, I see the woman who gave up on life when I needed her most. I see the woman who let me care for her when my world had fallen apart. I see the woman who couldn't find the strength to pick herself up for the daughter who begged her to. She's still that woman. She'll always be that woman.

Although the anger is still there, the resentment, the hurt as well, I feel more of something else today. Today I feel pity. For the first time in my life, I look at Patricia Holmes, and I see the broken woman that she is. I see someone who simply wasn't strong enough to weather the horrific agony that comes with having lost not one, but two loved ones to cancer. I see a woman who was knocked to her knees and couldn't find it in herself to get back up.

She's made bad choices, she's been weak when she needed to be strong, she gave up when she should've fought back—yes, she did all of those things. But this woman is my mother. For better or for worse, she's my mother and although she's not asking for it, I have the opportunity to forgive her.

And I likely won't get another chance.

I've done right by my mother. I've ensured that she's had the best care, I've visited her monthly, I've done the best I could for her, but it's always been out of obligation. I've never felt free to love her again. I was hurt, betrayed, and I was happy to hide behind the wall I built to shut her out. But the words of the priest I met in Rome resonate in my head, through my heart, showing me what I have to say, what I have to do.

He would never allow tragedy without purpose, never give a gift without a plan. He will guide you in it if you but ask Him. He waits for you to bring this to Him. Give Him your sickness. Give Him your child. Give Him your choices, and He will make your way straight."

The tragedy in my life has brought me here, to this moment. I'm dying, but I have so much to be thankful for. I don't have room in my life, no *time* for this kind of blackness anymore. There is only time for love.

Love and forgiveness.

Drawing from the love I have for my own child, the infinite capacity she gives me to pardon the sins of others, I move slowly across the room to kneel in front of my mother.

"Momma, I'm not trying to hurt you. I just wanted you to know that...that..." I force a swallow past the bloated lump in my throat and then begin again, tears coming out of nowhere to stream from the corners of my eyes. It's like a purging, a purging of all the dark and ugly wounds I've let fester, become gangrenous. "Momma, I just wanted you to know that I'm dying. I have a daughter that will never know me, and you're the only part of me in the whole world that she will have left. I w-w-wanted you to keep me alive for her. Tell her stories about me. Tell her how much she was loved, and how I took that love with me, to the grave and far beyond. Don't let her feel for one second the way I felt when I was young—alone and unwanted. Deserted. Be a part of her life. If not for me, then for you. She will be all that you have left, too."

I hold my mother's eyes for ten long, painful heartbeats before I give up, letting my chin drop to my chest and giving in to the urge to cry in earnest. Between muffled sobs, I faintly confess another reason for wanting my mother here. "I'm dying, Momma, and I just wanted to see you one more time. Just one more time. Is that so wrong?"

In the hush, I hear my husband's choked voice. "Oh Jesus!"

I imagine him running angry hands through his hair like he does, spinning away from the sight of his dying wife on her knees, begging for love. It hurts me that he has to see this, but it's something I must do.

But for the wet patter of tears on the back of my clasped hands, the room is absolutely silent.

Seconds tick by.

No one speaks.

I can feel the sadness, the hopelessness. It saturates the air like a physical dampness, a moist cloud that hangs over furniture and skin and hair.

Minutes, hours, days later, the first sign of movement is heard. It's the sound of Momma sliding off the couch and onto the floor, where she gathers me into her arms. I let her. I want nothing more than to let her. I fold into her softness, into her warmth and, together, we weep.

"I'm so sorry, my heart," she says, the words themselves a soothing balm to my aching soul. My mother hasn't called me that since right after Janet died. "I'm so, so sorry. Please forgive me. Please, Lena, please. Please don't go thinking that I didn't love you. I loved you more than anything. That's why I let you go. I was afraid to love you that much. I was afraid of what losing you would do to me." Her voice drifts off into the same whisper, like a mantra she repeats over and over again. "I was afraid. I was afraid. I was afraid."

I raise my leaden arms and wind them around my mother's slight shoulders, holding her close. "It's okay, Momma. We're all afraid."

"Say you forgive me. Please say you can forgive me."

I don't hesitate. I don't have the luxury of waiting or holding a grudge. It's now or never. "I forgive you, Momma. I loved you anyway. I always have."

Finally, after all this time, I recognize that it was more than mere obligation that took me to see my mother once a month for the last twenty-two years. It was hope, hope that maybe my mom would love me again. I thought my hope had died when I was a young girl, but maybe it was just buried under a lifetime of hurt and loss.

A bone-deep peace settles over me. It begins at the crown of my head as a soft tickle that sweeps away the pounding behind my temples. It eases onto my shoulders, brushing away the tension I hold there, and then it makes its way down.

Gossamer wings flutter through the rest of my body, washing away hurt and bitterness, anger and resentment, malice and ill-will. I'm left with nothing but love.

In my heart, I know I have only one last confession left to make. It's to Nate. Already I know that once the words are spoken, my soul will be at ease.

I'll be free.

I also know that I need to make that confession soon.

24

Wanted Dead or Alive

Lena

My mother stayed all day. She was there when I drifted off to sleep in the chair, and she is still here when I wake in the bedroom, hours later, as the sun is setting.

Hers is the face I see right after I see my husband's, leaning over me with a purposefully blank expression in place.

"I've got a delicious steak dinner blended up for you," Nate says, his lips curling up at the corners. "Broccoli, some bread, baked potato with extra butter— it's all in here." He holds up the canister I hadn't noticed him cradling. It looks like it contains vomit. It's food that will be administered directly into my stomach via the nasogastric tube.

"Why don't I *actually eat* with you?"

Nate's features widen in surprise, his eyes rounding, his mouth forming a silent O. "C-can you do that?"

"Of course, I can do that. I'll just have to chew really well." I know in the deepest part of my being that this will be my last meal with my family, and I want it to be as normal as possible. I know enough about last days and golden days to know the importance of making today special and memorable, even though it already has been.

"What about the…?" He doesn't finish his sentence, but rather sort of flips the tube that still dangles from my right nostril where it's taped.

"Help me to the bathroom?"

Nodding, Nate sets the container of nutrition onto the nightstand and helps me out of bed. When I stand, I glance over at my mother, Grace asleep in her arms, and I smile. "I love you, Momma."

Patricia Holmes simply nods. I don't take offense. I know my mother is probably overwhelmed and incapable of speech. I knew it wouldn't be easy for her, these last moments. They'll be bittersweet. Momma knows what's on the horizon for me. She's seen it too many times before.

With the help of Nate's sturdy presence at my side, I hobble past my mother and my daughter, pausing to kiss Grace on the top of the head. "My angel," I whisper, inhaling deeply before I continue toward the bathroom. Once there, I shoo Nate away.

"What if you need help?"

"Then I'll yell."

"What if I'm not fast enough?"

"You will be."

"What if I'm not?"

"You always are. I'll be fine. I promise." To emphasize my words, I pull myself up onto my toes as much as I can and I plant a kiss onto my husband's perfect mouth. I can't sustain the position long, the muscles in my legs trembling with that small effort. "Now go, you handsome hunk of man, before I take advantage of you with my mom right out there and embarrass us both."

"I honestly don't give a shit," he replies with a grin. "I'd take you anywhere, anytime." Even though he takes the bait and responds to my taunt as he would at any other time in our life, I see only a sad awareness on Nate's face. He knows that I don't feel like having sex. And I know that he knows. Yet neither of us acknowledges it. It seems easier somehow to pretend that things are as they have always been.

Even though everything has changed.

With a sweet kiss to my forehead, Nate backs toward the door. "I'll be right outside if you need me."

"I'll let you know if I do."

When the door is closed firmly between us, I lean against the sink and let my heavy head sag down between my arms. I take several cleansing breaths before I lift my eyes to a face that I hardly recognize reflected in the mirror.

What happened to the woman who stared back at me a few months before? When had I become this ghostly, sunken shell of Lena Grant?

Blonde tresses that used to hang in shimmering waves to just below my shoulders are dry and brittle and look more like hay than hair. Skin that used to hold a youthful glow looks sallow and paper-thin. Eyes that used to sparkle with life look dull and haunted.

I catalog everything from the dark circles under my eyes to the hollow cheeks, from the prominent collarbones to the bony shoulders poking out under my shirt. When did I lose so much weight? When had I begun to waste away? How has all this happened without me noticing?

Impulsively, I grab the nasogastric tube and pull it out, gagging as it passes the back of my throat. Without looking, I toss it into the trashcan and begin stripping off my clothes. I feel an almost frantic need to see my new reality while I'm still alert and oriented. I want to see what Nate sees, what my mother sees.

Less than a minute later, I stand naked in front of the full-length mirror that rests in one corner of the bathroom. In the shiny glass, I see the clawfoot tub behind me, luxuriously deep and inviting. I see the chandelier that Nate had rolled his eyes over when I pointed it out in a magazine. I see the pile of baggy clothes lying in a puddle beside the toilet, hastily discarded.

And then I see a body, a sick woman's body.

My lackluster eyes travel over the gaunt image. I see translucent skin stretched thinly over my chest, every rib visible. I take in the skinny arms that hang by my sides, the wrist bones protruding grossly. I see breasts that are still full and round from pregnancy, although I wonder why I'm not engorged and hurting since I'm neither pumping nor breastfeeding. At least I don't think I am. I can't *remember* if I am.

Or maybe, considering my condition, I'm taking medicine that I don't remember taking, to dry up my milk. Or maybe it's a side effect of one of the other medications I'm on. At this point, I can't keep anything straight.

Regardless, the one thing I *do* know is that I'm missing out on quite a few details of my life.

My gaze continues, on to the belly that is still swollen from pregnancy. I touch my stomach with trembling fingers, tracing the incision, pressing into the flesh above and below it. I feel the wave-like give of fluid just beneath the skin.

Ascites.

Despite the fact that my mind often swims with delirium these days, my years of nursing experience tell me what's going on. Gathering of fluid in the abdomen is common in people with liver disease. And I have the ultimate liver disease—stomach cancer with liver metastases.

Warm tears leave wet tracks down my cheeks as I evaluate the rest of my body. Legs that I've always thought were a bit too thick are now thin, the skin hanging loosely around the insides of my thighs. I turn to one side and note the disappearing butt that I'd been self-conscious of once upon a time. Funny how that works, because now I'd give almost anything to have them back, to be that *very* healthy woman again. Not this…this…shadow.

I don't know why Nate still looks at me as though I'm the most beautiful woman in the world. It's far from true, and yet that's what I see in his eyes. Every day.

Adoration.

Attraction.

Love.

Even through all of this, he's my knight in shining armor. I always knew I had a good thing in him, but I might not have known just *how good*.

When I once again face the mirror straight on, I give myself one more head-to-toe glance. All in all, one thing is very clear. The aesthetics confirm the mental diagnosis that pops into my head. They're as hard to *think* as they are to *hear*.

You're dying, Lena Grant. And now you can see it.

A soft knock at the door causes me to jump. "You okay, baby?"

Nate.

I don't know how to answer him.

With bitterness? *No, Nate, I'm not okay. I'm dying, and there's nothing anyone can do to stop it.*

With pretense? *I'm fine, babe. I'll be out in just a minute.*

Or with honesty? *I'm not sure. I don't even recognize myself anymore, and I'm afraid of what I see.*

It turns out that I don't have to answer him at all. When I don't respond, Nate opens the door and pokes his head inside. I can tell by the look of alarm on his handsome face that he was half-expecting to find me dead on the floor.

The relief I see wash over his features tears at my heart.

"I'm okay," I finally assure him, a wobbly smile tugging at my lips.

"What is it?" he asks, coming into the bathroom and closing the door behind him.

I start to cry. I can't seem to stop the small mewling squeaks that wheeze past the tight knot in my throat. "I don't even look like me anymore. When did this happen? How did I get here?"

"Oh, God, Lena!" he moans, dragging me against his chest to hold me close.

I know if he could, Nate would take it all away. That's what his arms say every time they come around me. They say "I wish" and "If only" and "If there was a way."

Only there is no way.

Not anymore.

"Where did the 'blaze of glory' go?" I whimper, losing the strength of will I've tried so hard to maintain.

Nate leans back and looks down at me with aching tenderness. "You did 'blaze of glory', baby. You're *still doing it*."

"N-no, I'm not. I failed."

"You didn't *fail*. You carried and delivered a baby while cancer ate away at your body. You've helped feed and care for her. You've given your husband hope every single day. You've laughed when you had every reason to cry, and you've gone out of your way to make sure the rest of us are okay when it's *you* who you should be worried about. Lena, you've done 'blaze of glory.' *No one* could do it better."

I'm distraught as I stare up into his eyes. "But look at me. I let it win, Nate," I croak miserably. "I let cancer win!"

I can tell my words hit home. I can see the pain that he works so carefully to hide. Like the curved back of the Loch Ness Monster, it appears for just a few seconds before vanishing back into the murky depths from whence it came. To a place that only Nate can see.

"You did this *your* way. You didn't let it win. You knew the risks, and you made the best choice *for you*. And you stuck with it. You did what you thought was right. I will always support you in that."

"But I should've fought, Nate. For *you*. *For us*. But I didn't. I-I was afraid. I was too afraid to fight. Even for you. And I'm so, so sorry, Nate. I'm so, so sorry."

Devastation softens my knees.

Regret weakens my limbs.

As this last confession leaves me, so does the last of my energy. I crumple like crepe paper. Faster than my melting body, Nate catches me. He always catches me.

Always.

"It wasn't because I didn't love you," I tell him brokenly, allowing him to sweep me up into his warm, comforting arms. I just don't have the strength to stand. Or fight. Not anymore. "It's because I was weak. And scared."

"You're not weak, Lena. And it's okay to be scared. I'm scared, too."

"But you didn't give up on me. *I* did. I gave up, Nate. Can you ever forgive me? Please say you can forgive me, Nate. Please!"

I turn my face into the curve of his neck. I feel the thump of his back hitting the wall behind us as he relaxes onto it, looking for some support of his own.

His voice is torment.

It is agony.

It is anguish.

"Don't do this, Lena. Don't torture yourself. You're one of the strongest, bravest women I've ever known. You did what you thought was best."

"I chose wrong, Nate. I chose wrong."

His next words are quiet.

Hesitant.

True.

"I bet Grace wouldn't say that."

Grace.

Our daughter. A piece of each of us in the form of the most beautiful child I've ever seen. I wouldn't trade her for all the years in the world. For a thousand lifetimes. For a million healthy bodies.

She's all we ever wanted. The missing piece of our family. She will be the one who holds my Nate's hand not only when *she* needs it, but when *he* needs it. She has brought us healing and hope when there seemed to be none.

My jar was nearly empty before her. Now it is overflowing. She filled it. *She* is the light that I will take with me to heaven, the light I will carry with me for all of eternity.

A piece of me.

The best piece of me.

Thoughts of her bring perspective. Calm. Resolve. I exhale, my sigh sounding like her name.

Grace.

"No, she wouldn't. And she *is* worth it, isn't she? Worth all of this."

I imagine that the sheen in Nate's eyes matches the sheen in my own. There's so much love between us, and because of that love and the love we have *for our baby*, I know that we could never fully regret my decision. It was either my life or Grace's, and I know I'd make the same choice again if I could give Nate that little girl over and over and over.

"Thank you," I murmur, brushing my lips over his.

"For what?"

"For forgiving me. And for reminding me. This is the only way it could've happened. God's will."

Nate says nothing at first, only watches me silently as he processes my words, words so unlike the woman he's known for so long. I know it must seem foreign, but to me, it seems like a truth I've known all my life.

"Maybe you're right. Maybe there is a God, and this is His will."

"I'm right, Nate. He gave me the choice between my own life and yours, *hers*. I made the right choice. I would choose you two every time. Again and again. I guess I just...I guess I just lost sight of that for a few minutes. I...sometimes I don't feel quite myself."

Oftentimes, I don't. I feel like some strange amalgamation of the old Lena and a strange new Lena, of her old memories and her wildest dreams. Reality, for me, is an odd mixture of elaborate fantasy and unspeakable horror.

"I love you. All the different yous."

"And I love you for loving me that way. I know it's been hard. But it's almost over."

I hadn't intended to drop that bomb on him in such a casual way, but here it is, out in the open.

Nate tucks his cheek against mine, and I feel his sharp intake of breath. I know he's fighting back a surge of emotion. I recognize the signs.

"I will always love you. Every part of you. There will never be another one like you. Never. Not for me. And just so you know, I would do this all again, fall in love with you over and over, no matter how long we'd have together. You're worth it, Lena. You're worth everything."

His voice cracks at the last, and he pulls me tighter against his chest and slides his face down into the curve of my neck.

This time together, here alone, near the end... It feels poignant and powerful and somehow significant, like we are communicating more deeply than our words. Sentiment swirls around us, weaving in between the spoken things, tying them together with truth and honesty.

His heart is as raw and open as mine. We are naked to each other, nothing between us but truth. And I don't want this moment to end. Not yet. I can't bear to break the magic of it.

"Can you help me in the shower?" I ask tentatively.

I don't want us to spend my last hours mourning this way. I want to give my husband good memories, especially now.

I feel him nod.

Silently, he crosses to the shower and sets me on my feet as he reaches in to turn the spigots. As the water heats and steam begins to fill the room, Nate starts to undress.

There is a sense of finality in his every movement, as though he knows that this will be the last time he will remove his clothes for me, the last time he will touch me in the shower, the last night we will spend together.

I feel the same way, only I know.

I *know*.

Moving his hands out of the way, I set my fingers to work on the buttons of his shirt, slowly divesting Nate of his clothes. I cherish the feel of the soft cotton against my skin as I shift against him. I relish the smell of his cologne tickling my nose. I revel in the warmth of his closeness, searing me all the way to my bones.

If I'd had a last wish other than to see my daughter safely into the world, it would've been this: To spend these minutes alone with my husband, even if I'd never have thought to ask for it.

Finally, we stand bare, staring into each other's eyes. We stay this way for several heartbeats before we both turn at the same time and step into the shower.

Together.

One last time.

Every moment seems especially significant. Every look, every touch, every whisper of breath into the stillness is the last of its kind.

The last we will share.

With excruciating tenderness, Nate bathes me. He massages my skin with his soapy hands, making small circles that ease the tension in my muscles. He kneads my thin arms, rubs my swollen belly. He even gently cleans the irritated tip of my nose where it's been taped up for so long.

And when I'm too tired to stand, he helps me to sit on the tile bench and finishes, even washing the sensitive space between my toes. He worships every inch of me, kissing the arch of my foot, the bend of my knee, the curve of my hip. With every stroke, he tells my skin goodbye. He misses nothing.

Quite simply, Nate loves me. With his whispered words, with his careful hands, with his broken heart, he loves me. He tells me I'm beautiful, even now, without saying a word. And he tells me goodbye, too.

With every stroke, he tells me goodbye.

Afterward, as he carries me out of the stall to dry me off, I breathe into his ear, "I will love you forever. Dead or alive, I will be yours, wherever I am."

"And *I'll* be yours. Always."

Always.

That says it all.

There is nothing left to say.

****

Dinner is the best thing I've ever tasted. Every flavor explodes on the surface of my tongue, and every bite is like the first I've ever taken. It's more than a last meal. It's a last *experience*.

I take my time and chew thoroughly, not wanting to mar the moment with choking and hacking. Eating had never been a chore before, but has certainly become one recently.

Although *I* am thrilled to have eaten a quarter of the steak Nate grilled and nearly a third of the small pile of potato I scooped from the peel, everyone else eyes my accomplishment with concern.

The message is clear.

And they all know it.

Nissa stays to help clean up. She and Nate are in the kitchen when I spot a bright blink through the patio door and get a better idea.

"Nate! Nissa!" I call. Both come running, alarm carved on their faces. "Let's go catch lightning bugs. With Grace. And Momma. You can film us, can't you, Nissa?"

Although her smile is soggy, my friend nods enthusiastically.

Wordlessly, Nate collects an empty Mason jar from the cupboard and brings it out. He hands it to Nissa along with his phone and then stoops to scoop me into his arms. His expression is meant to be neutral, I know, but I can see the way his mouth is pinched at the corners.

Bittersweet.

I feel it.

And he feels it.

I rest my head on his shoulder as we all make our way to the patio. I look out at the view—my home, my yard, and the night—with eyes that strain to memorize every last detail. I take in the white rattan furniture I fell in love with on one of our trips to the beach. I take in the cheerful row of pink and red roses that sway gently in the breeze. I take in the perfectly manicured lawn that I can't remember Nate cutting this year, as well as the cobalt sky that is coming alive with the yellow flash of lightning bugs.

I've been happy here, with my husband, in our home. So happy. We've been so blessed, even when I couldn't see it that way, when I'd been more aware of what we *lacked*—a child. But I can see it now. I can see all the smiles, hear all the laughter, feel all the love. This is home. And I wouldn't want to die anywhere else.

When Nate moves to set me on a lounge chair, I pat his chest in protest. "No, I want to hold Grace while you and Momma catch them. Is that okay?"

I wanted to be the one to capture the little bugs for my daughter, but I know my level of fatigue is too great to risk it. It will likely be all I can muster just to hold my daughter out in the yard as the others do the catching.

He nods. "Of course, baby. Just let me know if you get too tired." Gently, Nate lowers me until my feet touch the pavers then reluctantly releases me, his fingers lingering as though each digit knows the opportunity for moments like this is coming to an end.

With a smile that I feel light me up from the inside out, I approach my mother and daughter. Grace is awake and sucking on her pacifier. When I lean over her and grin, Grace smiles and coos as though she knows that her momma is close and she can feel the laser beam of love coming at her.

I hope that's the case. I wish that I could bottle my love and leave it for my daughter so that she'd be able to take it out and let it warm her whenever she's feeling cold or blue. Since that's out of the question, though, I pray that the videos will suffice.

"Hey there, beautiful," I whisper as I take my child from my own mother's arms. Momma attempts a smile, but it looks more like a rickety grimace. I shift Grace to one side and press my lips to my mother's cheek. "Thank you for taking care of her today."

Momma makes no response, and I understand why. What is there to say? Nothing that hasn't already been said.

Turning and crossing back to my husband, the trio of adults steps out into the cool grass and walks toward the biggest cluster of light. I can't stop the giggle that bubbles up as the grass tickles my feet. It's as though I can feel each individual blade as it drags across my skin. My every nerve and sense seems hyperalert, and

I'm committing it all to memory, a memory that will soon burn out like the glow of these lightning bugs.

Tonight, I know I will not only chase the lightning bugs, but I will do as my father did, and I will follow them as well. On to where they never stop shining.

On to heaven.

"Get that one," I say to Nate, tipping my chin at a lightning bug that's close enough and low enough for him to reach. He stretches out one long arm and taps the bug, which then lights on his finger. Nate holds it out to Grace and me, the slow, steady wink of light almost hypnotic in the night.

"Look, Gracie!" I tilt my daughter toward her father and then look back at Nissa, who isn't far away, filming us. I smile at my friend through the lens. Nissa waves, and I see a tear slide down her cheek to pause on her trembling upper lip.

"Say hi to Nissa, Grace. She'll help you with all your clothes and makeup and jewelry. All the fun, girly stuff." I take my daughter's tiny, chubby hand and wave it at the camera. A lightning bug appears between us as if by magic, its belly flashing yellow in the dark. "Oh! Oh! Get this one, Momma!"

Obediently, my mom grabs the little bug and places it in the palm of her opposite hand then holds it up for my inspection.

"Perfect," I declare, a blend of overwhelming happiness and pure agony burning the backs of my eyes.

I watch as my mother places the tiny insect into the jar Nate holds then he closes the lid quickly so that none can escape. Pointing out which ones for my husband and mother to catch, I watch the jar fill until the glass appears to be a sparkling beacon of sun in an otherwise sunless sky.

When the jar is becoming too full to contain the insects as they add new ones, I walk to the last low-flying lightning bug I can see, and I let it settle on the tip of my finger. I hold it to my little girl's face and murmur, "Don't go to bed with dirty feet or an empty jar. Say your prayers every night, and never stop chasing the lightning bugs. Never stop. I love you, Grace. Always."

I pull my daughter in close and kiss her forehead, her eyes, her cheeks, the tip of her perfect little nose. I inhale, smiling at the way the sweet baby scent makes even the fresh night air smell better. I know that if it were possible to carry the memory of aromas with me to heaven, I'd take this one and Nate's. They're the two best scents in the world.

Just as my knees begin to feel weak and strangely numb, I feel the big hands of my husband cup my shoulders from behind. So perceptive. So caring.

"How about we take these inside with our little one?" He bends to brush his lips over the shell of my ear and chills break out, pebbling the flesh of my arms and legs. I know there's one more thing I want from this night—to watch my child fall asleep in the glow of the lightning bugs.

"Yeah, I'm ready." I let Nate turn me back toward the house. I glance at my mother who's standing just behind me with her arms wrapped around her body. I wonder if she's cold or if she knows, too. "You're staying, aren't you, Momma? For a little while longer?"

My mother nods in that closed-off way that she has. I can't expect my mom to be one hundred percent the person she once was; I'm just happy that I get to see *this much* of the woman who raised me.

"We'll put Grace to bed and then be back out. Why don't you and Nissa wait in the living room?"

Again she nods, this time following quietly along behind us, as though she's afraid to move too fast.

Content that my mother is being included, that she isn't going to demand that Nate take her back to the institution right away, I will my tired legs to move forward.

Steadily, I make my way across the yard, over the patio and through the house, cradling my daughter tightly against my chest. I'm determined not to let her go, not to give this last bit of care over to my husband. I need this.

One last time.

When I bypass Grace's room, Nate asks, "Where are we going?"

"I want to hold her so we can watch the lightning bugs together. All three of us," I answer simply, my voice breathy with my exertion.

Once in our room, I hear Nate close the door. I walk to the bed and sit on its edge until my husband comes around to hold Grace while I situate myself on my side. When I'm comfortable, I hold out one arm, and Nate lays our daughter next to my chest. I curl around

Grace, enveloping her with a mother's love and warmth.

I watch as Nate sets the glowing jar onto the nightstand and then positions the phone where he can record us all in the bed. When he's finished, he climbs in behind us and pulls me and Grace into the curve of his body.

"Take her to church, Nate. Promise me you'll take her to church. Don't let her be bitter like I was."

There is no hesitation in his response. "I promise."

"I want you both to be able to understand."

"Understand what?"

"This kind of love," I explain. "It changes everything. It's why my father prayed like he did. It was for *love*, for *me*. I understood it the moment I knew I was pregnant with Grace. Instantly, I knew the kind of love my father had for our family and for me. That's what's in the jar. Not bugs or light, but tradition. Family. *Love*. My father wasn't just playing with me or keeping up a summer ritual. He was filling my jar with his love." I pause, sighing in relief, basking in the very love of which I speak, the magnitude of it. "That kind of love...it's the kind that sends people in search of a God they stopped believing in. It's the kind of love that keeps us going, makes us pray, gives us hope. The kind of love that saves us. You've given me that, Nate. You and Grace. You saved me. My jar was empty after my father died. Until I met you. *You* filled it up again. And I need to know that you'll let Grace fill yours. I need to know that you'll be okay when I'm gone."

When I'm gone.

"Lena, I..." Nate's voice is low and hoarse, like his throat is as bloody and inflamed as his heart.

I wait wordlessly for him to finish. I can almost hear the battle taking place. He wants to argue that this isn't the end, but he knows he can't. He can't argue the truth. This *is* the end. And we both know it. It's in the air. In the calm. In the acceptance.

What he chooses to say instead makes me smile.

"You're my peanut butter and waffles."

"Your what?"

He nuzzles the back of my neck as he repeats his words. "My peanut butter and waffles. *Only* the most delicious breakfast creation since French toast. But I didn't know that until I tried them. I had no idea what I was missing. But then, after that first bite, I didn't know how I'd ever lived so long without them. Or how I could possibly live without them again. You're the peanut butter and waffles of my life. I don't know how I ever lived without you. Or how..." His words trail off as though he can't get them out, as though some part of him still can't bear to speak the words aloud.

"Shhh, Nate. It'll be okay. I promise."

Nate wraps his arms around me and squeezes. I wonder if he thinks that if he holds me tightly enough he can somehow keep death from stealing me away from him.

But I know better. I know, and I believe that he does, too. Deep down.

We enjoy one another for several minutes, reveling in the feel of what it's like to be in each other's arms, warm and safe and alive. A family. A whole family.

Then, in the quiet sanctuary of the room we've shared for so much of our life together, I share with *my* family the end of a ritual that my father had started with me a lifetime ago.

I feel in many ways that I've come full circle.

Tracing a finger over my daughter's sleeping profile, I whisper, "Goodnight, stars. Goodnight, moon. Goodnight, lightning bugs. Come again soon."

Holding fast to one another, the Grant family rests. In the silence that creeps in to fill the room, I hear the comforting familiarity of my husband's voice. "I love you, Helena Grant. More than I've ever loved anything or anyone." Although I hear the timber of his words shift and waver, crackling with emotion, I feel my lips curve in tranquil happiness.

"As I have loved you, Nate," I reply. "As I will *always* love you."

The soft flicker of firefly bellies, the joyous bundle in my arms, and the warm presence at my back lull me away from reality and into the fluid recesses of my mind. Past and present mingle in a confusing cocktail of memories.

I feel the vitality seep from my body, forced out by a fatigue I can no longer fight.

I'm done.

Finished.

There are no words left unsaid, no deeds left undone. Nothing that has to be seen to before I give up my battle.

I have only peace. Deep, soothing peace, like an endless midnight ocean that beckons me to come and float, to allow the current to sweep me away.

And so I do.

I let my mind stretch back to days gone by, to the beginning, and to the end, and I bask in reminiscence for as long as I can hold on.

I let my mind drift…

25

You Give Love a Bad Name

Lena

Nineteen years ago

"It's hard to explain. It's like there was just this instant connection between us. Like...sparks. It was awesome!" I exclaim, half-swooning as I remember the hot guy I met at the bank. My friend and coworker, Regan, laughs and rolls her eyes. I rush to add, "I know it sounds hokey as hell, but I'm *serious*."

Regan looks skeptical. "I'm sure you are. You're also a drama queen."

I slap my friend's arm playfully. "I am not!"

"Ummm, are, too."

"Am not!"

"Are, too, but let's get to the important stuff like what was his name? Are you going to see him again? And does he look like he'd be good in bed?"

"God, Regan!" I know I'm blushing furiously. While as a nurse I'm very comfortable with discussions about sex *with patients*, I've never been at ease discussing *my own* sex life. With *anyone*. "You think I could let him buy me dinner first, or should I just go back to the bank and jump his bones?"

"If you're really asking me, then…"

"No, I'm not. I know exactly what you'd say."

We both laugh. Regan is the type that does exactly what she wants, when she wants. She explains herself to no one. Although I envy her bravado, I could never be quite as…free as Regan. It just isn't in my DNA.

"So? *Are* you going to see him again?"

I sigh. "I doubt it. I mean, it's not like we exchanged numbers or he asked me out or anything. I was there getting pre-approved for a loan for Pete's sake. I'm sure he has more respect for his job than to hit on a customer." I turn sheepish eyes up to my friend. "Dammit."

"Well, that just means you'll have to drop by to ask him something else then. And *you* can ask *him* out."

"I don't know. What if our moment was just in my head? What if it's just desperation or wishful thinking or a nine-month dry spell affecting my brain?"

Regan is no longer looking at me. Her eyes are trained at a point somewhere over my head.

"Uh, Lena, tell me again what he looked like?"

My mouth turns up at the corners, and I stare off into the distance as I think about the loan officer, Nathaniel.

"He was gorgeous! Short, black hair, jewel green eyes. Jaw made of steel, strong chin. Lips to die for. A smile that would melt a woman's ovaries at ten paces."

"Was he pretty tall?"

"Very. At least six three or so. Wide, wide shoulders, narrow waist. He was wearing this suit... Charcoal with a white shirt and an emerald tie that was probably the exact color of his eyes. Jesus, he was beautiful."

My toes tingle with the memory.

"And what did you say his name was?"

"Nathaniel, *I hope*," comes a velvety voice from behind me.

I whirl around so fast, I nearly topple my chair. I come to a sudden stop when I meet the laughing jewel-like eyes I'd just been describing. The sexy loan officer I met the day before is standing at check-in, not two feet away, smiling at me.

Good Lord, that smile!

I sit, gape-mouthed, and stare at him for several seconds, my cheeks undoubtedly beet red. I say nothing, *do* nothing.

I'm at a loss. A total and complete loss.

Finally, it's he who breaks the humiliating silence. And with a voice, I'd forgotten, feels like satin sheets sliding over my skin.

"Was it?" he prompts when I continue to gawk mutely at him.

"Was it what?"

"Was his name Nathaniel?"

Then it clicks. He heard my every word, or at least enough to make me want to die on the spot. "Oh God!" I moan, dropping my burning face into my suddenly-damp palms.

Within seconds, long, cool fingers wrap around my wrists and tug gently. And for the second time in twenty-four hours, I'm struck by the nearly-tangible connection between us. It's electric.

Lightning down my spine.

A buzz in my head.

Tingling in my toes.

It's an invisible circuit that stretches from his body to mine, and someone is cranking up the energy.

"It-it was," I eventually manage to eke out from between my parched lips.

"Good. I'd hate to think I was the only one who felt this."

"This?" I ask, dazed.

Nathaniel's thumbs brush the sensitive skin on the inside of my wrists, sending tiny shock waves ricocheting through me. "Yeah, *this*."

I let out a breathy laugh. I'm relieved and embarrassed and exhilarated and...giddy, all at once. "What are you *doing* here?"

In the space of three unnerving heartbeats, it occurs to me that he might've come by to talk with me about my application. This visit might be work-related for him.

If that's the case...

Somebody should just shoot me now.

I'll have to move. Change my name. At the very least I'll have to go to another bank and apply because I'll never be able to look this guy in the face again.

And *that* would be unfortunate as hell!

With his next words, however, I know I won't have to worry about that.

"I came here for you."

I came here for you.

For you.

He came here for me.

My pulse flutters wildly for a few more seconds, but then, oddly, it settles down to a steady, heavy beat within my veins. Although I might be a tad prone to dramatics as Regan suggests, I'd swear that I can feel the presence of fate. Here. With me. Physically, like a reassuring hand on my shoulder.

And just like that I know.

Some part of me *knows*.

One minute I'm a nervous, mortified mess and the next, I'm as calm and at home as I am with friends I've had for years. Suddenly, I feel as though I've known this man for most of my life.

Or maybe that I will know him for the rest of it.

Like the flip of a switch, I go from awkward to confident, from frenetic to flirtatious.

A grin plays with the corners of my mouth, and I eye him through narrowed, teasing slits. "Do you do this for all your customers?"

"Not a single one."

"Did you have to look up my name again?"

"No. I didn't *forget* it."

"Did you get lost on the way over here?"

"No. I used GPS."

"Coke or Pepsi?"

"Coke."

"Favorite time of the day?"

"Right now."

I can't help the smile that breaks out across my face or the way my belly flips over at his answer. "Do you like Bon Jovi?"

"Love them."

"Favorite song of theirs?"

"'You Give Love a Bad Name' because, at the moment, I'm feeling particularly shot through the heart."

I laugh at that. "If I ask you to dinner, will I have to fill out another loan application due to conflict of interest?"

"If you do, I'll help you."

"What's your favorite kind of food?"

"Anything that doesn't include raw fish."

"Pick me up at seven?"

"Only if you're okay with goodnight kisses at the beginning of a date."

I beam. "I wouldn't have it any other way."

"Then I'll see you at seven."

With that, Nathaniel, the hot loan officer, releases his hold on me, but even then, I doubt he'll ever release his hold on my heart. I can feel him digging in, maybe to stay. Forever.

I sure hope that's the case, because I've never looked forward to seven o'clock so much in my life.

26

Something for the Pain

Nate

I sit on the edge of the bed I've always shared with my wife, and I listen to her mumble. It sounds like she's recounting parts of the conversation we had the day I'd gone to ask her out.

Despite the boulder that has settled over my chest, I smile at the memory.

I'd taken a chance that day. I'd known I could be written up if Lena had found my behavior inappropriate and decided to report me, but I was young and cocky and thought it was worth the risk. At least that's what I told myself on the drive over to the clinic where she worked.

And I was right.

It had been.

Nineteen years ago, I met the girl of my dreams. She walked right through the door of my first job and explained that she wanted to get pre-approved for a home loan. I watched her eyes sparkle as she spoke proudly of landing *her* first job as a nurse practitioner. I listened to the excitement in her voice as she explained that she wanted to buy a small house rather than renting an apartment. I smiled at the animated way she used her hands when she talked. And with every minute that ticked by, I wanted more and more to ask her out. She was beautiful, smart, and there was something about her that drew me like a bee to honey.

It wasn't *only* that she was gorgeous, which she was. It wasn't *only* that she had brains, which she obviously did. It was something else, something I couldn't put my finger on.

I can now, though.

She was the one.

The one.

I'd known from the moment I met her that she was it. Something in my gut told me. Something in the way I wanted to smile when she smiled. Something in the way I wanted to know everything about her. Something in the way I *needed* to see her again. *Needed to.*

It was different.

It was right.

She was right. *So right.*

Whatever people want to call it as they scoff—insta-love, love at first sight, kismet, fate—I believe in it. I knew early on that I was hooked. We were perfect together. From that very first meeting, we were perfect.

And now, all these years later, as I sit by her deathbed, praying she'll regain consciousness yet knowing she won't, I know I'll never find another like her. I don't even want to try. I'd rather be alone for the rest of my days and live on the memory of her than ever try to replace her. It simply can't be done.

I take my wife's cold hand, rubbing the pale, pale skin with my fingertips, holding it tight as she jerks and twitches, and I whisper, "Are you remembering us, baby?"

The hospice nurse told me that hearing is the last thing to go, so I talk to my unresponsive wife often. For three days, I've hardly moved from the bedside. When Grace isn't sleeping, I hold her and feed her at Lena's side. Sometimes we even get in bed with her and play until Grace falls back to sleep.

I do everything by my wife's side, with our daughter present as much as possible. I can't bear the thought of her dying alone. I want her to feel the presence of the two people who love her most. If she can still feel *at all*.

The absolute absence of anyone from *my* family makes me wish things had been different with my parents before they died, and that I had siblings. I could've used not only their emotional support, but their physical assistance as well. Since my life revolves around Lena and our bedroom, it's hard to keep up with much of anything else. Nissa comes over every day to help out. But even more help than my wife's best friend is Lena's mother, Patricia. I don't know how I'd manage without her. She offered to stay. Until her daughter passes.

And I let her.

It's what Lena would want.

The night that we caught lightning bugs had been the last time Lena's eyes were open. It had been her "golden day."

The final words spoken between my wife and I had been declarations of our love as Lena held Grace and the two drifted off to sleep in front of a jar of fireflies. Or lightning bugs, as my beautiful wife called them.

I'd known it was coming, but still I'd been unprepared. When nearly an hour had passed that night, I tried to wake her so that she could go out and tell her mother goodnight, but she wouldn't rouse. I hadn't been *too* alarmed because her sleep has been extremely deep since her illness took a turn for the worse. That's why I thought little of it.

It was Mrs. Holmes who first realized what was happening. She knew it when she went in to kiss her only remaining child's cheek before she left.

I watched her bend and press her lips to Lena's forehead and then her temple and, finally, her cheek. Then she stepped back, tears leaking from the corners of her eyes, and pronounced, "She's gone, Nate. She's… gone."

I'd wanted to argue, to tell my mother-in-law that she was wrong. Wrong! That Lena is hard to wake these days.

But I didn't.

I didn't want to upset her. I knew Lena wouldn't want that. So I held my tongue and waited. I knew time would tell.

And it did.

The next morning, Lena didn't wake. The next afternoon, she didn't wake. The next night, she didn't wake.

The day after that, hospice came. That was the moment when I knew without a doubt that Lena's mother was right. This is the end. My Lena isn't coming back.

It was the sweet nurse, Donna, who explained that Lena had ordered their services before when she was... "Well...before," she'd said with a kind yet sad smile. Nothing else needed to be explained.

Donna has been a wealth of information and help to me and everyone else who loves my wife. She knew all sorts of tricks to keep Lena comfortable, like putting in a catheter and giving her oxygen. Although it seems counterintuitive to me to do these things for someone who isn't responsive, Donna explained the different physiological processes that are taking place and why they need to be addressed.

"We want to keep her as comfortable as possible. She didn't want to be in pain. I know *you* don't want her to be in pain. And this way, when her body is ready to let go, it can. She's at rest. At peace."

I had to leave the room after that conversation. It was all becoming too real.

Time is up.

My wife, my soulmate, the person I've loved above all others, is dying. Her body is holding on by a thread, and still, I can't bear the thought of letting it go. Letting *her* go.

But that choice is soon taken out of my hands.

On the eleventh day of Grace's life, Helena Holmes Grant, mother, wife, sister, daughter, friend, and nurse passes away.

Her pain is over, her struggle at an end. Now only *I* need something for the pain. But I know, as surely as I blink and breathe, that there will be no way to ease it, no drugs that will help me.

There is nothing I can do to stop the pain.

Not for the rest of my days.

27

Always

Nate

The days both creep and speed by, alternating between things happening so fast I feel out of control, and moments passing so slowly time felt never-ending. The hardest parts, I quickly learn, are the ones that crawl by at an excruciating pace.

The second Lena stopped breathing, her body going eerily still, had felt like hours. I sat staring at her, willing her to breathe, to open her eyes.

Only she never did.

I sat there wondering what to do, wondering how to go on, how to move forward. How to live without the other part of myself.

I held her hand for long moments after she died. I stared at her face, memorized her every feature. I cataloged every tiny detail from the peaceful expression to the flawless skin. I wept silent tears of grief and gratitude, glad that she'd gotten to go exactly as she'd wanted—her way. With a blaze of glory, a glory called Grace.

In that odd moment when I was able to look beyond my sorrow, I could see the courage and the splendor of what Lena had done and how she'd done it. She paid the ultimate price. She suffered and bled and cried. And she gave her life for another's.

My wife was amazing in life, and she'd been amazing in death.

I stroked her soft hair, caressed her cool cheek, kissed her stiff lips, and whispered into an ear that could no longer hear. "You made death beautiful, baby. Just like you."

When Patricia found me sitting with my dead wife, she called the hospice nurse, and within an hour the house was full of people. They were quiet and respectful, efficient and thoughtful, and they worked like a well-oiled machine. I couldn't imagine how many times they'd done this to get so good at it and, at that moment, I didn't really care. I only cared about *this* time and *this* body.

Lena's.

My wife's.

I watched with glassy eyes and a numb heart as they cleaned her up, removing the catheter and washing her body with caring hands. I picked out clothes for them to dress her in to transport her to the funeral home, and when they lifted her lifeless form onto the stretcher, I bent to give her one final kiss goodbye.

"I love you. Always."

They asked me to leave the room as they rolled my wife out of the home we shared. I did as they asked. I didn't get to see them take my Lena away.

Out of my home and out of my life.

Forever.

******

I'm grateful for Nissa and Patricia's help when it comes time to make arrangements, but I'm more grateful for the little bundle I can hold in my arms. Having Grace with me, holding her, is like holding a piece of Lena. I hadn't realized, *truly realized*, exactly what kind of gift Lena had been giving me when she decided to trade her life for Grace's.

But *she'd* known.

Lena had known.

She'd known that she would be giving me joy and purpose, *a reason*.

And that's why she did it.

So, together, Grace sucking sweetly on her pacifier, we make Lena's final arrangements. We choose a beautiful white oak casket with a white silk interior. I can hardly look at it for fear that I'll breakdown as I picture my beautiful wife lying dead within it. But I make it through the morning, even if a bit robotically.

I speak with the funeral director and pick out items and words and songs that will best honor Lena, each one stealing another piece of my soul. I keep my mind and my eyes on my daughter as much and as often as I can, though. She keeps me tethered to the world rather than allowing me to slip peacefully into the dark oblivion that hovers constantly at the edges of my consciousness.

If it weren't for my child, I have no doubt that I would've just shut down. Sold everything and moved to an isolated cabin in the mountains where I have to do nothing more than mourn the loss of Lena for the rest of my days.

But I can't do that.

I have a tiny, helpless life to nurture and care for. Lena saw to that. She gave me a lifeline.

She knew.

She *knew*.

****

Days and nights pass in a blur of sleeplessness and despondency. The only person I want to see or speak to is Grace. The others I just tolerate as I have to and walk away from when I can.

If the days surrounding Lena's death were a midnight sky, events that happen during that time are merely flashes of lightning in the dark.

Selection of the casket.

Flash.

Writing her obituary.

Flash.

Seeing my kitchen overflowing with food, yet not remembering a single visitor.

Flash.

Dressing my daughter in a tiny yellow dress.

Flash.

Carrying Grace into the funeral home.

Flash.

Seeing my wife lying at rest against the fluffy white silk lining of her coffin.

Flash.

"Amazing Grace" sang by a stranger.

Flash.

A pastor's words over an empty grave.

Flash.

Freshly turned earth seen through the tinted glass of the limo as we pull away.

Flash.

The desolate feeling of coming home to an empty house.

Flash.

No Lena.

Flash.

No Lena *ever*.

Flash.

Now, as I change Grace's clothes and then my own, memories of the funeral flit through my mind, things people said, folks I saw and have no real recollection of. Just a vague, foggy memory.

She looks beautiful, Nate.

You did such a good job, Nate.

Everything is just as she would've wanted it, Nate.
The flowers are exquisite, Nate.
She'll be missed, Nate.
I'm so sorry, Nate.
I'm so, so sorry, Nate.
Hollow words echo through my mind, disappearing into the distance like thunder from a fading storm. The only real, concrete thought that demands permanent space in my brain is the simple question: What now?

What now?

What now?

The last thing I remember from the day of Lena's funeral is lying on our bed, our daughter asleep at my side, and listening to Bon Jovi sing "Always".

****

Days drag by, each one passing in an almost identical fashion to the one before. I know I'm hanging on by a thread, a thread of dust and bone.

I'm self-aware enough to realize that I'm not doing well. From the outside, I probably look like any other man trying to cope with being a single dad, but from the inside...I'm practically dead. The one thing, the *only thing*, that keeps me hanging on is Grace.

My daughter.

My wife's gift.

I can't bring myself to change anything about the house. Several people who managed to catch me out and stop me for a minute to talk have given me their best shot at advice. Most of it's total shit.

Clean out her things as soon as you can. It'll help.

Keep just enough around to remind you, but not enough to drown you.

Talk to her if you want to. It'll help you heal.

If you do nothing else, at least move her clothes out of the closet.

I let it all flow in one ear and out the other. I know they're all trying to be helpful, anxious to see me put myself back together. And most of their suggestions are designed to help a grieving person move on.

That's where the disconnect happens, though.

I have no desire to move on.

Ever.

I'm not being unrealistic or masochistic; I'm being honest. With myself, with anyone who might've bothered to ask. I lost the only woman for me, a significant piece of my *soul*. My version of moving on will be to raise our daughter to the best of my ability, equip her to weather the trials of life and chase her own happiness. And then, eventually, I'll have to let her go. Let her grow up and find her own way. *That* is my version of moving on. *That* is what I want out of life— to do right by my daughter, to do right by my wife.

I'll include Lena as much as I possibly can in the rearing of our child. That's the only way I can keep her alive. And I *have to* keep her alive *somehow*.

Letting her go…

Saying goodbye…

Forever…

…it's unthinkable. So I don't think of it. I can't. I don't give a shit how unhealthy the "experts" say it is.

I can't do it. I just…can't. It's the one thing I'm not strong enough to do.

****

Days turn into weeks.

Weeks turn into months.

The most I can manage is taking care of my daughter and doing a few hours of work from home for the bank. I'm grateful they've been so accommodating.

Back in the early days of my career, I did some portfolio assessment and financial planning. Luckily, the bank I left when Lena got sick has been kind enough to give me a few new clients who need wealth management services. It isn't particularly taxing work. I can do everything I need to do from home. It's the perfect arrangement. At least until they hire another full-time person. That wasn't stated, but it was understood.

I'm okay with the situation. It gives me something to do when Grace is asleep, keeps some money coming in to supplement the investments I've been living off, and it's allowed me to keep one foot in the working world. I know I can't hide out forever. I'll eventually have to return to life and living. I'm just not in any hurry to do so.

That arrangement is why, on a Tuesday morning, nine months and four days after Lena died, I'm able to see my baby girl take her first steps.

I'm working on my laptop in the living room, quietly tapping away while Grace sleeps on a blanket a few feet away. She's surrounded by a mountain of toys she'd been busy playing with. I have to lean up and straighten my back just to see her. It's the squeak of a stuffed bear's belly that draws my eye, just in time to see Grace crawling out of her makeshift pen.

I smile at her, setting the computer to the side as I prepare to crawl toward her. She stops at the coffee table to pull herself up, which she's been doing for a couple of months now. But then, much to my surprise and elation, Grace lets go and takes an unsteady step toward me.

Her expression assures me that she's as shocked as I am, but she manages to take three more wobbly steps toward me before she just sort of crumples down onto her diapered butt like a train running out of steam.

"Gracie! You did it! You walked!" I exclaim.

Hurriedly, I snatch my phone from the sofa before I rush over to pick her up and take her back to the coffee table. I position her where she looks comfortable, and Grace stands there obediently, smiling around the fist she's chewing on in an effort to ease the ache of the teeth that are coming in.

After making sure she's stable, I slowly back away and get down on the floor, aiming my phone right at my daughter before clicking the record button. "Come to Daddy, Grace. Come on, baby. You can do it."

She watches me, still holding onto the edge of the coffee table, the tips of her fat little fingers blanching with her efforts. At first, she completely ignores my request. She reaches for the edge of a magazine and tries to pull it off the table, much more interested in *it* than *me* at the moment.

When she realizes it's too far out of her reach, she turns her attention to a red block letter, in the shape of an A, from her enormous stack of toys. She eyes it, and I wonder if she's debating whether it's worth the effort to crawl all the way back over there to get it.

Eventually, she makes up her mind that it's not and looks back to me for a little more encouragement. "Come on, Grace. Come to Daddy."

I shut off the video and restart it at least six times. I'm nearing resignation when Grace finally decides that *now* is the right time. Then, just like that, she lets go of the table, flexes her tiny fingers, and wobbles toward me.

On her feet.

I capture the whole thing on my phone, and for the first time in nine long months, I laugh. I feel the subtle stirrings of *real pleasure*. I love my daughter more than anything, especially now that Lena is gone, but my grief has been so deep, it's affected my ability to enjoy the little things. I care for Grace diligently, I love her profoundly, but on the inside, I'm broken and no other love can fix that.

Her first steps, however, mark a turning point.

The first step toward healing.

The first of a few.

From that day on, Grace and I interact on a whole different level. She's walking surely and chattering constantly before I know it, bringing true joy back into my life. She does it as effortlessly as her mother did.

Before I know it, spring has arrived.

****

Spring brings with it a renewal, as it's wont to do, but for me, it's a renewal of pain. The warming of the weather, the blossoming of the flowers, the leafing-out of the trees—it all forces ghosts out of hiding, and I become haunted by images of my dying wife.

I find myself watching her videos more and more often, turning inward, withering a little more each day. I know it isn't a good path to be on, but I'm helpless to stop it.

I just can't let go.

I sit alone in my bedroom floor most nights, watching Lena's beautiful face, listening to her beautiful voice, and remembering our beautiful life. The balmier the nights become, the closer I get to the anniversary of her death, the deeper I fall into depression. Grace brings me joy, of course, but even my bright, beautiful, intelligent daughter can't thaw what's frozen within me.

But as she did in life, my Lena is determined to save me, even in her death.

It's a Sunday in late May when I feel her for the first time.

Grace and I'd gone to church this morning, something I found an easy and soothing habit to adopt, and it had left me thinking even more about Lena. It's yet another instance I wish my wife could be with me. I know without a doubt that if Lena had had the benefit of holding a miracle in her arms, having something tangible to join her to her God, she wouldn't have struggled with Him the way she did.

Lena found her peace eventually. But it came at quite a price.

Grace and I decided to spend the rest of the afternoon at the park and then go out for dinner. Nissa and Mark had invited us over, but I politely declined. I didn't feel like being social. I never did, actually. Not anymore.

So as usual, I throw myself into my daughter, into her world. It's a soothing escape into love and away from memories.

It's later in the night when Grace totters through the house and wants to go into the pantry. I assume she wants to pick a different after-dinner treat.

But that's not the case.

"What do you want, little girl?" I ask when Grace putters around aimlessly from shelf to shelf. She grunts once, that petulant sound that I love and try not to smile at because I know I shouldn't encourage it. "What?"

Patiently, I let my daughter make her way through the small room. Suddenly, as though she just remembered what she wanted from the shelves, Grace turns. I watch with wide, curious eyes as she walks to the back corner of the pantry, leans against the wall, and points straight up.

My eyes travel up, up, up to the only thing above my child's head.

"Mines," she says, tilting her head back to look at me, to make sure I'm paying attention to her.

Slowly, I reach up onto the nearly-empty corner shelf. With curiously numb fingers, I take down the only thing that is anywhere near where my daughter is pointing.

It's an old empty Mason jar.

With holes poked in the lid.

In my chest, I feel an ache so sharp and painful that I have to reach out and steady myself on the shelving as I struggle to suck air into my throbbing lungs.

The last time I saw this jar was when it was full of lightning bugs and sitting on the nightstand. My wife was curled up against me, reciting an old rhyme to our baby. I don't remember freeing the lightning bugs, although I must've. But it had to have been Patricia or Nissa who washed it and stowed it away because I honestly can't remember putting it there. Or even *seeing it* for that matter.

Yet here it is.

Finally, I exhale one shaky puff of air and look down to where my baby bounces at my feet. What would bring her here? How could she possibly have known this jar was here?

I wrap my stiff fingers around the cool glass and take it off the shelf. I stare into the empty jar. I see my own face reflected on the shiny surface, but more than that, I see that it's not empty at all. Among the four slightly rounded walls of this container rests one of my life's most precious memories. Inside this jar there is love and family and a beautiful legacy that my wife wanted to share with our child. This moment, this moment where my child brought me here, will be added to it, as will all the laughs and squeals and yawns that we put in it from here on.

And it will never be *too* full. It will never overflow.

And it will never be empty.

My eyes sting as I squat down in front of Grace and hold out the old jar. "Is this what you want?"

Light brown eyes, so like her mother's, light up, and she reaches for the container. I let her take it from me as I hold her still and steady. As she studies the jar, I drop my forehead onto the side of her head, and I breathe.

More deeply than I have in months, I breathe.

I inhale the soft baby scent of her. It soothes my insides even as I conjure up a crystal-clear image of my beautiful Lena. She's laughing, holding Grace close to her chest as Patricia and I chase lightning bugs around the backyard to put into this very jar.

I remember it like it was yesterday.

I've watched the video of it so many times. I know every word, every step, every expression by heart.

I grab Grace, securing the jar with one of my much bigger hands, and carry her from the pantry. I waste no time in heading for the patio. Although I haven't seen a single firefly yet this year, something in my gut tells me what I'll find.

I yank back the curtain, fling open the door, and there, filling my backyard with their cheerfully winking bellies, is a sea of lightning bugs.

Grace squeals a shrill, happy delightful sound, and I stop. Stop right in my tracks and just stare out at the display.

There are hundreds of them. Maybe thousands. I don't think I've ever seen so many in one place. But they're here, in my backyard, on an early spring night, and I know it's no coincidence.

As I stand taking it all in, a single luminescent insect floats gracefully onto the patio. Instantly, it catches my eye. I watch as it, almost purposefully, drifts in a lazy pattern that leads it directly to me, and then lights on the back of my hand.

Tears pool in my eyes as I watch the soft flash of the bug's underbelly. It sits perfectly still, as do I, as though something as mysterious as the night is passing between us.

And it is.

It's mysterious and healing and awe-inspiring.

In a strangled voice, backed only by the sound of my daughter's gleeful squeak, I whisper to the little bug, "Hi, baby. I've missed you so much."

28

Pictures of You

Nate

Twenty-three years later

I pat the last piece of tape across the twelfth box and set it aside. It still makes me feel a little tight in the chest to think of my baby girl moving out, getting married.

Growing up.

I realize this is something I've dreaded for a long time now.

It's time to let her go.

Since my beautiful Lena died, Grace has been the center of my universe. Over the past twenty-three years, every star in the vast sky of my life is a moment, an event, a milestone involving Grace.

Crawling, walking, reading, writing. Her first words, her first tooth, her first day of school. Her first slumber party, her first boyfriend, her first broken heart—there are literally thousands of bright spots in my existence since Lena died and at the nucleus of every single one is Grace.

Her life, her love, her laughter, keeping her safe and helping her find her way were the only objectives in my life. Everything else came in at a very distant second. Or maybe even third.

In the beginning, I didn't think I would ever be able to recover from losing my wife. It was touch and go for a while, but the night of the lightning bugs…well, that seemed to start me on the right path. Just like I'm sure Lena knew it would.

After that, healing began. Slowly. Too damned slowly, but still, it began. I remember Lena telling me one time that if you put away a memory long enough, it will eventually fade. That's how she protected herself from her mother's abandonment after her father died. She tried to put the memories away so they'd fade and cease to be painful.

Maybe that's why I worked so hard to *never* put my memories of her away, to keep them as fresh as I possibly could. I never wanted them to fade. But the truth of the matter is, whether you put them away or not, they fade. Time and age make sure of that.

And so, while I still remember many things about Lena and our marriage like they were yesterday, a portion of the pain finally faded.

Finally.

Over the years, it's gotten easier to breathe and laugh and live. But that's as far as I ever *wanted* to move on. Lena was the love of my life. My one and only. Grace was my life after her, my whole world, and now, at sixty-five years old, I'm not sure how I'm going to fill the remainder of my days when she's gone.

When she's gone...

I pant, suddenly short of breath. Sometimes, just the thought of letting her go...

Of losing the only other love in my life...

A stab of pain pierces me between the ribs and strikes me right in the heart. Closing my eyes tightly, I grit my teeth and force myself to take deep breaths despite the ache as I massage my sternum with the heel of my hand. I wait until it passes.

Any other man my age might fear he's having a heart attack, but not me. I've suffered pains in my chest from around the time Lena died until now. It literally hurts me to think of her, but I enjoy it in a perverse way. It never fails to take me back to the place where I felt closest to her right before she died. It's like reliving a lesser version of her death all over again, but in doing that, it seems as though I just saw her a few days ago.

That alone is worth the pain.

It also makes me anxious for the day when I'll see her again, for real. I can almost picture her if I concentrate hard enough.

So I do.

It's *that* thought, *that* image, the one where I can see Lena's face reflected on the backs of my eyes, as clear as it was when she was still alive, that makes the pain go away. It's as if God Himself is promising me that one day it won't hurt anymore.

One day, I'll really get to see her again.

Until then, hopefully Grace will give me a grandchild or two, but not for a while. I'm not selfish enough to pray for one right away. I want her to get settled in her life, in her marriage before she dives into adding so much more responsibility to it.

I smile as I imagine my sweet, intelligent, funny daughter bloated with pregnancy. She'll look *even more* like her mother than she already does.

And that's a lot!

When the ache subsides, I resume my task and stack the last few boxes beside the door, turning to look back at the room that Grace has occupied almost every night of her life. All except for her college years.

Those were tough as hell!

I hadn't been away from her for more than a few hours since the day she was born. Even when she'd slept over at her friends' houses growing up, she'd always wanted me to pick her up early. Like *sunrise* early. So I always did. I'd take her for breakfast, and she'd tell me all the gossip she'd learned through the course of the evening.

I've been fortunate in that we've always had such a good relationship. I can't imagine how hard it would've been if we hadn't been close. Without Lena…it would've been a catastrophe!

But we have been. And still are. Even after she started spreading her wings and became her own woman, we've remained close.

Pride bubbles up in me. I used to sit in the rocking chair in Grace's room when she was tiny and listen to her breathe. I'd try to picture her as a teenager and as a young woman. I'd try to imagine what kind of man she'd marry, where she would want to live, what she'd choose to do with her life. I should've known, being her mother's daughter, that she'd be drawn into service for others. She's every bit as caring and nurturing as Lena, and she's grown up hearing stories about her mother from everyone who knew her. I suppose it was a no-brainer that she'd end up being a nurse, like her mom. She even got her first job in an oncology unit and loves it.

Just like her mom.

If I remember correctly, her exact words were, "It fits me like a non-latex glove, Daddy."

I smile.

My Grace…

My *saving grace*, as I call her.

And she is. Still. After all these years. I can't fathom what my life would've been like after Lena without my little girl. I'm glad I didn't have to. And I have one person to thank for that.

Lena. My beautiful, beautiful Lena.

"Daddy?"

Grace startles me from my musing.

"In here," I call in answer.

My throat lumps up for a second. She even *sounds* like her mother since she's matured.

Seconds later, Grace appears in the doorway. Her smile is wide and bright and full of sunshine. My heart swells with love and pride. "Wha'cha doing?"

"Packing up the last of your things."

"Daddy!" she chastises good-naturedly. "I told you Robbie and I would do that tonight."

Dusting off my throbbing hands, I shrug my stiff shoulders. "No big deal, honey. I wanted you two to be able to relax. This is your last night before all the wedding craziness starts."

"People get married every day, Dad."

"That's a fact. *But* how many of them do it in Rome?"

"Probably a lot of Italians."

I can't help grinning. "Smart ass."

She sticks out her tongue pluckily and, for about twenty seconds, I consider kidnapping her and running away, anything to keep her my little girl forever. But I know that time is past.

Gone.

Over.

I have to let her go. It's as much a part of life as death is, and *that* is something I've become intimately familiar with.

Grace's eyes cloud with concern. "Are you sure this won't be...too much for you?"

"I'm positive. I wouldn't miss this for the world. And the seats are surprisingly comfortable."

"I don't mean just the flight. I mean the whole trip. Rome... All the memories."

I cross the room and lay my hands gently on my daughter's shoulders. "Gracie," I begin, using one of my pet names for her, "I couldn't ask for more. Your mother..." The lump in my throat inflates like a hot air balloon. I have to clear it before I can continue, but even then, I can hear the emotion straining through my vocal cords. "Your mother would be thrilled. And I can't think of any place I'd rather be than a city where I spent so many wonderful days with her. I'm looking forward to it. I promise."

Her smile returns tentatively. "Okay. If you're sure."

"I'm sure."

She pops up on her tiptoes and kisses me on the cheek. I want to take her in my arms and hold on to her, hold on tight and never let go. But I can't. I can't risk her getting a glimpse of my true feelings on all of this. I don't want her to know how hard this has been, and *will be*, for me. But I'll get through it. For her. For my daughter.

Much like my wife, I would do anything for Grace.

"Where's the little chick?" comes a second female from somewhere in the vicinity of the kitchen.

"Back here!" Grace says in a louder voice.

Within half a minute, Nissa appears in the hall. She walks up to Grace, slings an arm over her shoulders, and hauls her in for a smacking kiss on the cheek.

"You packed yet, kiddo?" she asks.

"Daddy just finished, *even though* I expressly forbid him to touch any of this."

Both Nissa and Grace both turn their disapproving gazes toward me, but in Nissa's I see the laughing tolerance she's always had for the way I indulge and spoil my little girl. "Thick-headed as always, I see," Nissa says, shaking her head. Then she looks back to Grace. "No, I meant for your trip. You know *the honeymoon.*" She wiggles her eyebrows, and a sly grin plays with the corners of her mouth. I can remember finding her wearing just such an expression as she sat with my wife, having coffee early in the mornings. I woke to find them that way countless times.

I push that thought out of my head in favor of what's happening right now. "Oh no!" I say firmly, holding my hands up to stop what might be a disaster.

"Oh no, what?" Nissa asks, her features arranged in her most innocuous fashion.

"You are *not* helping her pack for her honeymoon!"

"And why not?" Nissa's hands go to her hips. I know what that means. Grace does, too. If the finger comes out...

"If you recall, I got to see *firsthand* what kind of sh— stuff you pack for Europe."

A mixture of happiness and deep melancholy swirl through me.

Europe.

Lena.

Lingerie.

Kisses in London, Paris, Rome, and several more countries than I ever thought I'd kiss my wife in.

"Nathaniel Grant, you ought to be ashamed! Do you seriously think I'd pack things like that for my little Gracie-Lou?"

I say nothing, just eye her suspiciously. I don't *think*. I *know*.

Finally, she concedes. "Fine," she huffs, muttering under her breath. "Spoilsport."

I smother a grin.

As she has for years, Grace sweeps in to mediate. "I have everything I'll need, Aunt Nissa. It's fine. Really."

"Are you sure? Because after Mark and I split and I married Thad, he let me take his credit card for a spin and, girl, let me tell you. I bought some pretty nice stuff. You sure you don't want to come take a look?"

"Aren't you needed at home?" I ask, pushing through the door to take Nissa by the shoulders and aim her toward her own house, which she kept in the divorce and then remodeled for her new husband. She was adamant they live in *that* house, in *this* neighborhood. She wanted to be close to Grace, something I'll never be able to adequately thank her for.

"As a matter of fact, I *do* need to get supper on."

"Then by all means," I say, giving her a nudge, smiling in spite of myself.

Nissa blows Grace a kiss over her shoulder and reminds her, "See you at the airport, kiddo. Call if you need me."

And then she's gone, the back door slamming shut, leaving me once again alone with my daughter.

"That woman... She's a bad influence," I murmur halfheartedly.

Grace knows me too well to believe that, though. "You love her just as much as I do," she teases, smiling up at me.

"Yeah. She was a good friend to your mom. And she's been good to both of us over the years."

"Maybe you should take it easy on her, Daddy," Grace advises. "I think she's empty nesting. I'm the last of us to go off and get married, you know."

The last of us.

Grace grew up with Nissa's children. It was like having a ready-made family. They love each other like siblings. I know if Lena could see how it all turned out, she'd be pleased.

Thrilled, even.

I can almost see her smile...

"Daddy?"

"What? Oh, right. Yeah, I'll take it easy on her. As long as she doesn't send you to Rome with stripper clothes."

Grace gives me her brightest, most Lena-like smile and tells me as she's walking away, "I make no promises."

I just shake my head and watch her go.

****

Rome.

Jesus, I think silently when I unlock the hotel room door and step inside. The rush of emotion hits me like a physical blow. I can practically smell Lena.

Shaken, I wonder if it was an enormous miscalculation on my part to think I could handle staying in the beautiful suite I shared with my wife all those years ago. I'd thought I might feel comforted, might feel her presence stronger, but this...

I stumble forward and drop down onto the closest chair, a Queen Anne-style one sitting at the edge of the living area. The room has been redecorated, but it's still so much the same that when I glance up at the window, I can envision with disturbing clarity my wife standing there, looking out at the incredible view. I feel closer to her all right, but I also feel closer to the loss of her. Like it just happened, the anguish of it that poignant.

It staggers me.

Or maybe it *daggers* me.

Right through the heart.

An increasingly familiar pain ripples behind my breastbone, and I fist my hand in my shirt right over my heart. I squeeze my eyes shut. I wish I knew exactly how many days, weeks, months, or years it will be before I'm reunited with my wife. Maybe that would make it easier, knowing. Seeing an end in sight.

Or a beginning.

I don't want to hurt my sweet Grace, but she's grown up now. She'll be busy with her own life. She doesn't need the added worry of her old man clogging up the smooth runnings of her existence.

I'd love to see how she ends up, see her children, see her become even more like her mother, but I also miss my Lena. Still miss her so, so much.

As soon as the discomfort eases, I rise to unpack the laptop I brought. I power it on and pull up the extensive photo and video collection it holds. I find what I'm looking for quickly—the folder simply labeled LENA.

Scrolling through, I find the range of dates I'm looking for then I scan that section for the one entry in particular. When I spot it, I click to open it.

It's a short video of my wife speaking to our daughter. At the time, I'd been asleep in the other room of *this* suite. Unbeknownst to me, she'd just found out she was pregnant and had already begun recording messages to the child she wasn't sure she'd even be able to bring into the world. If she'd asked me then, on that very day, I would have told her that I had no doubt she could. And *would*. To this day, I've never met a stronger person than my Lena.

Circling the pointer over the play button for several seconds, I take two deep breaths before I click it. There's a slight pause, and then I see my wife appear on the screen in front of me, big as life and twice as stunning. Behind her, framed by the window like an expensive painting, is the Trinità dei Monti. I know that if I walk over and pull back the curtain, I'll see the exact same view, right down to the angle. If I'm careful enough, I could probably even stand where she stood. I won't do that, though. I won't risk giving that scene, that moment, *her* moment any other meaning.

It was Lena's.

And Grace's.

I realize, however, that I would've given anything to see her standing where she stood. Right now. Even just one more time.

Exhaling loudly, my eyes scan my beautiful wife's face as she begins to speak. Her happiness, her pregnancy, her burgeoning hope was already showing in the faint pink of her cheeks. Although I've watched every millisecond of footage at least two thousand times over the years, it never stops my arms from breaking out in chills when I first hear her voice. It's as though she's in the room with me.

Only she isn't.

She never will be again.

And that loss, that cold, hard realization never fails to crush me anew.

"Hello, my beautiful child," she croons softly, smiling into the camera. "I just found out about you today. I don't know if I'll ever get to see you to tell you this in person, but I hope *you* get to see *this*. I want you to know that you made me so happy today. You changed *everything*. For the better. Already. I don't even know if you'll be a boy or a girl, but I feel complete today.

"I've wanted you for all of my life. I've dreamed of feeling you kick for the first time. I've dreamed of holding you in my arms for the first time. I've dreamed of what your face might look like—your smile, your hands, your little feet. You'll be perfect, I know. I know in my heart that you'll be the most perfect thing in the world. The best thing I've ever done. And I'll die happy if I can see you just one time before I go." I can see where Lena was trying not to cry, and my gut twists. "I love you. Today. Tomorrow. Always."

I watch the screen long after Lena's face has disappeared. As I always do when I replay the videos, I feel so homesick I'm nearly nauseous with it. But it doesn't stop me from hitting play over and over and over again. It's the best kind of homesick I can think of. And the pain, while it still hurts, it's less sharp than it once was. Time truly does heal.

But it can't make me forget her. And it can't take away my desire to be with her again.

Nothing can.

Finally, some time later, I stand and kick off my shoes. Carrying the laptop, I walk into the bedroom and stretch out on the bed. Lazily, I search for one of Lena's longer videos, and I hit play.

The last thing I see before I doze off is my wife's striking face, her laugh ringing in my ears.

****

A more incredible wedding ceremony I can't imagine. The flowers, the cathedral, the music, the atmosphere…it's like one of the fairy tales I used to read to my precious baby girl when she was just a few years old.

I might be a tad biased, but I also think the bride is the most breathtaking sight I've ever seen. Aside from her mother, of course.

Grace and Lena… The two could've been twins. Or at least really similar sisters. The resemblance is uncanny. The biggest differences are Grace's chin, which has a touch of me in it, and the shade of her hair. It's a darker blonde than her mother's. Otherwise, she is Lena made over.

From the beginning, I prayed that she would be. I wanted, *needed* to see Lena after she died. It was the one request I'd been granted. It makes it hard to look at my daughter sometimes, but impossible to look away. And today is no exception.

Pride and a bittersweet mixture of love and loneliness well in the center of me when my little girl appears in the doorway across the vestibule. She crosses slowly toward me and then stops a few inches away.

"You ready?" she asks. Her eyes are sparkling like pale chocolate diamonds, and her cheeks are flushed with the glow of pure happiness. I remember what that feels like, and I hope my only child can have the privilege of enjoying that for several decades to come.

"You look…exquisite. I can't believe this is my baby Grace standing in front of me. You look so grown up. So much like your mother." As much as I try not to tear up, I can't stop the moisture that floods my eyes. I blink through the burn as I smile down at my daughter. "I wish she could be here to see you."

"I do, too, Daddy."

For a few seconds, the world falls quiet around us, allowing father and daughter to share their pain, to remember the person missing from such a joyous occasion.

I've known this day would be hard. I've expected it. Nothing has ever been exactly perfect since Lena died. I've had some near-perfect moments with this child of mine, fun times with family and friends, but there is always something missing. From every room, from every event, from every sunset and sunrise, there is always something missing.

My wife.

My other half.

My Lena.

When the music on the other side of the doors changes, Grace takes a deep breath and laces her arm through mine, turning me toward the aisle. That's our cue.

"You might be giving me away, Daddy, but I'll never be far." I pat my baby's hand, love overflowing the confines of my heart. Much like Lena, Grace always manages to take care of me. Even though it's I who's been supposed to take care of *her*, our roles have been reversed in some ways, right from the start. Her laugh picks me up, her voice soothes me, her presence gives me purpose, and often, her words speak directly to my soul. It's as though she knows what I'm thinking and feeling, and she seeks to comfort me.

Just like Lena.

The majestic double doors part slowly. The dramatic display further lends itself to the feeling of being in a living fairy tale. I want nothing less for my saving Grace.

Squaring my shoulders, I face the church that stretches out in front of me.

The ceremony is traditional and touching. I'm absolutely certain that I'll still feel the beauty of it until the day I take my last breath.

The reception is as lively as one would expect it to be in Italy. More people show up for it than I expected, but I'm pleased for Grace's sake. She seems to be having the time of her life. My only hope is that things will get better and better for her. Minute after minute, day after day. Year after year.

The wine flows freely, the laughter rings loudly, and happiness is the theme of the day. Conversation is easy, and my daughter is perfection flitting around in her off-white Stella McCartney wedding dress that had given me sticker shock for a month and a half. But now I can see that it was worth it.

My Grace...she is worth everything.

Just before nine, an unusual fatigue begins to plague me. No matter how tired I am, though, I refuse to excuse myself early. I wouldn't miss throwing birdseed (Grace didn't want the birds to choke on rice) at the newlyweds for all the hours of sleep in the world.

Hours later, as I fling my lacy pouch of pellets, I'm especially grateful that I powered through when I see Grace depart from the line of well-wishers and head straight for me. She already nearly knocked Nissa over, sending Nissa into a flurry of sniffling half-laugh, half-crying hiccups. Now it's my turn. And I can't be sure I won't react the same way. Wouldn't that give my Gracie something funny to remember?

With shimmering eyes, I watch her hurl herself toward me and throw her slight body into my arms. It's another moment I know will be forever seared into my brain. The way she smells, the way Rome sounds, the way I wish Lena was here.

"Thank you for today, Daddy. I couldn't have asked for a better father. You're more than any girl could possibly deserve."

My heart swells and pulses with adoration.

"I love you, pipsqueak," I say gruffly, using another of my favorite nicknames for her, determined not to embarrass us both by crying.

I've had many pet names for her over the years. Grace loved having her dad call her different things. When she took an interest in something, it somehow ended up being part of the new name she chose for herself, like the year she discovered squirrels. We'd watched an animated movie together where the main character was a squirrel named Pipsqueak. Grace had demanded that I refer to her only as Pipsqueak for weeks. I was glad to see that phase go, and only a few of the names withstood the test of time. Pipsqueak was one of them, though. And during her teenage years, I'd enjoyed using it to tease her. It had quickly become one of my favorites. And hers again after she grew up a little more.

"Love *you*, Dad."

Grace kisses my cheek, and I tug at the long blonde tresses that fall down her back. Reluctantly, I let her go when she pulls away to go and rejoin her new husband.

That might be the hardest part of the whole night—letting her go.

But I did it.

I let my baby go.

I have to, and I know it. I can't keep her around to fend off the suffocating silence that fills the house when she isn't there. I can't keep her around to help distract me from the grief that still gnaws at my soul when it's too quiet or my mood is just right. I can't keep her around to keep *me* from falling apart. She needs her own life, and I want her to have it, even if it means heartache on my part.

"Grace!" I call before she ducks her head into the waiting limo. Her head pops up, and her light brown eyes meet mine. "I left something at the hotel front desk for you."

"Daddy!" She gives me the look that says *You already spent too much money!*

I wave her off. "It's not expensive. Just something I wanted you to have as you started off on *your* life."

She nods and blows me a kiss. In my head, I catch it and tuck it into the space closest to my heart, right beside the place where Lena still lives.

Where she will always live.

I don't wait for the crowd to thin before I make my hasty exit. I don't doubt that people will stay and party, enjoying the music and the bar until the wee hours, but I've already paid the service to take care of everything, so I'm comfortable retiring for the night.

Stuffing my empty hands into the pockets of my tuxedo pants, I stroll slowly along the curb, back toward the hotel.

The street still teeming with people, I'm far from alone, yet I've never felt more isolated. More lonely.

I take in the sights.

Remember.

Think.

Mourn.

It's such a bittersweet day, it seems that's all I can do. Everything will change now. Again. Only Lena's not here to save me this time. And neither is Grace.

By the time I arrive at the hotel, I'm unbearably exhausted. It's been a busy day. Another turning point in my life.

I ride the elevator to my floor and walk to my room on rubbery legs. Once inside, I cross to the window and look out at the view, the view that frames my wife's head on the video I watched earlier. Alone, in the void of the room and the emptiness of my life, I give in to the urge to weep. I don't do it often, but sometimes...

I make no sound.

I make no move.

My body doesn't shake or tremble. It simply bleeds clear drops of liquid that spew from my heart, but leak from my eyes.

I'm tired. So, so tired. I've done what I promised my wife I'd do—I raised our daughter. I've been there for her, provided for her, loved her, supported her, and now I've given her away. I finished my race, and now I just want my prize.

Lena.

A deep, excruciating pressure grips my chest. I gasp once, twice, and in that time, I know that this is something different. This pain...it means something else.

I feel no fear or uncertainty. I feel no sadness or regret. I feel only peace. Beautiful, blissful, warm peace.

I turn from the window and stumble to the couch. I collapse onto the soft cushions and lean my head back, closing my eyes against the pain radiating into my left arm and jaw. Moments later, when I open them again, I'm not surprised to see the most beautiful face of my sixty-five years of existence. Her face is within inches of mine. Close enough to touch.

My Lena.

I smile and reach out a hand, every molecule in my body sighing in relief. "Hi, baby. I've missed you so much."

EPILOGUE

Grace

In the attic, one day in the future

As I cradle the old Mason jar, my eyes mist over with tears, the remains of a sadness I never quite overcame. The night of my wedding, my father had a massive heart attack. He died in the hotel room that he'd shared with my mother decades prior. It was fitting.

I know he loved me. More than anything on Earth, he loved me. But I also know he welcomed death. He'd always felt separated from the other part of his soul. I didn't understand that at first—the agony he seemed to live with every day—but after I'd been married for a while, I finally came to see why he felt that way. My dad's heartache lessened over time, but it never quite went away.

Until he died.

Then he was at peace.

I drag my bent thumb over the inscription on the bottom of the jar.

I love you, baby girl. More than I could ever tell you. Don't go to bed with dirty feet or an empty jar. Say your prayers every night, and never stop chasing the lightning bugs.

My sweet daddy.

I recall the first time I saw it. Dad had left it for me at our hotel on the night of our wedding. It was a brand new Mason jar at the time. It had been heavily wrapped in tissue paper with a note taped to the front that said, "Although this jar is brand new, it's not empty. You started filling it tonight, Gracie. All your wedding memories are in here. Keep filling it up. Every day, fill it up as you fill up your life—with happiness and love and family. All the beauty of yesterday and all the promises of tomorrow are kept in here. It will never be empty as long as you have love. Never. So go and start your own traditions, but never forget the old ones. Love you, baby girl. Be happy."

Catching lightning bugs in a jar—he'd kept that one going for my mother. And I kept it going for my kids. From the beginning, Robbie and I caught fireflies with our children. Those memories are some of my most precious. Robbie and I watching our children and our grandchildren fill this jar with laughter and bugs and family tradition. The beauty, the *importance* of this simple glass container is something I didn't understand until I got older. It's about so much more than just fun summer nights. It's about life. And priorities.

It's about love.

Now Robbie and I are getting older, frailer. We've seen children, grandchildren, and now great-grandchildren come into the world. A fuller life I couldn't imagine. Unless I'd been able to share more of it with my parents. That's the only gripe I have. I'm happy that they found their peace; peace, for them, was just different than most of us think of as ideal. They showed me some valuable lessons while they were here, though. You never know when the angels will come to take you home. You just pray that you get in as much living as you can before then.

We love.

We laugh.

We hope.

And we keep filling our jar.

That's what we did. All of us in my family. We did while my mother lived. We did while my father lived. And we have since they've been gone.

I don't doubt that my children will do the same. And their children. And their children's children. Then one day, we'll all be a whole family again. In heaven. But until then...

With great effort, I rise from the chair, my knees creaking in protest. I ignore their groans as I've done for quite some time now. I'd much rather be the spry young thing that I once was, but I'm making my way toward the end, not the beginning. So until my day comes, I'll keep getting up. I'll keep laughing and loving and living the life that my parents and my handsome Robbie and I always envisioned. Filling my jar. And I'll keep catching lightning bugs with my kids. And their kids. And *their* kids, which is what I'm about to do now.

Because that's what we do.

We keep going on until we go on no more.

I fold the jar into the bend of my arm, holding it against my side like a football made of crystal. I don't trust my aged fingers to grip it as I navigate the tricky steps. I figure this is the best way to ensure that it—and I—make it back downstairs in one piece.

As soon as my foot touches the hardwood at the bottom of the last step, I hear the excited squeals of my *great*-grandchildren. My heart swells to near bursting, and I'm overcome with the gratitude that I get to share this tradition with yet another generation. I hope it never fades, no matter how many kids of kids of kids my line has. I smile, knowing it would thrill my father to no end that I was keeping the chase of the lightning bugs alive. Even more, it would thrill my mother.

For a few seconds, I see her face. Lena Grant. She's smiling at me through the flat, bluish screen of a monitor. I grew up seeing her that way. She was my mother, a bright spot in my life, even though I don't remember meeting her in person. She's proof that we can live on long after our bodies have given up.

A different face bursts through my mother's, this one real. Molly's sweet, shining countenance causes the image of my mom to tremble and shiver, then disappear like ripples in a pond. My great-grandbaby is who I see as I step out into the backyard, into the waning light.

At four, she's the youngest of all my great-grandkids and the spitting image of her grandfather, my son. As she stares up at me, her eyes wide with exhilaration, I see the brilliant eyes of my husband looking back at me. That single trait of his runs strong in our family. He's proud as a peacock that his genes are so robust. He often teases and clucks about his manhood. Like I have for sixty-some years, I just roll my eyes, but he always makes me smile.

I look up and see the object of my ruminations sitting in an Adirondack chair, throwing a ball with my eldest. The scene warms me, as it always has. Gratitude runs through me like the crystal clear waters of a mountain creek. I need to thank my Robbie for loving me. I've said it dozens of times over the years, but it always needs saying. That man and his love... Well, they changed my life.

One day, I'll get to thank my parents, too. When I get to heaven, I'll go straight and thank my father for staying with me as long as he did. He shaped the woman I am today.

Then I'll find my mother. I'll hug her, for the first time since I was only a few days old. I'll hug her, and I'll feel her touch and see her smile, and I'll thank her for giving her life for mine. For teaching me about sacrifice before I could even spell. For showing me what a woman will do for those she loves.

Anything.

The answer is anything.

A woman will do anything for the people she loves.

And as long as she has love, her jar will always be full.

DEAR READER

As you may have guessed, this story is very personal to me. Although Lena's tale is her own, it was inspired by events in real life. *My* life.

It all began with the love between my parents. Their love was true.

Deep.

Lasting.

Just like Nate and Lena's. It was *real*.

My parents would've been married for fifty-three years if my father had lived for twenty-four more days. But he didn't. He couldn't. His body just couldn't make it any further. But that doesn't mean their love died.

It didn't.

It will live on to inspire and comfort the rest of us until *we* are long gone, too. Love is like that.

It lingers.

My father died on December 4, 2015, of stage four esophageal cancer. While this story is completely fictitious and Lena's cancer is a slightly different variety than Dad's, they suffered in much the same ways. We, my family and I, watched my father fight a war he couldn't win. We watched him struggle to get his food down, battle to keep his disease under control, and all the while he lost more and more weight. We saw the toll the cancer took, how it crept in and ravaged everything it touched. When it's widespread like this, into the liver particularly, it affects more than just one body system, especially sensitive ones like the brain.

Several of the scenes in *The Empty Jar* were directly inspired by events that I personally observed.

I lived them.

I stayed up many a night with my father while he rearranged things on the counter and worked on projects only he could see. He, too, was getting his affairs in order. He once told me that he had too much to do to die. I think that's why he worked so hard in his last days, even though he never left the house and never completed any of those tasks. He wanted to leave everything in good order for those he loved most—us.

In addition to the confusion, my father suffered the failure of one organ after another until he, too, slipped peacefully into a coma. As long as I live, I'll never forget those days.

I cried over him when he wasn't watching.

I prayed over him while he slept.

I told him over and over how much he was loved.

Like Nate, I spent most of my time by his bedside. I wouldn't trade a single minute of it, though. I got to hold his hand as it turned from warm and pink to cold and pale. I got to speak to him long after he stopped speaking back. I got to spend precious moments with him right up until the day he died.

Death is a long, tragic road for those of us left behind, but it can be a blessing for those sick ones who are hurting. As hard as it was to let him go, death was a blessing for my dad. Watching him suffer was unspeakably painful, more so for him, I know. And while artistic license was employed to specifically tailor some parts of this story, the bulk of it is completely accurate, even the horrific parts.

Especially the horrific parts.

Cancer is an evil nemesis.

A killer.

A thief.

It tried to take my mother, too, who was diagnosed with cancer in January 2015. She is still with me, though, and I'm deeply, profoundly grateful for that.

As much as cancer takes from us, it can't steal our love or our memories. Like these characters, I'm thankful for every day that I was given with my sweet daddy. I treasure those memories like the world's most expensive jewels. There *will* come a day when I won't need them anymore, though. There will come a day when I'll get to hug him again. Maybe we can even chase lightning bugs in heaven. Who knows? But until then, I'll just keep writing.

Knowing him and loving him made me who I was up until December third.

Losing him made me who I became on December fourth and every day after.

Thank you for sticking with this, for reading something that is pretty out of character for what I usually write. Some things in life change you. They affect you so profoundly that it's hard to remember the person you used to be. That's where I found myself after Dad died. And that's why I had to write this book. I wanted to write something that *matters*, not just to me, but to others.

This is my heart, my soul, my pain and my healing all wrapped up in a bow called *The Empty Jar*. I *needed* to write this book. It was all I could think about for weeks, and now that it's done, I know in my heart it's the best thing I've ever done. It's the thing I'm most proud of in all of my works. I hope my dad would be proud of it, too. Proud of *me*. Nothing would make me happier.

If you enjoyed this story, if it touched your heart, brought a tear, reminded you of what's important in life, **please tell a friend.** I'd love nothing more than for this book to help someone, somewhere, out there in the world. For it to *matter*. It sure matters to me, and it sure helped me. But there's only one way that it will make it to those who need it most. And that's up to you, my amazing, incredible, wonderful readers. You change lives. You may not believe that, but it's true. You changed mine. And I've seen you change others by coming out in support of what you love. So if you loved *this* and would pass that love along, maybe leave a review as well, I'd be forever grateful. Hopefully someone else will, too.

Thank you.

Truly.

Sincerely.

Always.

Michelle

ACKNOWLEDGEMENTS

First, I'd like to thank my sweet husband for bearing with me since 2015 when my mother was diagnosed with breast cancer. That set the pace for one of the worst years of my life. She fought her battle and then rolled right into helping Dad fight his. She's the Lena in my life. I just hope that I can be her Grace.

But back to my hubby...

You've been patient, loving, kind, helpful, thoughtful, and more understanding than I could've hoped for. Aside from my father, you're the best man I've ever met. I'm blessed to have you in my life, and it was YOU who showed me how lost Nate is without Lena. That's how I'd feel without you.

Lost.

I love you, baby.

Always.

Next, I'd like to thank my best friend and crit partner, Courtney Cole. How you put up with me, I'll never know. Thank you for reading this book (more than once) and for your always-valuable input. I wouldn't have wanted to walk this writerly road with anyone else. I love you like family. You are definitely in my jar!

I'd also like to thank Kat Grimes. You are like a ray of sunshine. Your kindness and encouragement never fail to brighten my day. You make my life a better one and the world a better place. You are also definitely in my jar.

I'd like to thank Marion Archer. You always have the best insight! Thank you for squeezing me in and for being a sister in the ways that matter. You're in my jar.☺

And Paige Smith. Thank you for working with me on such short notice. I can already tell that you're going into my jar.

Lastly, I'd like to thank each and every reader who embraces this story. You may not know it, but you're in my jar now, too. Because your love of my work *matters to me*. You are in my jar. Always.

A FINAL WORD

If you enjoyed this book, please consider leaving a review and recommending it to a friend. You are more powerful than you know. YOU–the words from your mouth, the thoughts from your heart, shared with others, can move mountains. You make a huge difference in the life of an author. You have in mine. You do every day, which brings me to my gratitude, my overwhelming, heartfelt gratitude.

A few times in life, I've found myself in a position of such love and appreciation that saying THANK YOU seems trite, like it's just not enough. That is the position that I find myself in now when it comes to you, my readers. You are the sole reason that my dream of being a writer has come true and your encouragement keeps me going. It brings me unimaginable pleasure to hear that you love my work, that it has touched you in some way, that it has made life seem a little bit better for having read it. So it is from the depths of my soul, from the very bottom of my heart that I say I simply cannot THANK YOU enough, which I say a lot of in this post.

For the full post, visit my blog at http://mleightonbooks.blogspot.com. You can sign up for my newsletter or find me on Facebook, Twitter, Instagram or Goodreads via my website, www.mleightonbooks.com

ABOUT THE AUTHOR

New York Times and *USA Today* Bestselling Author, M. Leighton, is a native of Ohio. She relocated to the warmer climates of the South, where she can be near the water all summer and miss the snow all winter. Possessed of an overactive imagination from early in her childhood, Michelle finally found an acceptable outlet for her fantastical visions: literary fiction. Having written over a dozen novels, these days Michelle enjoys letting her mind wander to more romantic settings with sexy Southern guys, much like the one she married and the ones you'll find in her latest books. When her thoughts aren't roaming in that direction, she'll be riding wild horses, skiing the slopes of Aspen or scuba diving with a hot rock star, all without leaving the cozy comfort of her office.

Other books by M. Leighton

All the Pretty Lies
All the Pretty Poses
All Things Pretty

Down to You
Up to Me
Everything for Us

The Wild Ones
Wild Child
Some Like It Wild
There's Wild, Then There's You

Pocketful of Sand

Strong Enough
Tough Enough
Brave Enough